Run to The Rio

RUN TO THE RIO

Joe Egan

Also from Joe Egan

Kate is Late
Jude is Rude

Losing Lee

To my son C, may you one day be the good man.
To M and I, for your endless faith in me.
To you, the reader, for reading my stories and
supporting my dream.

Table of Contents

Chapter 1

Mia walked into my office on a Wednesday. Ash Wednesday, to be precise. It was also, coincidentally, Valentine's Day. She had the smudgy black thumb outline on her forehead, a universal sign among Catholics that she had received the sacramental ash in the hours prior. She walked through the revolving, poorly constructed plexiglass door of Westco's regional headquarters holding a plastic Tupperware container. From the corner of my office, I could make out her figure as she strolled into the company's command post.

Mia sauntered over in my direction and kissed me a few times, the latest a little longer for effect. "How's your day going, my love?" She handed me the container. "I brought you lunch today."

"You are the best." I grinned. "Ten years together and you never cease to amaze me. As for my day, it just got a whole lot better."

She blushed a little. Of course, our romance had blossomed far beyond the initial attraction and honeymoon phase, but Mia's devotion to me shone every single day. Acts like these became commonplace in our marriage. I'm convinced I married the best woman in the world.

"What'd you bring?" I rubbed my hands together rapidly in anticipation of the homecooked meal.

"Oh." She blushed again. "Nothing too much. Just some enchiladas and tamales."

"That's a hell of a lot better than the fast food I was going to order." I laughed. "Thanks, Mia."

I put my hand on her back and led her down to the break room where the employees at Westco typically dined.

"Anything exciting going on today?" Mia asked me. "I need to hear something good. Francisco is driving me up the wall today."

"Where is he right now?" I asked. "Daycare?"

She nodded. "I dropped him off there for an hour. Kristin said she would watch him for a bit so we could have lunch together."

"That's so nice of her," I smiled, "and to answer your question, nothing too exciting. No new business today."

"That's no good, *mi marido*," she laughed. "How will we pay for the boys' school?"

I reached out to touch her belly. She was three weeks shy of her due date, and she still looked as pretty as the day I met her in 2008. She was of above average height, had dark skin, a brownish green tint to her eyes, and a face that could only be described as home. Her slightly frizzy hair was a De Leon trademark. Her accent still sounded a tad foreign, and even though she grew up in New Mexico her tone was reminiscent of her parents and their Mexican roots.

I, on the other hand, had the palest skin in Colorado. Mia says my blue eyes got her. I had the strong personality, the amiability needed to land a girl like that. I was in my early thirties, my once thick mahogany hair beginning to thin. My cheekbones appeared and vanished based on what the scale read. I stood five-ten, three inches taller than Mia.

If she wore heels, she would match or even surpass my height. It presented a real catch-22 for me because I wanted to be taller, but she looked absolutely stunning in heels. She had a way of causing this born-Minnesota boy to melt.

I motioned toward the fading ash on her forehead. "How was Mass?"

"It was good," she answered. "Father Montgomery had a great homily. He talked about the future and what God has in store for us, and you know, *mi marido*, it made me excited to see where we're going. How was Mass this morning?"

"It was good," I grinned again, "and do you mean geographically speaking or our family?"

She slapped my hand playfully. Even though I claimed I didn't, I loved when she smacked me in a fun-loving way. "You know what I mean."

I did. Recently, I'd been approached by the regional head of my company, Bart Thompson. My numbers as a regional sales manager at Westco had been stellar as of late, and Bart had offered to make me head of the executive sales team. The only catch was that I'd need to relocate to the company's headquarters in Minneapolis, Minnesota. Mia and I had begun to establish ourselves in Denver, so we were torn. We had friends, were parishioners of a traditional Catholic church, and our two-year-old, Francisco, really enjoyed the mountain hikes we frequented on Saturday mornings. Though Minnesota was the state in which I grew up in, it is flat as can be and less interesting to me in many ways than the topography of Colorado. My disdain for my home state might also be the product of childhood memories, but the mountains trump the plains in my mind. Being further away from her parents in New Mexico troubled Mia, too. Thompson told me I'd need to inform him of my decision to accept the promotion or not in the next week. Mia and I had not yet so much as explored many pros and cons. Coming together to decide seemed a journey miles away.

"So, let's talk about it now," I proposed.

Mia looked skeptical, to be sure, but she nodded anyway. I took a bite out of the first enchilada and was speechless. Even years later, her cooking never ceased to amaze me.

"I still can't believe how good of a cook you are," I confessed. "We can talk about Minnesota some other time."

She chuckled. "Stop flirting and trying to avoid the conversation, Scott. Let's talk about it." She set down her enchilada and folded her arms. This discussion was happening now, regardless of my preference.

"All right, all right." I got serious then and took a deep breath. "I believe this is a fifty-fifty decision. We do this together."

"Of course. Pros and cons," Mia said. "What are they?"

"I'll be the realist then. An obvious con is we lose what we have here," I started, "and we do love Colorado. Frankie loves the walks, and I get that. But other than that, Mia, I don't see any other reason not to. The money..." I truly did believe that.

"A thirty thousand dollar raise is what people dream of, *mi marido*," she answered, "but think about Francisco."

"I know, I know," I responded, "but he's two. He'll make new friends, and we'll find some new hiking trails."

"And what about *me*?" Mia replied. She placed her right hand on her stomach.

"God willing, we wouldn't have to move in the next few months. The baby will be okay—born here in Colorado—and everything is going to work out. You'll be fine by then." I shrugged my shoulders as a gesture of apathy.

Her face became flush then. She leaned back in her seat to convey her hurt. "And how do *you* know I'll be okay? Have you ever given birth before? Have you ever moved a month after giving birth? What about my recovery?"

"Mia, I don't mean—"

Her tone raised. "No, answer me!" A few of the folks eating in the large Westco break room took notice.

"Mia, that's a dumb question and you know it," I said.

Her normally warm and rational demeanor disappeared like a whisper in the wind. She knew I was embarrassed so she lowered her tone. "I said *answer me*," she demanded.

"No, I have never given birth. That's obvious."

"That's right. Every child is different, just like every woman's recovery." Then her eyes faded into sadness, and she started to cry. I stood up from my side of the table and walked over to comfort her. She put her head on my shoulder, and I could feel my gray sweater becoming moist as it clung to my skin. I know Mia had been having a rough go around during her second pregnancy. Almost every morning over the last two months began with her sobbing in my arms as she detailed her terrifying nightmares and painful kicks our soon-to-be son had doled out. She continued, "I'm sorry, it's just the hormones."

"Don't apologize. It's going to be okay, Mia," I consoled her, "and in three weeks we're going to have a beautiful baby boy."

She rubbed her eyes and then gazed up at me with wonder. Something was on her mind. "What do you think about Marcos?"

"As a name?" I smiled. "It's perfect."

"Marcos Scott," she said.

My grin grew even wider. "Now what gave you the idea for that?"

She laughed. "I'm so sorry we can't celebrate Valentine's Day together this year."

"That's okay," I comforted her. "It's my fault with work stuff. Besides, didn't we agree this was a Hallmark holiday?"

Mia laughed again. I looked at my watch, and I swear that hour with my wife had passed faster than the speed of light. It happens every time.

"I have bad news," I stated. "I need to get back to work, dear."

"I understand, *mi marido*," Mia said. "I'm glad we could do this."

"Me too. Thank you so much. Give Francisco a big hug for me, and I promise we'll talk more about it tonight, okay?"

She nodded and stood up from the table. We left the nearly empty break room, and I walked her out to the plexiglass door and let her out of the security gate so I could resume my Wednesday. I was so proud of her, for what she was enduring, but that pride was interrupted by the note waiting for me back on my office window. It was etched on a yellow Post-it, words only Bart Thompson could write so easily: "Scott, see me in my office. Urgent."

Truth be told, I knew Westco's sales team was sketchy. At a company get together last month, Bart drunkenly let out that a fellow employee had been questioned for security fraud. Not to mention, there was a co-worker of ours named Keith Stephens who was a loan shark and ran an underground gambling ring. I fell for the trap once, but I promptly paid back. Local legend has it that Keith was involved with the Satrione family, a notorious crime gang in Denver that has been in control of the area for almost a century now. Rumors in the office ran rampant that Joey Satrione, a higher up in the family business, once sent Keith a human finger in the mail when it was acknowledged that he didn't pay his debts. Apparently, Keith, who is one-eighth Italian, so admired Joey's tenacity in pursuing him that he begged to join the Denver crew. That's right: A man was sent a finger by a known mob associate and in return asked to join his gang. Last I heard, Joey said yes, and Keith was loansharking out of the casino and Jack's Burgers just outside of downtown. Keith Stephens is a sociopath. So is Joey Satrione.

My heart thumped sharply as I raced across the east wing of Westco's Denver regional headquarters. I would not call it a sprint, per se, but I was nearing an inappropriate level of stride as I strolled into my boss' office. I read the name plate situated in the middle of the door: Bart Thompson, Jr. I don't know why, but the junior part ticked me off every time I saw it. What a pompous prick.

I inhaled a prolonged breath as I entered the room. "Hey, Bart," I spoke nonchalantly. "What's up?"

He laid his soft brown eyes on me. For a man who stood so physically imposing at six-foot-four, especially to someone noticeably shorter like me, Bart's countenance could only be explained as unharming. Though I had yet to witness it, the man looked as though his tear ducts could burst at the drop of a hat. Unfortunately, the unintimidating appearance did not match his demeanor. He leaned back in his swiveling chair, halfheartedly looked in my direction, and began, "Sharpe, I know I told you I needed an answer by mid-next week in regard to your move."

I nodded. I felt my very light skin become void of color. "Yes?"

"Things have changed, Sharpe," Bart played it calm, "and I'm sorry about the situation. It's not a good one for any one of us, but I need an answer in the next twenty-four hours."

"What? In twenty-four hours?" I exclaimed. "I haven't even finished talking to Mia yet, and as you know—"

"Yeah, yeah," he interrupted and put his hand out to dismiss me. "I know you have a second one on the way." He crossed his arms, and those sad eyes pierced me. He doubled down on the aggressive route. "But this is the way things are now." Hostile doesn't begin to describe his manner. I remembered Bart himself had three kids, and an ex-wife, but I knew for a fact she had full custody and he had no sympathy toward employees with families. The only situation in which he could spend time with his own children were if the visits were supervised by a state worker. Then again, it'd be a cake walk in court to prove this guy was a dud of a father. All he did was work. I never even heard him mention his kids' names or how old they were. He lived in a million-dollar mansion all by his lonesome self, five bedrooms unoccupied except with the ghosts of what could have been had he favored fatherhood to workaholism. Gray streaks clouded his previously brown hair, a real shame for a man who had just recently turned forty.

"What do you mean, 'the way things are'?" I demanded to know. "What changed?" My fists were out of view and clenched in a ball of fury.

"Corporate told me something happened with your potential predecessor," he admitted. "You know, HIPAA and all that mumbo jumbo. The privacy stuff. Basically, I can't tell you." His words were panicked, and he knew he was screwing me. He hadn't looked me in the eye over the last thirty seconds.

"When would we have to move?" I demanded. "I absolutely deserve that much."

Bart shrugged. "We'd move you in a few weeks, I think."

"You're kidding me," my mouth was agape, and I placed my fists on each hip to convey the frustration. "What will I tell Mia? She's due in three weeks!"

"Well, you can tell her that this was always a possibility." He smiled at that last point.

Though he was technically right, that answer infuriated me. He had mentioned once or twice over the last month that timing could change, but to give me one measly day to decide on the future of my family was far too big an ask. I thought about my sons and what kind of upbringing we'd give them. In Denver, our life was better than good, but the promotion to Minneapolis would send us into another class entirely, and that meant financial security for my family. A seesaw played on a loop in my mind.

And so, with all the restraint in the world, I selected my next words carefully. "Fine," I said. "I'll give you an answer first thing tomorrow." I shook his hand, almost out of obli-

gation, and worked up the courage to say, "Thank you, sir."
What a lie. I hated this man's guts.

My first thought was to sprint back to my office and give
Mia a call at home, but I didn't want to frighten her.
Besides, she probably wasn't even home yet; she had to pick
up Francisco from daycare to head back home to Thornton,
the suburb in which we resided.

It was a delicate conversation as is, and she deserved to
hear about it in person. After all, this was our life and her
mind—and body—was already anticipating a significant
change on the horizon.

Chapter 2

Mia was born April twenty-fourth, 1990, in Albuquerque, New Mexico. Hers was a working-class family of immigrants. Her father, Ramon De Leon, originally from Hermosillo, Mexico, ran a convenience store in their homeland and that was his trade. Standing at a modest five-foot-six and a bit pudgy, Ramon had patchy facial hair on his round face and almost always sported his signature white cowboy hat. What he lacked in stature he more than more up for with resounding courage and an enormous heart. Mia's mother, Adriana, was also a first-generation immigrant from nearby El Alamito Buenavista. Although she had a pretty face and a well-defined jawline, her expression often carried an air of emotionlessness. When she caked her face in makeup, her body would glide through the desert almost like a ghost. The two, who could not have been more different, met in 1982 and hit it off right away, promising each other a better life than either had as kids in the state of Sonora. They had dreams of a big family they could provide for, and so they shared with one another their ambitions: a simple, not extravagant, but structural life in the United States of America. It was within their grasp, they decided. That is, if they made the leap together.

About two months after they first met, Ramon and Adriana began to plot their escape. It took months of planning. They needed food and they needed money. Rumor had it that the United States was cracking down on illegal aliens, especially those who came from beyond the southern edges of the border. They knew it would be an exceedingly challenging endeavor.

First, the two would need to marry. Being that Adriana's family, the Alonsos, were devout Catholics, her parents insisted they tie the knot in the church rather than go downtown and elope. And so, the De Leons and the Alonsos converged for one hot Hermosillo summer day. Ramon would later say this was the best day of his life, even if every single one of Adriana's family and friends questioned his intentions. She had many sisters who were skeptical of his every word. The wedding was special, no doubt peculiar, but to Ramon and Adriana it was just another checkmark off the list to get to the United States. They loved each other, and they loved the life they saw with one another. Being married made logical sense.

And so, within a year of becoming acquainted with one another, Ramon and Adriana set off on foot for their 175-mile journey to America. The couple's quiet exit from their homeland came as no surprise to Ramon's family in Hermosillo, as the De Leon clan was not too fond of him. He was a man of few words, quietly harboring the belief that the socioeconomic challenges facing Mexico were overwhelming. They looked at Ramon as a rebel and they were content when they came to terms with his leaving. Adriana's immediate family included nine brothers and sisters, and it would be days before any of them would even discern that she and her husband had left. To claim she and Ramon's departure was received well from the Alonsos would be a downright falsehood. Word around town, started somewhere within the Alonso compoumd, was that Adriana was kidnapped by her new husband. The cowboy took the angel, they said. Ramon warned her that friends of hers would turn their backs on her. But Adriana didn't care; she was hopelessly in love with her man.

The sack the two prepared for the ten-day journey included just enough rice, beans, and water to make it to the border. Adriana brought a bit of her art supplies as well. They had saved 1,500 pesos, the equivalent of just over 200 United States dollars, and Ramon had given the keys to his Hermosillo convenience store to his one dear friend, Felix, whom he confided in his master plan. He informed Felix to let people know not to worry, for he and his wife had gone on vacation to Punta Chueca. The Gulf of California was a premier spot to hang out on the beach, so folks around Hermosillo might've bought the excuse for a short time. But almost no one in town believed it. They still thought Ramon kidnapped the girl. Felix ended up with the shop keys, which was what he wanted all along, so everybody won.

Dust storms and extreme heat were the chief deterrents of the newlyweds' trek. Eventually, Ramon and Adriana made their way into the United States just east of Nogales, Arizona. It was summer, and the desert suffered through a long drought. From Nogales, they found a bus up north to Phoenix and decided to stay there for the time being. For weeks, they slept in the streets downtown, across the way from the forty-story Valley National Bank Center. Ramon got a job working as a janitor at a local high school, and Adriana soon became pregnant with their first child. She was so overwhelmingly sick with symptoms that she couldn't last the long days at the sign factory at which she was employed. The De Leons had no insurance, so they visited an immigrant doctor in Phoenix in secret.

Ramon spoke to Mexican co-workers of his newfound freedom but wisely neglected to mention he and his pregnant wife had crossed the border illegally. He knew better, for he had heard too many stories where folks like him were plucked from apartments in the middle of the night, detained, and sent back to Mexico. He befriended a fellow Sonoran, Luis Alvarez, and the De Leons were invited to his family's Christmas celebration in 1983 when Adriana was seven months pregnant. Ramon accepted, and the four of them—the De Leons and the Alvarezes, Luis and Silvia—headed east to Albuquerque, New Mexico to celebrate. It was the first time the De Leons had left Arizona since their entry to America.

Long story short, Ramon and Adriana loved Christmas 1983 in New Mexico so much they only returned to Phoenix so Ramon could do the respectful thing and quit his job at the high school in person. They had found a new home in which they would make their family. The Alvarezes were sad but said they'd visit frequently.

Besides, the De Leons were now 650 miles northeast of Hermosillo. No one could catch them if they tried.

Chapter 3

I'm not a perfect man, but I like to think I conduct myself in a matter that is commendable. I make good money and I have a great marriage. And yet, I have secrets. Secrets that could ruin my marriage, secrets that would force Mia to no longer believe I was a worthy husband or father.

I am referring, mostly, to my affinity for the bottle. I have other faults, but my drunkenness is my greatest. In a sadistic, cold-blooded sort of way, I love my secret life. Nearly every night without fail I get drunk, and no one will ever know. The hour or two after my wife and child doze off into slumber has become my favorite part of the day. Because she is the primary homemaker, Mia wakes up before I do and gets Francisco out of bed to feed him breakfast. We chalk up me sleeping past seven o'clock to the stresses of work. On any given day, I can slurp down a twenty ounce cup of black coffee and be out the door without a single Sharpe detecting my hangover.

Though Mia does know I enjoy a drink from time to time, the extent in which I am living is a total mystery to her. She doesn't know about the tremors. She doesn't know about the bottle I keep in my drawer in my Westco office reserved for the hard days. Of course, that's how it started. Over time, it has revolved into a daily routine and now I have to replenish that bottle in the desk every week. Mia is either extremely naïve or loves me to a fault. The more I look at her, the more I hate myself. She could do so much better.

My friends joke that I am the only man on the face of the Earth that would simultaneously drink Stranahan's whiskey with Coors Light beer. My older brother, Simon, who lives in Kansas City, calls me "a true Colorado man", attributing it to the fact that both Stranahan's and Coors, with their origins, trace back to the Centennial State.

My mother was a raging alcoholic. Her mother before her loved booze, too. This thing, this disease, is in the Sharpe family blood. I have known about this fact my whole life. The only difference is that I can function. No one at work knows about the ten drinks I have a day.

I don't want to tell Mia. I don't need to. If she notices my work or personal life suffers, I will be more than happy to admit it. In her opinion, Mom epitomizes the definition of "alcoholic", not me.

--

I grew up between the towns of Carver and Jordan, Minnesota. Each town is populated by several thousand and has a distinct small Midwest town feel to it. Jonathan Carver Parkway is the gateway to and from Carver and Jordan. The bluffs that lie between the two and the Minnesota River are beautiful. During the summer, tall, thick deciduous and coniferous trees dominate the horizon, creating a lush green landscape. The only areas devoid of trees are the blue waters of the lakes and river and the northern portion of the Minnesota Valley National Wildlife Refuge. The area looks more Appalachia than Midwest and is a hidden gem outside the Twin Cities.

Before you get into Jordan city proper, you cross Highway 169, which along with Highway 212 is the easiest way to travel west into South Dakota or east into Minneapolis. Jordan in recent years has become like the rest of them, welcoming you now with the iconic golden arches of McDonald's and a blue Holiday gas station sign you can see for miles from the west. The bones of the town's history are still there, but corporate America is catching up. Carver, on the other hand, swears off chains other than the Casey's gas station on the east side of downtown. That will change in the 2020s as the population skyrockets in the town nearest west of Chaska. Even today there are new construction neighborhoods popping up everywhere. I don't mean this in the Clint Eastwood "get off my lawn" way, but the area is changing. At least teachers now are advising students to only use one space after a period.

When I grew up, the towns were historical. Gorgeous yellow Chaska brick-clad buildings adorned both cities, and it's not an exaggeration to say their ambience evokes the feel of the early twentieth century. I remember descending into downtown Carver as a child and seeing the coolest looking old buildings. People don't want that anymore, I guess.

My family lived in a modest abode in the forest one half of a mile from the main road, Jonathan Carver Parkway. The home, which no longer exists, was made of distinct masonry. I remember obsessively running my fingers along the grayish, rigid mortar paste between the red bricks. Dad would often "time" us while we ran around the home, checking on his stopwatch to see if we had shattered the "world record". I believe it took about twenty "Dad seconds". In hindsight, it was a great way to tire out his kids before bedtime.

In front of the home stood a majestic white pine, the state tree of Minnesota. The backyard greeted you with maples that turned into a red hue when the latter days of September hit. Summers consisted of fishing for pinheaded sunfish and skipping perfectly shaped rocks off the often still blue waters of the river. One summer, my brothers and I were gifted a canoe. We would get in the car and drive to Horseshoe or Long Lake and navigate the bajeezus out of that canoe into every inlet on the lake. Our feet would become so muddy that my father would require we rinsed them off and towel-dried them before we could come back inside the house. Hiking was an activity Dad partook in especially. Now that I'm older I understand there were times he just wanted us to leave the house, to protect us from the horrors inside.

I knew at age six that Mom was an alcoholic. She bounced from job to job, offending one employer to the next. At one plant, she shouted at a group of Kenyans a racial slur; at another, in the presence of her superiors, she called her Italian nemesis Joe Delucci an "only good for cooking ziti wop". I think she forgot *The Sopranos* was fictional. Though we lived in a semi-remote forest outside of the Twin Cities, she had a big reputation. People didn't like her.

What really bothered me most about Mom was her penchant of violence. When she was drunk, she would throw objects or cuss at us. Simon, Spencer, and I were all victims of her brutality. Simon was once hit in the mouth with a glass plate. One of his molars popped out, and the plate shattered on the ground. A vivid childhood memory is etched in my mind, the three boys scouring the ugly black-and-white tiled kitchen floor in search of Simon's missing tooth. I think only one of us stepped on glass, thank God.

Poor Dad was a hardworking mechanic, and he knew people around and between the towns were whispering about his wife. I could not imagine the abuse he took. Once when I was in a Philadelphia pub with Mia, some frat bro poked fun of her Mexican accent and told me, "She was lucky she was hot." I clocked him in the face and was just fine with being permanently banned from the joint. That abuse was so minor compared to what my father went through. Day after day, the townspeople jeered, and Mom's sickness worsened.

When Mom tried to get sober in the late 2000s, around the time I went to college, it was too late. She had already lost Dad. She had lost us. The last I had heard from her was a phone call a few years ago. She was living in northern Colorado in a remote cabin, and she had started a memoir about her life. In fact, in the span of a year, she told me she had gotten married, won the lottery, been arrested for burglary, and began writing her autobiography. Mom claimed she had kicked the booze on the phone, but I could tell based on the rapid pace in which she was speaking that she had to be on some substance. She'd traded one addiction for another. I wondered if painkillers had claimed another victim. Maybe she had hopped aboard the Oxycontin train like so many during that time. Her new husband, whose name escapes my mind, was a California hippie with a drug dealing conviction. When Mom revealed to Simon her new husband's identity, my brother did enough internet research to write a dissertation on the guy. That is how we found out about his perpetual legal troubles.

I had accepted the inevitable reality that the next phone call concerning my mother would likely be someone informing us of her passing. Well, it would be that or her asking for money. I wouldn't put it past her. It made me mad she didn't even know the name of her own grandchildren. If we spoke for fifteen minutes on the phone a few years ago, I would be willing to wager less than thirty seconds were devoted to me or my family. Mom is self-absorbed. Mia had told me tales of Adriana's unrelenting fidelity to her family, and I was jealous. I never had that.

At this juncture, the only way in which my mom plays a significant role in my life is through rationalizing my own drinking. I may have an addiction, but at least I didn't abandon my family like my mother. While I do undoubtedly have issues with alcohol, I can, at the very minimum, say that I haven't irreparably damaged my marriage to Mia. Mom both abandoned her family and destroyed her marriage to Dad. She walked out. I'm not planning on doing that. She is the real drunk, not me.

I'm obviously biased because I grew up there, but I want my family to move to Minnesota. Westco's headquarters is stationed thirty minutes from where I grew up, in the suburb of Edina. I could raise my sons to be fans of the Twins, Timberwolves, Vikings, and Wild, not the Rockies, Nuggets, Broncos, and Avalanche. We could be Gophers and not Buffaloes. Heck, maybe we could even live out in the sticks and skip rocks and fish like I did. Life would be so much simpler, and perhaps I'd even put the bottle down there.

Chapter 4

Times were tumultuous in their first decade in America, but eventually the De Leons settled in a little three-bedroom rambler in the West Mesa neighborhood of Albuquerque. Ramon and Adriana were now living the American Dream thanks to Luis Alvarez and a little hard work.

Ana was born two months after the De Leons moved east, and her birth proved to be a financial burden for the family. In his adult life, Ramon knew of one trade—that of the convenience shop owner. After working as a day laborer and janitor for a few years, the stubborn man finally saved up enough money to purchase an Allsup's convenience store in Albuquerque. To fund the venture, he had to sell almost everything the family had, including jewelry, Adriana's art, and a fair share of his pride. One possession Ramon held onto was his old Polaroid camera. It was selfish, sure, but he knew Adriana would be crushed if he pawned it, so he kept the picture taker.

Though she always supported his goals, Adriana took issue with his idea to own the convenience shop. She begged him to reconsider the purchase in their native tongue, "*No puedes hacer esto, Ramon.*"

Adriana explained that they had left Mexico, and Ramon could do anything in this free country. Why would he settle for the same job he had down south?

The man knew what he had to do for his growing family, and despite his wife's plea he decided to send the check for the down payment. The bank called and let him know it wasn't enough, as there was another buyer interested in putting down more cash. Ramon sulked, knowing his dream was gone for the time being. So, he went back to day laboring and saving. It was then that the magic of he and Adriana's marriage started to plummet. She was pregnant with Mia, their second daughter, but the two of them couldn't have been further away from each other spiritually. Their initially strong bond in faith began to fizzle, and they stopped talking about important things with one another. Adriana was really upset that Ramon had gone behind her back, and almost as upset that his dream could not be fulfilled for the time being. Long, drawn out morning conversations under the rising sun on the front porch with hot cups of coffee soon became passing glances.

This trend continued well past Mia's birth. Mia would later say that as a youth, she would take advantage of the fact that she and Ana knew they could get away with mischief because it was clear their parents were not on the same page. If Ramon said she could not go play with her friends, Mia would get the affirming answer she needed from her mother. It was a game of cat and mouse of sorts, and the kids always got what they wanted.

One foggy November evening, when Mia was two, Ramon came home drunk and announced to Adriana that he had kissed another woman. The mistress was a friend of theirs named Therese. Adriana and Therese had been a part of the same quilt making class from the year prior and the former had invited the latter into the De Leon home on more than one occasion. Ramon explained that he and Therese bumped into each other at a West Mesa bar, had a drink together, and she leaned over and kissed him, and he reciprocated for a moment before pulling back. Adriana was understandably crushed. Not only did she feel betrayed by her husband, but also by another she considered to be a dear friend. Adriana told her husband, though, she was proud that he admitted his mistake. She asked Ramon how long the kiss was and if it meant anything. She wanted to know, in essence, if her husband had any feelings for Therese. Ramon vehemently denied this and reiterated his desire to continue forth with his marriage to Adriana. He told her he loved repeatedly.

The ensuing months proved to be very arduous. Any trust between the two had been effectively shattered. Whereas Ramon spent the following winter trying to make amends, Adriana wanted no part. She felt herself withdrawing, jumping out of her marriage and diving into a new world of books and television that she had neglected ever since the family came to America.

The two of them decided to give marriage counseling a shot. A way for them to be closer, they had both convinced themselves. The sessions—paid for out of pocket—helped. The therapist, also a Catholic, convinced Ramon to confess his sins. And so, Ramon went to his home parish, San Juan Catholic Church, and had a memorable confession with the priest, Father Pedro.

"Forgive me, Father, for I have sinned," he began. "My last confession was, you know, six months ago. I was unfaithful with my wife who is another woman, and I am sorry."

"Unfaithful with your wife who is another woman?" the priest replied.

"Oh no, I'm so sorry," Ramon explained. "My English is not so good. Forgive me for that, too."

"Were you unfaithful?"

"*Si.*" Ramon nodded through the confessional.

"I want you to say a rosary for your wife," Father Pedro gave him his penance, "and when you finish every decade, I want you to pray for your wife's healing throughout this. I want you to *really* pray for her. Make every Hail Mary count."

"What do you mean, *really* pray for her?" Ramon asked. "Isn't that what I already do?"

"You do not feel bad for yourself anymore. None of this slouching. I see you through the confessional. Stand up straight," the priest demanded. "Honor her. Cherish her. Whether you feel it or not, you owe it to her. You vowed in front of her, in front of Christ, and your community, for better or for worse, to be there until death do you part, did you not?"

"I did."

"So be a man about it." Ramon was impressed by the priest's candor.

"Thank you, Father." The confessor folded his hands. "*Gracias, gracias.*" He prayed the Act of Contrition with purpose in every word.

Father Pedro smiled. "Your sins have been absolved, my son."

"Amen."

Ramon walked out of the church feeling like a brand-new man. He went home, kissed Adriana, and fell to his knees and sobbed. He begged for her forgiveness. She said she needed time to exonerate him, and he understood. He doubled down on his promise to her, that he didn't desire anything else in the world but marriage to her.

This became Ramon's new mission in life, to win back the woman he fell in love with all those years earlier in Hermosillo. Meanwhile, little Mia had just turned three, and even in her young age she noticed a change in her *papa*. He showed up every night for dinner, at six o'clock sharp, and became a more present father and husband. After three long, dreary years, Adriana gave her blessing to Ramon to purchase a convenience store. The search took only a few days. The prospective store was an Allsup's. The only concern would be falsifying documents to obtain the store. Ramon was not a legal American citizen, so he had a friend of Luis Alvarez draw him up a fake identification. He also purchased a 9mm pistol for self-defense. Ramon knew it was illegal to own one as an immigrant. Despite the happy front, he was anything but innocent.

The man was simultaneously overjoyed, nervous, and content. Uncoincidentally, he went back to church that same day. Through the striped confessional, Ramon recognized Father Pedro's voice.

"*Padre, padre!*" Ramon shouted. "I know I'm not supposed to say who I am, but I confessed months ago to my infidelity." Typically reserved, his voice echoed throughout the halls of the church.

Father Pedro, also a man of few words, could not have been more unprofessional. He burst out laughing, and Ramon sat frozen in the wooden chair. It wasn't the introduction Father expected, and it was not the reaction Ramon expected. "My son, why have you come in here and uttered your past sins? Don't you know the Lord has already absolved you of them?"

"*Si, si, padre*," Ramon replied, "but my wife, she's happy again."

"That's wonderful," Father Pedro said. "What have you come to confess today?"

"I just came to tell you—"

The priest interrupted Ramon, "So nothing to confess? Just to gloat?"

"*Si.*"

"It sounds as though your work has just begun."

"What do you mean?" Ramon asked.

"It means confession is the only the beginning to the way. You must lead this life every single day. Christ calls us to do this. Now go, my son," the priest said. "Go and keep up the good work. And, sir?"

"*Si*?" Ramon stopped in his tracks.

"Come back when you have sins to confess," Father Pedro laughed. "This is a confessional, after all."

"God bless you, *Padre*."

Chapter 5

That Wednesday afternoon dragged on after that exchange with Bart, and I spent most of it pacing in my office wondering how the heck I was going to broach this subject with my pregnant wife. I sensed that she would not entertain the idea of it at all, even when I stressed the urgency of our resolution. We reached all our decisions fifty-fifty, and the feeling to me was that we'd most certainly disagree on this one. If we even got to the point of resolution, that is.

On a record player Mia gifted me several years ago, I played several classical musicians I liked—Chopin, Tchaikovsky, to name a few—to relax my body as I prepared myself for one of the tougher conversations I would ever have in my life. A co-worker I liked, Kenneth, a member of Westco's business development team, stopped by my office to chat Broncos football for a little bit, and that killed some time. He may have been focused on whether signing a good quarterback was a top offseason priority, but I couldn't stop thinking about Mia.

Kenneth left, and I remembered the handle of Colorado whiskey I hid in my bottom drawer. I rolled over to the desk, grabbed the old brass handle, and yanked it all the way open. Hidden underneath loose plastic bags and an outdated framed photo of Mia and twelve-month-old Francisco was the glass bottle.

I swiped it and quickly lowered the shades that led from my office to the main area of Westco's headquarters. I presumed no one was watching, but it didn't hurt to be safe. I was all alone. After screwing off the lid slowly, I pressed the bottle against my lips and took a swig. Then, I sipped another ounce. I took three gulps of the whiskey before I knew it, and the burning sensation lingered in my throat. I looked at the digital clock on my desk—ten minutes past two—and did a quick calculation of my blood alcohol content. I could drive at five o'clock, I convinced myself.

Ten minutes went by, and that bottle lingered in my hand. *Just one more sip*, I thought. I repeated the routine from minutes earlier and found myself two swigs deeper. I had drunk more than six ounces at this point, and knew I was doomed. No way could I drive home at five.

As is the tradition, my heart throbbed at the thought of someone entering my office. I staggered over to the door and locked it, pretending to be consumed by the rigors of work. It was all a lie, of course. I grabbed my headphones and stared blankly into my laptop. Surely no one would bother me now.

I was uncharacteristically distracted on my drive home that day, cutting other motorists off and seldom paying attention to what was going on north of downtown on Interstate 25 towards our home in Thornton. To further hammer that sentiment home, I was pulled over in my Acura halfway through my commute. My heart sank as I realized the potential insurance ramifications, and I decided to be completely transparent with the police officer.

Crap, I've been drinking, I remembered. Surely, the consequences were not limited to just insurance at this point. I did the math in my head: I had six drinks about four hours earlier. Surely, my BAC was more than the legal limit, .08. My calculations deduced I was treading right around that number. Thank the good Lord it was five in the evening and not ten.

Just like out of a Hollywood film, the cop, donning sunglasses, tapped on my window lightly with his baton. I rolled down the sucker and he began to speak, "License and registration, sir." He could not have been out of the police academy for more than a few years; in fact, he looked physically like one of the interns at Westco, Todd, a racquetball buddy of mine.

I feigned a smile and handed him the documents he requested. Compliance wasn't typically how I dealt with authoritative figures, but I knew now wasn't the time for more trouble as my conversation with Mia was at the foreground of my thoughts. Not only that, but I was still a little tipsy.

He glanced over my papers and continued, "Do you know why I pulled you over today?"

"Recklessness?" I asked.

The officer nodded his head. "Not only were you speeding and weaving through traffic best you could, but you failed to signal any turn through the last half mile," he said, motioning back towards the downtown Denver skyline. "I know this because I've been following you. I got you going 78 in a 65."

My mind was so consumed with my drunkenness, my imminent conversation with my wife, I had not even noticed there was a squad car behind me the last thirty seconds! "Sorry, officer," was all I could muster. It was good enough for him not to notice.

He bobbed his head again and headed back to his Town Car. Being that it was February and a tad chilly, I rolled the window back up to avoid the piercing wind of the Colorado winter. I sat there wallowing in my pain as I saw hundreds of other vehicles drive by. I could be in Thornton by now. A few minutes went by, and the officer hadn't come back yet. Was this a bad omen?

Slowly but surely, the cop waddled his way up to my car, tapped on the window again, and I rolled it back down. "Mr. Sharpe, how many speeding tickets have you had in your life?"

I was not in the emotional state for games. "I don't know?" I shrugged my shoulders before answering, "Five? Six?"

He nodded. "Six by my count. Makes sense a man your age and driving condition would've received that many by now."

"Excuse me?" I groaned. "'A man my age'? Do you have any idea how 'old' I am?" I felt somewhat sensitive about the fact that I looked a bit older than my age because I smoked a pack a day throughout my twenties, and the longevity of my tobacco use took a toll on my face, causing wrinkles in some spots. Well, that and my drinking. I quit cigarettes about three years ago for good when Mia's mother Adriana gave me a hug and politely asked if I had just returned from the casino. The odor was that bad apparently. Cigarette smoking had become taboo in the 2010s, and I told myself I'd get one of those new vape machines if the urge to smoke ever returned. Thus far, it hadn't. Although, this incident with the cop might drive me to purchase one.

The officer laughed. "Older than me, that's for sure," he remarked. "What do you think? I saw your license. You're a little too old to be racking up speeding tickets. Anyway, here's another one for your collection!" He tore off his newest ticket from his little notepad and handed it to me. He chuckled some more as he made his way back to his squad car.

I was enraged. As much as I'd like to say I'm a model citizen, my anger towards folks in charge has always gotten me into a bit of trouble. Once during my childhood in Minnesota, I confronted a teacher, expressing my dissatisfaction simply because she didn't give me an A for what I perceived to be the best essay in the class. Another time in my youth, a baseball coach and I exchanged cuss words merely because I complained about being benched. Never mind the fact that I struck out four times in the game and caused two errors. In hindsight, I was completely wrong each of these times, and I tried to make peace with my inner anger. Sometimes it just seemed to come out of me.

The last thing I needed at that moment was a speeding ticket. I was so angry heading home I nearly crashed into a parked Lincoln Continental kitty corner from my home. The man in the driver's seat, grasping a newspaper or a comic book of some sort, panicked and started up the car. He thought I was going to plow into him, and part of me wished I would have. My life was slowly beginning to unravel.

Chapter 6

Ramon continued working hard at the neighborhood All-sup's, and eventually became known as "*hombre de la tiendita*", which translates to "little shop man" in English. He played every role in the place, including owner, manager, and janitor. He was as hardworking as any man in America. This was his dream, what he had set out to accomplish a decade earlier crossing the border with Adriana. In 1995, she became pregnant with their third child, and the couple found out at the immigrant doctor's ultrasound that they were having yet another girl. Ramon was thrilled; he always enjoyed being a girl dad and after Mia, his second, was born, he never really pictured himself as anything but a father to sweet little girls.

Adriana would have preferred a boy but understood God wanted another De Leon girl among them. She wanted to see Ramon with a son, to teach him to play sports like baseball and *futbol*. Instead, he'd have another daughter who would recognize him every December underneath the fake Santa Claus beard or dress him up and put makeup on him as a rite of passage of every daddy-daughter relationship.

It was in those days that Ramon and Adriana dreamt of a triumphant return to Mexico. The visit would only be for a short while, they had convinced themselves, and then the

De Leons would come back to their rightful home in Albuquerque. They knew, underneath it all, that the risk of deportation was not worth it, and so they opted to stick it out in the States. Not a soul from Hermosillo knew where they lived in America. Word had reached back to their hometown, probably because Ramon told Felix in confidence, that they now lived in the free country. Adriana often was sad that she could not communicate with her relatives back in El Alamito Buenavista. She would tell Ramon she was homesick and lonely, that all her friends in quilt making class didn't want to get involved so they dropped her from their lives. Apparently, the onus was more on Ramon than Therese during their two-second affair.

Adriana explained to Ramon that she felt as though her world revolved around changing diapers, teaching the girls, and watching old films.

Though Adriana had given her blessing, she eventually—and honestly—warmed up to the idea of Ramon owning the convenience store. It was a modest life, sure, but it gave them everything they needed: food on the table, a roof over their heads in the West Mesa area, and most importantly, money to care for their children. Never again would they have to worry about mud floors or storms ripping off their roof. They lived in a primarily Hispanic neighborhood, where nine out of every ten residents spoke Spanish at home. In some strange way, it did feel like Mexico to Ramon and Adriana. Their daughters were certainly adjusting well to their surroundings, making friends and excelling in elementary school and preschool. Though it was a tumultuous journey there, life was relatively good for Ramon and Adriana.

--

One day in the mid-1990s, months after the De Leons' third daughter was born, a white man sprinted inside the Allsup's that Ramon owned. He wore a black cowboy hat, suit, tie, and sunglasses. The shades were especially curious, simply because it was fifty degrees and cloudy in Albuquerque that day. Ramon noticed that oddity and chalked it up to the man acting *loco*. He thought nothing of the situation initially, but when the man huffed and puffed, Ramon paused his sweeping for a moment. He gazed over at the outsider and noticed the holster on the man's hip. He was packing heat.

The stranger approached Ramon and whispered, "Where's the ATM?" There was a rasp in the man's voice. He sounded like a cowboy in an old Western film and resembled one. He had a long, wispy mustache with unkempt ends.

Ramon, perhaps a little nervous due to his inexperience of feeling uneasy in his store, pointed shakily in the direction of the cash machine. The strange man walked around, pushed a few buttons on the computer, and the ATM dispensed one bill. He walked back over to Ramon and, in a surprising twist, passed him by. The man opened the door to leave the Allsup's, and the broom in Ramon's hands shook. Something felt a little bit off.

Hours later at nightfall, when Ramon was spinning the keys of his shop on his index finger, ready to lock up, he heard a loud crash coming from the back of the store. He hadn't heard anything like it before, so he was nervous. He recalled the sketchy man from earlier in the day and assumed the worst, that the man was trying to break in. As he tiptoed the perimeter, he prayed to God for his safety. He thought of his children, especially baby Maria Elena, and Adriana. After what seemed like an hour, he reached the back wall of the store and whipped his head around the corner to capture a glance. What he saw was a towering fourteen-point elk that had to have been about ten feet in length. The wild mammal was illuminated by the spotlight in the rear of the store. Though only Ramon's head was visible to the animal, who was looking to the east, the elk slowly moved his head in the direction of the man. Before he could disappear, the beast made eye contact with Ramon. He stumbled when the behemoth identified him with his yellow-brown eyes, and suddenly his whole body was exposed in front of the wall. Ramon thought it to be strange there would be an elk so close to civilization, as he had never seen one this nearby. He knew they lived in the Sandia Mountains and further up north in the state, but never expected to spot one in the heart of Albuquerque. The majestic creature was extremely muscular, and its brown upper body was a stark contrast to the rest of its tan frame.

Eye contact between the two beings lingered for about ten seconds; the elk had a keen sense of sight. Ramon had read quite some time ago in *National Geographic* that the best way to avoid an elk attack was to slowly back away until you were out of its sight. The man's whole body was exposed, so he moved away at a leisurely pace from the elk and back behind the wall.

Once out of the elk's vision, Ramon De Leon sprinted to his car and turned over the key. He tried to catch his breath and take a moment to process what he had just seen.

His palms were sweaty, and his breathing was labored. As he turned east on to the main road, Ramon came parallel with the animal.

The elk, having not moved an inch, stared as Ramon cruised into the night.

--

The very next day, the same man—donning the same coal black cowboy hat, suit, tie, and sunglasses—entered the same Allsup's in the same speedy manner. Ramon again found it to be peculiar but gave no extra thought as the man scurried over to the ATM machine upon entering the store. He may have needed cash two days in a row. Ramon didn't see a problem with it.

While the owner was checking out one of his regulars, Don, he noticed out of the corner of his eye the white man's holster. Ramon got a shiver down his spine, and wondered just like the day before if the man would use it.

Ramon thought to himself that he ought not to judge and that there was only one who could. He decided to shift his attention back to Don, to let his mind escape the judgement his brain had furiously latched itself onto.

In all honesty, he just couldn't forget the stranger. Ramon suddenly remembered his own self-defense mechanism, the 9mm pistol he had purchased. The weapon was kept locked in a safe at his feet underneath the cash register. While reaching for the pack of Lucky Strikes Don had requested, Ramon slyly knelt to unlock the safe. He punched in the code, 0708, commemorating his wedding anniversary with Adriana from more than a decade earlier.

He twisted the door open and placed the pistol on the shelf directly below the register. It was preloaded. He flicked the safety off. He was prepared for any sort of confrontation.

When he arose, Don was still talking and now the white man stood directly behind him. Boy, Ramon wished Don would shut up. The De Leon patriarch loved Vicente Fernandez as much as the next, but to stand there and talk about his latest album for five minutes was difficult to endure, and not just because of the scary figure situated behind him. Ramon gulped and handed Don his cigarettes.

"*Gracias, mi amigo,*" Ramon said as he finally shuffled his acquaintance to the side. The man in the cowboy hat approached him, glared over at Don, who was slowly sauntering out of the store, and shuffled his feet a bit. This muddled Ramon. It appeared as if the man was waiting for Don to leave.

Once the bell rang to signify Don's exit, the cowboy casually glanced around to confirm the two were alone. With his right hand, Ramon held onto the butt of the pistol. The sketchy man noticed something was amiss, and his left hand swung near his holster.

"How can I help you, sir?" a shaky but firm Ramon asked.

"I'm going to tell you how things work around here," the man swung his body ninety degrees so Ramon could once again see the holster.

"Oh?" Ramon felt the beads of sweat from his forehead fall slowly down his nose and cheeks. Something had to give.

"You're a man of God, I take it?" He motioned to the hanging cross draped around Ramon's neck and shoulders. The terrified man nodded.

"You're aware of the parable of the lost sheep?" Ramon bobbed his head up and down once more.

The man, still wearing his sunglasses—presumably, to hide his identity—told the story anyway, "It's in the holy gospel according to Matthew. A shepherd has 100 sheep, and one goes missing. He goes and looks for the lone sheep and tells the other ninety-nine to stay put. When he brings back the one sheep, he praises him. The moral of the story is God welcomes back sinners."

"I know the story." Ramon stayed calm despite the obvious hostility. Lost in all this eeriness was that the man in the black hat was impressed with Ramon's English.

"The point is, you're going to give me all the money you have in the world," the man continued. "Everything in the register, and everything you can give me on a card. If you don't, I will kill you. When I leave—and go astray, like in Matthew—I will ask for God's forgiveness, and he will welcome me into heaven."

"There's one problem with your 'story', friend," Ramon retorted.

The man with the holster laughed. "And what's that?" he huffed.

"You're committing sin knowing you will have to beg for forgiveness," Ramon continued. "That's premeditation. God will not open the gates for you so easily."

"And how do you know that?"

"I believe."

The man in the sunglasses huffed. "You believe in what you know, not in what is the truth. God knows the truth. I know the truth."

"How do you know the truth?" Ramon challenged him. "To come into *my* shop and say these things. You're comparing yourself to Him."

"The truth is you're an illegal."

Sweat beads dribbled from the shop owner's forehead, slow like molasses in January. "You have no evidence of that, *machista.*"

"Your English is pretty good, I'll give you that, *Rico.*" The man tipped his cowboy hat. "Pretty good for an illegal."

"You don't know that."

"I do."

"It does not matter what you think you know about me," Ramon spoke softly. "I am not giving you the money. This is my shop, and you will not harass me here."

"Well then, there's only one thing to do," the man smiled, and pulled out the gun from his holster. At the same time, Ramon revealed his 9mm in his hand.

The two men pointed their guns at one another.

Chapter 7

"I want a cigarette," was the first thing I said to Mia the moment I walked into our home. We bought the three thousand square foot home back in 2013. It was nice, furnished well, but chiefly we made the purchase five years ago to own the surrounding land. The house was just a nice attached bonus. A creek lay about one hundred yards behind our modest ten foot by ten foot deck. The city would never build back there, and so we had planned on staying awhile in the home until we outgrew it. Or, that is, until we moved to Minnesota, which was suddenly an option.

Mia's eyes shot at me, then Francisco, and then she mouthed words at me so the boy would not hear.

"Daddy! Daddy!" Francisco shouted. "What's a sig-ner-ut?"

His mispronunciation filled me with a profound sense of guilt. I picked him up and said, "Sorry, son. Don't listen to Daddy. He had a bad day. Say, did I hear someone was a good boy today at daycare?"

Immediately, Francisco's attitude changed. That's the spectacular thing about having a two-year-old boy, that he's always on your side no matter what, and he loves you unconditionally when you walk through the door. "They" might say dogs are man's best friend, but clearly "they" haven't met a two-year-old boy.

Francisco was the son I didn't deserve. He was a sweet, scrawny toddler with olive skin and dark brown hair—a nice mixture of Mia and me. He was in the eightieth percentile of height, said his pediatrician, and stood nearly three feet tall. He eagerly awaited the call to join the preschool ranks, going as far as asking us to purchase him "school books". I asked him one morning what exactly a "school book" was, and he said a school book was what Dora the Explorer carried in her backpack.

Mia knew something was up after the sarcastic comment. Her normally warm face became icy and her eyebrows arched. "Is something the matter, Scott?"

"Yeah," I confessed. I turned my head the other way to avoid her smelling the liquor on my breath. "At some point, when Francisco is down, we need to talk."

"Talk about what?" she tried to whisper so our son could not hear. "Urgent?"

"Work wants a decision by tomorrow," I muttered.

Her brown eyes grew in size. "What? Okay, this is officially *loco*."

She instructed Francisco to go make busy for a bit in the playroom, and our two-year-old followed his mother's orders. He usually did, especially if it meant he could play with the stuffed rhinoceros he affectionately named Gray. Shockingly, he christened the toy almost immediately after learning his color wheel.

"You're too good to me." I smiled.

She crossed her arms and rolled her eyes. "Start talking."

"Well," I began, "Bart told me that he needs an answer about Minnesota first thing tomorrow morning. He didn't delve into details, but he did mention there's some sort of HIPAA reason behind it."

Mia appeared confused. "I thought you had more time?"

"So did I," I returned.

"You know what you have to do," she answered.

I sincerely did not in my heart of hearts, but I understood my wife's point. "I don't know, Mia. It's a big move and we love it here in Denver—"

Her eyes began to well up. "You have to take it, Scott."

Again, Mia was too good to me. This meant she'd have to give up her life, her friends, just so we could consider a slightly cushier life in the place I grew up.

"Should I ask for more money?"

"That would be helpful," she said. "We'd need a lot for moving. Have they said if they'd pay for moving expenses?"

"They won't," I answered.

She shrugged and said, "I say ask for more money. You never know."

"I don't know if he has the authority, but I will."

Half that night, I tossed and turned not knowing how Bart Thompson would react to my demand. I woke up the following morning especially early and kissed my wife for more than a few seconds. I knew in her hands she held the Bible, and she was clasping her rosary. Unlike most mornings of the last two months, Mia did not inform me of her newest nightmare, and I did not pretend to play dream therapist. There was a calm but eerie presence that day in our bed. We may not have uttered more than ten words to each other since we woke. Our words were spoken in the passionate kisses we planted on one another. I sat up, walked into the shower, and stood there for a second as the water heated. I had an important day ahead of me. Was I making the right decision?

I hopped in the car twenty minutes later and set course going south on Interstate 25 for downtown Denver. To my east, I could see the outlying suburbs that welcomed orange sunrises, and to my west stood the frosty Rocky Mountains that showcased premature sunsets. Because it was February, the peaks in the distance were sprinkled with milky snow and it seemed an omen for the icy reception I could receive from my boss.

Colorado is a lovely place to live, but at the end of the day family will always bring you home. My brother Spencer and his wife lived in the suburbs of the Twin Cities, as did my father. Having never resided more than a six-hour drive from her parents, Mia was a bit anxious. But I knew we'd make it work.

--

Bart Thompson got straight to the point once we met. It was just past eight o'clock and I had strolled into his office mere moments after I saw him make his way into his Westco abode.

"Sharpe," he said as he unfastened the top button of his blue blazer. "I must admit, I did not think you'd be in here this early."

"Well, sir," I began. "To commence this whole conversation, I'd like to say thank you to you, Bart."

His eyes widened. "What for, Sharpe?"

"For the opportunity, of course," I answered. "When I joined Westco a number of years ago, I never did believe I would make it this far in the company. When Mia and I got married and I needed a job, you were there for me, Bart. I never want you to forget that—"

My boss interrupted, "It sounds an awful lot like you're going to reject the offer, Sharpe."

"On the contrary, Bart," I assured him, "I would like to take you up on the offer. On one condition, of course."

Bart's eyes beheld a blatant, intentional look of sourness. "What condition is that?" He laughed.

I looked him dead in the eye, just like I'd rehearsed with Mia the night before, and declared, "I'd like a raise."

His confusion increased tenfold. "How much more? For the record, this is not something I had considered and don't mean for it to be an open debate."

I cleared my throat and responded, "$30,000. You know, to make it a round $250,000 per year."

Bart grimaced and stood up suddenly, clutching one side of the chair. I could see his white knuckles, a classic sign of frustration. I knew I had him roped in. "You have gonads, Sharpe. I'll give you that. But my answer is no."

I was not about to let up on my master plan. I thought about Mia; I considered Francisco and our soon-to-be second son. My eyes honed in further on his. "You need me, Bart. You would not have asked me to take this promotion if you didn't need me to take it. You know I've had the best numbers of anyone in the Denver branch and—"

His cold eyes lingered on me, and he almost whispered, "Enough."

But I would not back down. "Bart, I know what goes around in here, and I promise I'd never in a million years sell out your—"

"What do you mean 'what goes in here', Sharpe?" I blushed, realizing it was imprudent to bring up the fraud and mobster connections of Westco's higher ups.

"Nothing," I gulped. "Nothing."

His face turned beet red. The man, in the firmest way, demanded, "Get out of my office, Sharpe. Now." He pointed towards the door to shoo me out. I obliged.

I sheepishly walked back to my office, knowing full well I should not have brought up the insurance policy fraud and mob interrelation. I felt that even more so when Bart walked over to my office shortly afterward and swung the door open. He slammed it shut behind him and closed the shades, like I would when hosting my solitary drinking parties.

"You're going to pay for what you said," he glared at me. "You don't get to talk crap about this company. Especially when you yourself have benefitted."

I felt a shiver run down my spine. The exchange began to feel like a threat, and I didn't know what my boss meant by the threat.

"Pay—pay for it," I gasped. "What does that mean?"

"It means you can't come into my office and talk about your stupid claims. And that's what they are, Sharpe: *claims*. There's no reason anyone would truly believe what you say." He lowered his index finger, which was pointed at me, and sauntered out of my office.

"Bart, I know I benefitted," I said, "but, but—those things were minor—"

"You mean borrowing money from Satrione at the casino and drinking at work?" Bart's face turned almost purplish, and my heart sank. "Don't think I don't know. If you bring me down, I am most certainly taking you with, you prick."

Chapter 8

Ramon considered his family as he faced off with the man in front of the counter. He had not come this far just to go down like this in an Allsup's convenience store. He remembered Adriana, Ana, Mia, and Maria Elena, and all their smiling faces. He needed to be there for his family. In that moment, perhaps the most important of his life, he chose them. So, he squeezed the trigger, point blank, and the two men gasped simultaneously.

The sketchy man dropped his own firearm. He grabbed his chest and uttered, "Not like this." He fell to the ground, and a pool of gore slowly encircled his expiring corpse. It was a gruesome scene.

Immediately, panic reared its way into Ramon's cranium. *I have just killed a man*, he acknowledged. *What now?* If he called the police, they would undoubtedly raise questions about his citizenship. He took in a few deep breaths, four seconds in and four seconds out. Knowing he had established his business under a fake passport with no problems from immigration, Ramon wanted to make the call himself. If anything, the problem here was the gun. It wasn't registered. What would he say if questioned? He knew what was right, what the good man would do, and so he picked up the phone.

Two Albuquerque squad cars showed up three minutes later. Ramon again panicked a bit and assured himself the false documents he had submitted were indistinguishable from legal papers. America was the problem, he had convinced himself. It wasn't his fault he was illegal.

He could see the two cops talking outside, and one of them lit a cigarette. The other, who sported an impressive goatee, stamped out his own butt and opened the door to the Allsup's. He covered his mouth immediately upon seeing the amount of blood on the floor. Ramon had been so caught up in covering his own tracks that he forgot just how gory the scene was.

"Did you call in this one?" The cop plugged his nose.

"*Sí*," Ramon nodded. "I am the one who shot him."

"What happened?"

"He came into my shop and pulled the gun out," Ramon stuttered. "I had no other choice, sir."

The cop's head swung around to the south side of the store. He noticed the video camera and motioned toward it. "Can footage corroborate your story?"

"Corroborate?" Ramon had never heard that word before.

"Can video camera footage," the cop said just a little too slowly, a little too condescendingly, "back up your story?"

"Yes." Ramon answered the question confidently. In the back of his mind, though, he knew his fingers rested on the gun as soon as the man approached the counter. Would that come back to haunt him?

The officer fiddled with his goatee a bit and asked, "Is the gun registered?"

"Yes." Ramon had no choice but to lie.

The policeman could not stop looking at the dead body that lay before him. Ramon had also never encountered quite a scene and was in shock. "I need you to come down to the station with me, make a statement."

The second cop walked in and had a similarly disgusted look on his face. "Let's close this place down," he demanded. "Bring our detectives in and wipe this scene." He walked over to Ramon, looked at him in the eyes for the first time, and said, "Okay buddy, chop chop. You're closed for now."

"I need to call Tito," Ramon pleaded. Tito was the night manager, the one who took over every evening when Ramon went home to his girls. "He might come in if I don't call."

The two cops shrugged and the one who entered first said, "Sure, that's all right."

After a short call with his employee Tito, who suddenly found himself with the night off, Ramon hopped into the first officer's Lincoln Town Car. He had never been in a police vehicle before, not even in Mexico. He marveled at how similar the interior matched the depictions in the movies. The prisoner partition, the glass, the way a cop's radio buzzed; it was all the same.

Once they arrived at the police station, Ramon was let out by the officer. "What's your name, sir?" the cop asked.

"Ramon," he stood up straight and told the truth. "Ramon De Leon."

"You own that place?" the officer inquired.

"Yes, sir."

"You want to step inside the station with me?" he asked. "We need to ask you some questions."

Ramon gulped. In his heart of hearts, he knew the possible ramifications of walking into that station. He might be sent back to Mexico. Surrounded by police and seeing no better option, Ramon nodded and followed the man inside. The cop opened the door for him and led him down a hallway. The more progressively they moved inside, the darker the corridor became. It was freaky. After a left turn, Ramon heard what sounded like a machine press running behind a closed door. At at the end of the hallway, there was a lightbulb on the ceiling, and the police officer grabbed the dangling string beneath it. The sticker on the outside of the freshly illuminated entryway read "Interrogation Room". The lead officer urged Ramon to go inside.

"Ramon De Leon?" There was another police officer already in the room seated, and he positioned a chair in the corner with the room's light shining on the lone spot. Ramon gulped again.

"*Si*, that's me," the timid man replied. Ramon's demeanor shifted wholly as he anticipated an ugly interrogation. "I am working on my English. It is getting better."

The detective ignored the sentiment. "Ramon, did you fire your gun at the victim?"

"Yes, but, but—he had one, too." Ramon's voice stuttered as the shock continued. "He came after me."

"But were you, or were you not, the only one to shoot?"

"Yes. Yes, I was."

Just then, a bald man burst through the door. He was in street clothes, but Ramon had to assume he was also a police officer because of the way he entered. The bald, pudgy man pointed at Ramon and whispered something to the detective.

"All right, all right," the detective muttered. He looked at Ramon and almost sarcastically said, "De Leon, at first glance the video evidence showed you were firing on self-defense. The victim had indeed pulled the gun an instant before you. That video right there may have saved you the rest of your days. You're a free man because of it."

Ramon was miffed by the detective calling the white man the "victim". He knew he was the one who had pulled the trigger, but in reality Ramon should have been the one called the "victim". The man held up *his* store, after all.

"Like I said, sir, I didn't do anything wrong," Ramon said, scratching his beard. "So can I leave now?"

"And like *I* said, you're a free man."

"*Gracias*," The language barrier prevented Ramon from wholly grasping the sarcasm. Suddenly recalling that the police had inquired about the registration of his gun at the scene but omitted the question at the station, a smile crept on Ramon's face. He breathed a deep sigh of relief. It seemed like there may have been a miscommunication somewhere, and he silently thanked God for his good fortune. He vowed to get the weapon registered.

As the police led him out of the station through the dark corridor, they made small talk. Once they approached the light of the lobby, Ramon asked a question, "So I know, what was his name?"

"Whose name?" the cop huffed. "The guy you killed?"

Ramon expressed his dismay with a roll of the eyes but eventually nodded in agreement. "Yes. I will pray for him."

"His name was Bart Thompson, Sr., sir."

Chapter 9

Boozing wasn't my only secret. I withheld the knowledge of that incident. I certainly didn't tell Bart, either.

In 1996, my wife's father killed my current boss' father. Thank the Lord Ramon was not my dad, because Bart Thompson, Jr. might murder me.

A few years ago, when he was a bit saner, Bart and I were having a conversation at Jack's Burgers, which I now know is a Satrione family establishment, about our upbringings. It turns out that he had a father who was near and dear to him in his adolescent years. He told me all about the late Bart Thompson, Sr. and how heroic he was and how he had fallen prey to a government conspiracy and died. It was days, in fact, before Jr.'s eighteenth birthday.

I inquired during our exchange, "All right, all right. I'll bite. What does the government say was his *real* cause of death?"

"Apparently, he turned into some bank robber of the Wild West. I don't believe it still," Bart replied. "They say he was killed at a gas station in New Mexico. I think it was an inside job."

My heart was beating like a wild animal trying to escape my chest. I just knew it was the West Mesa Allsup's, and I just knew Ramon De Leon was the triggerman. I had to confirm.

"What part of New Mexico?" I asked confidently. "My wife is from Albuquerque."

"Yeah, that's where it was," he responded. "At an All-sup's. They said it was some nobody Mexican shop owner."

"That's too bad," I said to him. What else could I do? Reveal the skeleton in the closet?

In the years following, Bart never detracted in his view that the United States government murdered his dad, his hero. So, I had my secret.

Mia had talked about the incident some, but never revealed the name of the man her father killed. I never spoke to Ramon about it, either. I spent hours scouring the internet. Finally, I stumbled upon a news article that noted "a convicted bank robber was killed in Albuquerque by a local shop owner," and that was just a blurb from the *Albuquerque Journal*.

The internet made me nervous. Always a small fear of mine was that Bart Thompson would walk into Westco on any given day and strangle me to death. Someday, he would deduce the family tie. That day would either be the day I was arrested or fired. Both were in play now that I had discovered he was a blabbermouth.

I would potentially get arrested because of the loan I took from the Satrione family. Again, Mia didn't know about that either. I would get fired because I ratted them out. Can employees who get arrested still receive their severance?

--

Last winter, the Westco sales team took a "field trip" to a casino just west of Denver, to the famous Whitehawk Casino. I brought one hundred dollars, per Mia's request, and lost all of it before our noon lunch. I had more lost hands than drinks. We were slated to be there for many more hours, and I was officially out of cash. Boy, was I an idiot for thinking I could make one hundred dollars last all Monday.

Stressed and feeling hopeless, I waltzed over to the bar. I ordered a double shot of Stranahan's whiskey. I swallowed it in three seconds. I ordered another, and downed that one within ten seconds.

As I was walking back, I turned around. One more couldn't hurt, I figured. There's no way I would ever ask a co-worker for a loan when I was sober.

I sauntered back to the blackjack table, the scene of my lost cash. I peered around the circle to determine who would be the most likely to loan me some moolah. Dave, a buddy of mine in the tech department, would be the first to fork it over.

"Times are tough at my house, and I would normally say 'yes'," he explained to me, "but I just can't today."

"That's fine." I groaned as I realized Keith Stephens was the only other Westco employee at the table. He had the Satrione family connection, though, and the tie freaked me out.

I decided it was worth a shot. After all, I had no business bothering the other two men at the table. The first guy wore a trench coat and claimed he was in town from Beijing on business. No, I did not want to ask this stranger for money. The second fellow was an annoying truck driver named Raymond who would not stop discussing the most mundane details of his route to San Antonio, which he called "San Antone" like he was a born and raised citizen of the city. No thanks. "Hey, Keith," the liquor inside me called out to my last hope. "Could I talk to you for a second?"

He stood up once the hand had finished, and I followed him as he shuffled away from the blackjack section. It was almost as if he was already apprised of my proposition.

I said to him, "I've heard you're a man who knows how to get things."

Keith smiled. He appreciated my *Shawshank Redemption* reference. In his best Morgan Freeman impersonation, he uttered, "I've been known to locate items from time to time."

Now both of us were beaming. I continued, "I'd like to play more blackjack, if you catch my drift."

"Scott Sharpe," Keith gasped. "I didn't take you for a gambler."

"Tonight I am," I slurred.

"Follow me." He yanked the cuff on my checkered blue shirt, and I followed. We headed towards the elevator, and he selected the number three button once the door had closed. Keith whistled to himself during the seven second wait.

He and I proceeded toward a room on Whitehawk's third floor, and he knocked on the forest green door of Room 316. A bespectacled man in a shiny black suit that stood at least six-foot-five answered, and he grunted to acknowledge Keith's presence. I gulped.

Keith straddled the chair-like structure typically used for placing luggage. "Well, you may or may not know the drill, so listen up." He opened an envelope on the side table, licked his lips, and started peeling off one hundred dollar bills. I'd never seen so many Benjamin Franklin faces at once. There must have been fifty of them. I'd bet there were many more in the additional manila envelope peeking out of his jacket pocket, too. I was in awe. "First off, how much do you want?"

"I'll take ten g's." The liquor that had been dumped in my stomach called out the number.

"Now we're talking," Keith stated. "With ten percent interest. That means you owe eleven thousand. You in?"

"Yes."

"Now I'm not messing around, Sharpe," Keith wagged his first and fourth fingers at me. "You know who I'm with?" The man in the glasses and the glossy suit glared at me. His left hand clenched into a fist, repeatedly striking his open-palmed right fist to stress the solemnity.

"Yes."

"The boss doesn't take kindly to people being late on their payments." Though I was wasted, I noticed the grave tone in his voice. There was no messing around with the Satrione family; he knew it and I knew it. Keith continued, "You catch my drift, Sharpe?" The tall man lowered his glasses and stared at me.

"Yes," I said for the third time.

"You better have my money next Saturday," he whispered. "I'm not kidding. Put in on my desk at Westco in a manila envelope and label it 'Sharpe'."

I nodded. *Think of how much we could make from this*, I drunkenly thought. It was a slam dunk win.

Keith handed me the cash and shooed me out of the room. I hurried to the elevator, pressed the L button for lobby, converted the ten thousand to chips, and sprinted back to the blackjack table. I placed one thousand in chips, and the dealer, a Native American fellow named Pahayoko, distributed the cards. I showed a seven and a six, and Pahayoko was showing a nine.

The odds told me to hit, so I did, and the eight of spades appeared. I hit 21 on my first blackjack hand. My heart thumped as Pahayoko flipped his card, an eight, to total 17. I won the hand, and the table cheered. The dealer handed me one thousand more in chips.

I should have cashed out; I should have quit. The funny thing about alcohol is that it doesn't care about common sense. Common sense might as well be that friend you know and don't regularly converse with but still send a Christmas card to every December.

I put down one thousand in chips, drank another double whiskey shot of courage, and won again. Eventually, I was ten thousand up. As the day went on, I continued to win. The drinking never stopped.

After Westco's crew finished dinner, I sprinted to the roulette table. I realized I had no idea what time it was. The Nuggets, Denver's NBA team, were playing the Lakers on television, so I knew it must be at least seven o'clock in the evening. Other than that, I had no perception of time. With every drink, minutes melted away like a warm snowflake on the palm.

A few games into roulette, I stepped aside and ordered a tall glass of Stranahan's whiskey. No chaser necessary, I told the indifferent woman at the bar. There was a man arguing with a bartender about a wager they placed with each other on the Nuggets game, and I thought that was funny. I tried to imagine the pandemonium that would ensue in casinos once sports gambling attained legal status.

I noticed more and more that time of night the lack of co-workers around me. I was making new friends at every table; I believed at the time this was because I was the victor in many hands.

I ordered up another glass of Stranahan's, placed my ten thousand dollar bet on red and even, and a few seconds later the ball rested on red 12.

"I just won forty thousand!" I shouted, and the whole table erupted on my behalf. People I had met that evening were slapping high fives with me. I was the king of that room.

A few seconds later, as I placed one thousand in chips on black and second 12, the room faded into darkness.

--

I woke up with a throbbing head and an aching back. What happened? I grabbed my Rolex, adjusted my eyes, and checked the time. It was two-thirty in the morning. The Westco "field trip" had ended a few hours ago. I was contorted in a bathroom stall.

I searched my pockets. My cellphone indicated I had many texts and missed calls during my slumber. Among them was a message from my wife, asking my whereabouts.

That message came around nine o'clock in the evening. Since I had no more texts from her, I was willing to bet she had fallen asleep and not been too worried. My jean pockets were empty aside from the phone. Where was the money I had won? Oh, no.

As soon as I received a burst of energy, I pulled myself up and grabbed hold of the metal bar where the toilet paper roll laid. The bar snapped, and I was too drunk to care. I heard a man finish peeing and flush the urinal. It made me contemplate the length of time in which I was in the state. Being a handicap-friendly toilet, it was longer than usual, implying that it might have been a considerable amount of time since someone last, if at all, caught a glimpse of my legs. In these situations, men often resort to glancing at the floor beneath the next stall to ascertain whether they're alone or not. The presence of shoes become the telltale sign that you're not.

I swung open the bathroom door, proceeded down the left corridor, and was greeted by the unmistakable sounds of a casino: machine noises and the murmur of people engaged in conversation. The chaos served as a definitive marker for my whereabouts. Glancing around, I observed that the gaming floor wasn't necessary bustling with activity. Looking at my phone, I noted the time was two thirty-six. The smaller crowd made perfect sense given the late hour.

I proceeded through the floor and reached the hallway leading to the Westco room. Attempting to open the door, I jiggled the handle, only to find it locked. The stakes were high; my money was securely tucked away in my wallet in that room. Or at least I thought so. Memories of the night are blurred, shapes and colors blended together in a haze of uncertainty.

The pit boss would know. He or she had to. I went back on to the gaming floor, desperate to find the person in charge. I saw a woman wearing a collared black shirt with some sort of logo on it, and she had talked to two dealers in the preceding seconds. She was definitely in charge, so I flagged her down.

Cheyenne, her name tag read. She had to be the tallest woman in the place; at five-foot-ten, I was a clear three inches shorter than Cheyenne. She had straight brown hair, toned biceps poking out of her short-sleeved shirt, and wore a traditional Native American jacla turquoise necklace. I think she could have beaten me up in five seconds. I did not intend to find out.

"Hi," I started. "I need to get into one of the party rooms. My wallet is in there."

She sighed. "Why is the door locked?"

"I don't know," I admitted. "I got a little too into gambling and wasn't around when my group left."

Cheyenne laughed. "That's all?"

"I may have had too much to drink," I said. "Please, just help me."

"Wait here." The pit boss walked by me. She was still chuckling as she shuffled past me. I waited for a minute or two before it hit me; I had no idea how much money was in my wallet. It could be ten dollars or ten thousand. The last thing I remembered was watching Nikola Jokic and Jamal Murray, two Denver Nuggets players, connecting for a basket, and a man at the table declaring Murray would be a draft steal, that the Nuggets got a star at the seventh pick.

Even though he was Canadian, he was still welcome to play for Denver, the man said, and he began to belt out his best drunken rendition of the Canadian national anthem. When he began to sing, eyeballs from other tables swiftly turned his way. I remember it especially because the man was wearing a Jamal Murray jersey. I wondered if he was a family member of Murray. The basketball game being played would put the time between the hours of seven o'clock and half past nine. The real mystery was the length of time in which I passed out. Essentially, it could have been up to six hours. I didn't feel fully rested.

As I awaited Cheyenne's return, I noticed on the box score ticker that the Nuggets had won the game, and that the weirdo who loved the rookie was no longer in the vicinity of the tables.

The rude pit boss returned and said, "Come with me."

I brushed off my blue checkered shirt and complied. The brief moments during our journey to the party room seemed to stretch into a lifetime. As soon as Cheyenne opened the door, my eyes fell on my wallet. I gasped. It appeared as though my wallet was devoid of any contents. My clammy fingers instinctively reached for it, but before I could grasp it, Cheyenne forcefully swatted my hand aside. I mean it when I say she hit my hand with considerable force.

"I need to prove you are who you say you are first." Cheyenne stuck out her hand. In hindsight, I could've been any lunatic. I appreciated Whitehawk's commitment to safety, prompting me to verify my identity.

Cheyenne opened my billfold, and peering over her shoulder I could see it was not empty. Thank God I had not lost all my money the night before. She flung around, noticing my sneakiness, and shouted, "Get back, sir! Get back. I need to prove who you say you are."

I threw up my arms in defeat. "Okay, okay," I pleaded. "So ask me!"

"Name?" She was checking the faces to see if they matched up. Other than a haircut I desperately needed to preserve my old and balding look, there was no way anyone would think I was a different guy than the one in the license photo.

"Scott Sharpe."

The pit boss slowly gave me an up and down, and I felt a little violated. "What city do you live in, Scott?"

"Thornton." I played with my feet a little. The anticipation was killing me.

Cheyenne glared at me, handed me my wallet, and scolded me, "Don't pass out in my casino again."

"I won't." I was praying in my head that she would leave so I could study the wallet's contents. As luck would have it, Cheyenne left, and I opened my black billfold and gasped. Seven thousand dollars stared back at me. Relief washed over me; I had figured I lost all eight. That meant I only owed Keith one thousand plus the money I was looking at, plus interest.

Acquiring the money proved to be more challenging than it initially appeared. Given our joint bank accounts, Mia had access to all my banking transactions. There's no way I could just withdraw two thousand and get away clean. She knew our finances. So, I opened "a new Roth IRA" and deposited fifteen hundred. I'd eventually come clean to Mia, probably around the time I stopped drinking to excess.

However, much like many of my other undisclosed manners, I never did. My wife remains completely unaware that I borrowed money from the mob. More importantly, I had forgotten I'd borrowed ten thousand and not eight thousand.

Chapter 10

In a strange way, Ramon's life only slightly changed following the shooting. If nothing else, he had gained a little respect and "street cred" in the West Mesa neighborhood. Yes, it was a justified killing but that's what it was, a killing. Ramon's reputation turned to that of a killer. Cross him once and you'll end up like the dead *hombre* in Allsup's. There were whispers. People in West Mesa gossiped.

At home it made Ramon's oldest daughter, Ana, admire him a bit more. She was approaching her tenth birthday and, among the three daughters, was the only one of an age who fully comprehended the repercussions of what happened at the store. She asked a litany of questions, and for the most part her father answered the only way she thought he knew, with the truth. Ana was generally very sweet, so her father's answers startled her a bit. Of course, none of the girls were aware of the kiss their father had shared with Therese, the woman from Adriana's quilt making class. The local praise Ramon was receiving wore on Adriana because of the secret she held within. She was proud of her husband, of course, but no one else knew the pain this "hero" had caused years earlier in his wife's heart. She didn't think that was fair. The locals only knew of Ramon De Leon's good side. It angered Adriana.

A newspaper wanted to interview Ramon for his bravery and quick reflexes, but he didn't like all the attention. At the end of the day, he was a simple man. He hoped this would all blow over soon. But it didn't, at least not within himself.

Allsup's was closed for two days as police cleaned up the scene. The man from Hermosillo was officially cleared of all wrongdoing the day after the shooting. A pair of local news trucks and a few dozen Albuquerqueans stood outside the door during the closure, desperate to catch a peak at the crime scene. The cops wouldn't budge, though. One of the policemen who held him noticed the same thing Ramon did, that the detective referred to Bart Thompson, Sr. as the "victim". He apologized on his peer's behalf. Ramon appreciated that. He also tried to avoid the cops mostly because he was nervous they'd ask again for the registration of his gun. He didn't have it, of course, because it was purchased illegally.

On the third day, as Allsup's opened back up, Tito was the only employee left. The other two, both teenagers, were unnerved by the prospect of being shot at work and decided to quit. Ramon himself had opted to take a week or two to recover. He was still suffering from a bit of post-traumatic stress disorder, even if he did not know it. The De Leon patriarch had nightmare after nightmare the first two nights. The dreams consisted of the same man—who he now knew as the late Bart Thompson—and his message, that God will forgive him after any crime he committed. It seemed so wrong. Why was God punishing him? He was, other than his brief lapse in judgment at the bar years earlier, by all accounts a stand-up man. He was a member of the local Catholic church, and he volunteered frequently at the girls' school. How could God do this to him?

--

Ramon often wondered in the days following the shooting how it would have gone down in Mexico. In Hermosillo, there would have been a lot of unrest and lawlessness. Looters would have taken advantage, no doubt. Unless, of course, it was July. Those hot summer days in the city would frequently reach 110 degrees. Conversely, Albuquerque rarely rose over one hundred. It may have been too hot to protest in Mexico that time of year.

Meanwhile, Adriana remained homesick. As things died down from the fallout of the shooting and everyday life returned to normalcy, these feelings of loneliness intensified. In a strange way, she felt nothing towards her husband. She loved him, of course, but also felt detached after the shooting. Her frequent impassive expression now matched her demeanor.

She decided to talk to Father Pedro, in the form of confession, about her intrusive thoughts. Much like her husband's experience months prior, their conversation left a lasting impression. Father Pedro had that effect on people.

"Forgive me, Father, for I have sinned," she began, in Spanish.

"How long has it been since your last confession?" Father Pedro asked in his second language.

"Years, Father. Since I last lived in Mexico, at least."

"Welcome back," the priest replied with a smile Adriana couldn't see through the confessional. "What is it you'd like to confess?"

"Father," she began, "I am resentful of my husband. Everyone loves him. He's a good man, but he's made mistakes, and now everyone treats him like a hero—" Adriana paused as she realized she blew her cover. "Oops."

Inside the confessional booth, and unbeknownst to Adriana, Father Pedro tried to stifle the laughter bubbling up in him. He knew who he was speaking to, yet tried to maintain a calm exterior. "Tell me, ma'am, have you spoken to your husband about these resentments?"

"No." Adriana hung her head. "I have not."

"He needs to know you're resentful."

"I am a submissive woman by nature, Father," Adriana explained.

Father Pedro shook his head. "'I've commanded you to be brave and strong, haven't I? 'Don't be alarmed or terrified because the Lord our God is with you wherever you go.' That's from Joshua. Don't fear your husband."

Adriana knew what he meant. Her marriage with Ramon was always at its strongest when she was at her most faithful.

She approached Ramon that evening, and then came the productive conversations.

--

As the years went by, Ramon and Adriana continued to build the American Dream they sought after. Their marriage had been repaired, they loved and trusted each other once more, and they parented their girls together as much as they could.

In what seemed like the final step in becoming true blue Americans, the couple decided to finally become legal citizens of the United States. After all, their daughters were red blooded Americans by law, and what kind of example would that set for them if their parents continued to lie? All they had to do was live five years lawfully in the country and not get into any trouble. Adriana remarked they should have started this process as soon as they made Albuquerque their home.

Ramon had to admit to Father Pedro that he falsified documents to purchase his convenience store. He also had to confess they crossed the border in a way that was illicit. The priest was taken aback. He, like so many in the neighborhood, had assumed that Ramon and Adriana had always been by the book. Father Pedro, who was known for his harsh penances, asked him to say a rosary for each of his four daughters, to think about the terror he could have put each of them through had he been arrested. He also told Ramon he should be very thankful he and Adriana had never been caught, detained, and separated from their daughters at any point during their time in New Mexico. He urged the man to live a lawful life from this day forward.

Ramon thought long and hard about that last point. He knew the reason they didn't become citizens earlier was because they feared the ramifications of getting caught. But really, there were so many more things that should have scared him. Losing his family was something Ramon never wanted to even imagine. He thought back to when he killed Bart Thompson, Sr. with a bullet to the chest and that the cops never followed up to verify the legality of his gun. He also thought about the time a police car shined its lights on him and when he pulled over, the car zoomed by to capture the speeder ahead of him. That could have been Ramon. He could have spent ten years rotting in a cell in Mexico. He risked the lives of his children. He said a rosary for each of his girls with intention he had lacked from the years prior. No longer would he and Adriana fly under the radar as an illegals. Ramon De Leon was going to become an American.

And in 2007, after he aced the exam and rode out the necessary waiting period, Ramon did just that. To celebrate the occasion, he shaved his scraggly beard, wore his Sunday best, the only suit and bolo tie he had ever owned, and smiled as big as his overbearing cheeks would allow.

"Say 'cheese'," the clerk unenthusiastically huffed.

Ramon smiled. "Abraham Lincoln."

Chapter 11

"No raise." Bart Thompson flashed me a crooked grin and slammed his water bottle emphatically on the desk, echoing the authority of a gavel. At that moment, I'd never felt a stronger desire to deliver a forceful blow to his face.

Not only did he leverage threats based on my knowledge about the company's sketchy doings, he also brought up my office drinking and my loan. *There goes my theory that my drinking at work was a foolproof system.*

I wanted to sucker punch Keith Stephens, too. Where did he get off telling Bart about my drunken loan? I repaid the eight thousand with full interest within the specified timeframe with a manila envelope on his desk. His conditions were met. What was the point of sharing our transaction with Bart? Not that anything was worse than being in debt to the scariest bunch in Denver.

Shifting my attention back to Bart, I glared at him. "Let's negotiate."

"You've got some guts, Sharpe, I'll give you that." Bart laughed. "What do you want?"

I inhaled deeply, locking eyes with my boss. With unwavering resolve, I asserted, "Give me thirty thousand more or I won't go."

It was a standoff akin to *High Noon*. My Westco nemesis grumbled, "Fine." His concession made me realize he wasn't out to leverage what he had against me. In fact, he knew what I knew about *him* was potentially much more haz-ardous to his career. I'd get off with a slap on the wrist.

"Would you be willing to put that in a contract?" I decided to strike the iron while it was hot.

"Yes," Bart Thompson grumbled, and I could see the panic in his face. Aware of the value and the crucial evidence at my disposal, the sad-looking man understood the sig-nificant ramifications of losing me as a sales manager.

"Great." I contorted my face into a devilish grin. "Then Minnesota, here I come."

I was eager to share the news with Mia. The day unfolded slowly, as they do, with seconds morphing into minutes and minutes stretching into hours. Then it was five o'clock in the evening, and I was prepared to dash home. I slid into the driver's seat of my Acura sedan, accelerated onto Interstate 25 bound for Thornton, and replayed the conversation with Bart in my mind. I could not wait to tell my wife what a hero I was, that I had asserted myself and gotten the big raise.

I walked into our three-bedroom home—which, sud-denly, we needed to put on the market—where Mia was standing, waiting.

"Quick, *mi marido*." She shuffled along. "My water has broken. We need to go to the hospital now."

--

My, how quickly gears can change. There I was, excited to inform my wife that we could afford a slightly more lavish house, maybe a nicer vehicle, and there she stood, awaiting my arrival, conveying the imminent news that our second son was about to make his grand entrance into the world. Never mind the fact that the Sharpe's income was about to rise to two hundred and fifty thousand per year. God doesn't care about your plans, and he cares less about when you make them. My Thursday had not gone as I expected.

Mia and I planned for the moment her water broke. After all, we'd gone through it with Francisco. She instructed me to pack up the Acura, for it was showtime. I snagged the hospital bag, scooped up our first born, buckled him into his forward-facing car seat, and let Mia know a few minutes later that we were ready.

We arranged to leave Francisco at our friends Marty and Lara's house, as they had kindly offered weeks ago to watch him while we were at the hospital. Lara, being a stay-at-home mom, guaranteed us she could take care of our son for at least forty-eight hours. We would come get him on Saturday, we assured them.

I gave Francisco a big hug in front of Marty and Lara's house, and he looked at me in utter confusion. "Why you leave, Daddy?"

"Because your brother is going to be on Earth soon," I explained, and motioned back to his mother and unborn brother in the Acura.

"Will he come today?" my two-year-old son asked.

"Today or tomorrow," I said. "You'll have a new brother!"

"Yay," he responded with delight.

"Be good for Aunt Lara and Uncle Marty now, okay?"

"Can Wyatt play with me?" Francisco asked, referring to Marty and Lara's son of almost four.

"Of course," I said. "That's the fun of it, that you get to have a two-day sleepover with Wyatt."

"Great." Francisco smiled. "You leave now?"

Kids are the greatest. I laughed and passed him over to my friend Marty, who spoke to me, "We'll take good care of him. Good luck with everything! See you Saturday!"

The door closed behind me, and I hopped back into the Acura. It was time to get to the hospital. The journey was quick, covering just five miles from their house to the place our second son would be born. When we arrived, I texted my father and Ramon and Adriana, my in-laws. Everyone was very excited.

Mia was amazing, of course. After enduring labor for two hours, she persevered and, lo and behold, our second son entered the world. Within six hours of entering the hospital, a new human was born. Like an observant Catholic, Marcos entered the world the second day of Lent, on Feburary fifteenth, 2018.

"Marcos Scott," she whispered to me in front of our newly swaddled baby. "Like I said. What do you think?"

"It's perfect. He's perfect." I smiled. Glancing at my Rolex, I realized it was ten o'clock. "Why don't you pass little Marcos to me and close your eyes for a minute?"

Mia obliged and handed me our brand-new baby boy. Holding him in my arms, as his mother dozed off, I felt a sense of tranquility. Sure, there were scary things on the horizon for the Sharpes, but none of that mattered in this moment. The next two days were all about this little boy and his mother. Marcos stretched a little and yawned. His world revolved around eating breastmilk, taking odorless dumps, and snoozing. What a simple life that is.

As I sat there in the Denver Memorial Hospital on the rocking chair with my son, the peacefulness wore off and panic set in. How would I provide for this boy?

In that moment, it dawned on me that I hadn't updated Bart about the arrival of our son, considering he anticipated my return to the office in six hours. Swiftly, I grabbed my iPhone, unlocked the screen, and fired off a text message to my boss at Westco. It went something like this, "Hey Bart, Mia went into labor tonight. Baby boy born. Mom and baby healthy. Thanks, Scott."

That made me angry. The fact that there was this cloud of nervousness over my son's birth frustrated me. The sooner I could get to Minnesota, the better. I could get away from the evil of the Denver office and do my own thing as a sales manager. Plus, I told myself as I looked down at my second born, my sons would come to know their grandfather. We would have a safe life in Minnesota away from Bart Thompson, the Satriones, and all the others.

Despite the late time, I received a swift text back from my boss. It read, "Congrats. Talk soon. Bart."

--

On Friday morning, once we were settled in Postpartum Room 121, I decided to tell Mia. She had gotten some rest overnight and was admiring Marcos, who was cooing. Now was as good a time as any.

"I got the raise I asked for, honey," I explained. "Thirty thousand dollars."

"That is incredible!" Mia exclaimed, then quickly lowered her voice to a whisper, mindful of our half-sleeping, half-eating newborn. "I'm so proud of you."

I beamed, reveling in the pleasure of making her happy. I cherished the sight of her smiling.

"When would we have to move?"

"It's unclear," I admitted.

"Oh."

"We didn't get that far, and, as great as he is," I motioned toward baby Marcos, "the situation is now a bit more complicated."

"Why is that?" Mia asked.

"I mean, I'm not going to work for a bit," I told her. "That would be unfair to you."

I had always assumed I'd be able to take a few weeks away from Westco and be present for my family when my son was born. However, things around the office were a bit more complicated now. I'd try my best given the state of affairs.

Mia smiled. "That means a lot, Scott," she said. "I'm going to feed Marcos now, okay?" She lowered her shirt, and Marcos latched on.

I nodded. "Would you like some food? I think there's a Jimmy John's across the street."

"That would be great," she responded. "I could go for a turkey sub. Extra lettuce, please." Always one to be a health nut, Mia and green foods maintained a healthy relationship.

I kissed her on the forehead, then our son, and walked out of Room 121. I waltzed through the hospital parking garage, hopped in the Acura, and sped away from the hospital. I saw the Jimmy John's rather quickly and smoothly maneuvered into the parking lot.

As I shifted the gear into park, I noticed the building next to it, Rocky Mountain North Liquor. I hadn't had a drink in two days. A shiver cascaded down my spine. My head told me to go into the sandwich shop, but my legs were already on their way into the liquor store. I pushed the door, heard that awful beep, and slowly walked past the whiskey. The whispers of the customers began to bother me. I knew they were not talking about me, but the tingle in my back said otherwise. The colors of the whiskey aisle are nearly always strikingly brown. Even the brightest of logos cannot overtake the dominate hues of amber, beige, and chestnut. I have always been drawn to that color, that brown that reminds me of the last leaf falling off a Colorado maple tree.

Sweat beads shot down my forehead. I needed to come up with a plan, and quick. Mia was expecting me back; time was of the essence. I swiped a fifth of Canadian Mist, which would be enough to keep me good and drunk the rest of the day, and a container of Altoids from the front counter to mask the smell of my breath. The plan was in motion.

I picked up Mia's Jimmy John's order and headed back to the hospital parking lot. I parked the Acura in the subterranean garage in a spot blocked by an F-150 on one side and a Ram 1500 on the other. I took a deep breath, opened the brown paper bag, and pressed the bottle against my lips. The first sip of whiskey slid through my throat, and I gulped it down. The warm sensation in my body relaxed me.

After a few more pulls—about a quarter of the bottle in total—I popped an Altoid and sprinted back up to the birthing floor. Mia, who was feeding Marcos, smiled when she saw me. "Thank you for getting me Jimmy John's, *mi marido.*"

"You bet," I said. If only she knew.

--

The hours slipped away as my wife, still holding our newborn son, indulged in a post-sub sandwich nap. I let my drunk ride a bit, but I knew to maintain a calm exterior. My whole body was relaxed, and I had reached the perfect state of inebriation. Nothing could stop me now. Before I decided to check out for the afternoon, I figured I would take a few more pulls from the fifth since Mia and Marcos were sleeping together on the bed. I ran down to the parking garage and repeated the process. By now, half of that bottle was gone, and I was feeling pretty good. If my math lay correct, I was eight shots deep. On my way back to our room, I stopped by the kitchenette and grabbed a Blue Bell chocolate ice cream container, fully equipped with a wooden paddle spoon.

I stealthily returned to the room, evading my sleeping wife's notice. I flipped on the muted television, retrieved my phone from the counter, ignored a text message from Bart Thompson, studied a game of Words with Friends, and reclined my chair. I was comfortable. Life, I convinced myself, was good.

That is, until Mia woke up thirty minutes later. By then—somewhere around five in the evening—I had felt the strongest effects of the liquor and was hard pressed to move. I was walking down a gravel sidewalk in tipsy town. My sweet wife whispered to me while I lay in the chair, "Honey, can you please go get a nurse? If Dotty is here, I'd like it to be her. Marcos is having a difficult time latching."

I shook. "Yes, dear." I hopped out of the reclined chair and practically sprinted to the hallway to conceal my inebriation. It would be less danger to have Dotty the Nurse see me hammered than Mia, anyway.

I stumbled over to the nurse's desk and informed the two on duty of her situation. "My wife and son need some help in Room 121. My son Marcos was born last night, and they need some help."

One of the nurses was significantly taller than me, and the other could not have been more than five feet in height. I chuckled inwardly, appreciating the irony of their extremities. I nearly fell over but caught myself as my left knee barely skid the ground. I brushed off my shoulders. The two nurses were chatting amongst themselves, and one of them pointed at me.

"Sir," the shorter one spoke softly, "are you all right?"

I swayed a bit but composed myself in the blurry hallway. "Sure, sure." I nodded. "Never been better. My son, Marcos, was born last night. He's in Room 121, you see?"

The six-foot-tall nurse looked me up and down. "Yeah," she fidgeted with the key ring in her hand. "You mentioned that already."

"Did I? I think I would have remembered that." I played surprised. Had I also told them about Mia's problem?

The two of them anxiously laughed. "Sir? Can we take you back to your room?"

I stood up straight. "Sure," I said. "I'm in Room 121. My son was just born last night."

The short nurse retreated slowly to the desk, and I noticed out of the corner of my eye that she was pressing something on the other side of the table. "Give us just a moment, sir. We'll bring you back to your room. You'll be all right."

Was I discovered? Was I being paranoid? Incoherent thoughts entered my brain, and about thirty seconds later a figure came through the door behind the desk.

I could discern what he was by his buttoned-down, short-sleeve shirt; he was a security guard. He was vigorously chewing a piece of gum and fumbling around in his pocket.

He glanced up at me, motioned with his index finger, and stated, "Come with me, sir."

My head pounded rapidly. My heart thumped as we walked past Room 121. We took the elevator down to the first floor. The officer spoke to me, but I couldn't make out any words he was saying. I was still flying high as we made it into the lobby.

"So, what's the problem?" Security Officer Clarkston, his badge read, said. "Nurses told me you were drunk on the birthing floor."

"I am not drunk," I slurred. "I've had a couple of drinks—maybe one or three—but I am not wasted. I need to find Dotty."

"Uh-huh," The officer looked me up and down. "I'm going to have to ask you to leave."

"But—but," I raised my voice to a level that caught the attention of everyone else in the lobby, prompting them to turn their heads in my direction. "What about my wife and kid?"

"Come back when you're sober," the security guard was unsympathetic, "but until then, *get out.* We have a zero-tolerance policy here. You're lucky I'm not calling the police."

"Fine. I can walk out myself." I pushed through the swirling doors—wildly reminiscent of those at Westco—and took a deep breath of the wintry Colorado air. The mountains were in the distance and cars heading for different destinations zoomed by in most directions. I sat on a bench near the entrance for a moment. Clarkston glued his eyes on me from inside the hospital. We made eye contact, and he made a shooing gesture, as if to say the bench wasn't far away enough to satisfy his demand I leave the property. I stood up, stretched some, nearly fell over, and started walking west towards Martin Boulevard. He watched me stroll away for a moment, and when I swung my head around to look thirty seconds later, he was gone.

Recalling that the underground garage was adjacent to the hospital, I made my way to its entrance. I had remembered my half-drunk bottle of whiskey in the Acura! How glorious an evening I'd be having with the brown liquor and the Amor Towles novel I left in the back seat. Not to mention the newest edition of *Baseball Digest*, where I'd read, like every year, that my beloved Colorado Rockies would be good this season but not good enough to win the World Series.

Then I remembered Mia and Marcos. How could I spend the evening with them? There were two clear choices in my foggy brain. First, I could sober up and go spend the night with my family. It was the smart, logical option. Anyone with a brain would tell you that. Secondly, I could drink in my car alone and head back up to the following morning, either when I sobered up or that idiot Officer Clarkston was no longer on duty.

The sane man would have opted to sober up quick and head upstairs to Mia. He would apologize, and she would be upset. But at the end of the day, he would be able to spend the second night of his newborn son's life as a present dad. He would be able to look into the eyes of his wife and say with utter confidence, "I can do better, and I am sorry."

Too bad I'm not the sane man.

Chapter 12

I remember the first trip from Minneapolis to Albuquerque, 1200-some miles in the car. Throughout the expedition, which spanned seven states and two days, the topography changed remarkably, evolving from undulating woodlands to flat prairies and eventually giving way in the West to the expanse of a sandy desert. The vastness of these open spaces left quite the impression on me. I was just an unrefined kid from Minnesota who had no idea how expansive America is. Somewhere on Interstate 35 in southern Kansas just shy of the Oklahoma border, I realized just how remote that part of the world was. I was in awe.

Once we made our way into the Land of Enchantment on the second day, I noticed the desert taking shape. It was unlike anything we had back home, which was mostly tree skylines and green grass. Every mile we passed heading west on Interstate 40 was magical. The mesas and buttes of eastern New Mexico were outlined with red rock, resembling the rarest of New York strip steaks.

Why did I choose the University of New Mexico for college? Initially, I was drawn to the aesthetic of southwest campuses. They presented a stark contrast to the familiar scene I had grown accustomed to in the Midwest. The buildings, predominantly adorned by a brownish-beige hue, captivated me with their unique appearance. So, when my dad took me to see the campus, I fell in love immediately. Along with the attractive style of architecture, UNM had a distinct and quirky edge to it. If there was an empty corner or opening anywhere on campus, you can bet it'd have some sort of fountain or pond with a thousand quarters and countless wishes inside. I admired their style if that makes sense. I always wanted to attend a Division I school for the athletics as well. That day Dad and I rolled onto the campus, I became a Lobo.

--

In December of 2008, I was a senior at the University of New Mexico. At the time, I was a sly and cheeky twenty-two-year-old guy, and I took to dating as many girls as my schedule would allow. I was an economics major and spent a great deal of my days in the aptly named Economics Center on the northwest side of UNM's campus. I studied hard and partied hard. I went on many dates with the intent of finding the girl I would marry and start a family with.

The weekend before my final Christmas break in college, I went to a party on Princeton Drive, just south of campus. There I bumped into, and subsequently, chatted with a gorgeous freshman by the name of Mia. A little unique among Hispanic families, she told me, but it meant "mine" and her father liked the name. She was around five-foot six inches, had long, wavy brown hair, and a smile to die for. Boy, did Mia capture me the second we met. She was studying art and informed me she was from the west side of town. Our conversation of a few hours was magical. When it was time to say goodnight at two-thirty in the morning, I offered to walk her home. She accepted, and we set out the three blocks to where she lived off Lead and Cornell.

In those five minutes, I decided I liked her. I didn't get the same vibe from her, so I didn't ask for her phone number. I knew that was a mistake. I beat myself up in the coming days for not getting her digits. As cellphones were becoming more commonplace, I observed Mia frequently reaching for hers that night. In a landscape where half the students possessed mobile devices, this girl and I lay on the same side. I believed I missed my chance with her, and I felt disheartened. I asked friends about the girl with the curly hair named Mia, but no one knew who she was.

Five days later, one before I was slated to make the nineteen-hour trek back to Minnesota in my 2005 Subaru Forester, I was departing the Economics Building and heading south on campus. I was galloping over to Zimmerman Library to study when I saw her on those stairs. She didn't even notice me. I watched in slow motion as she approached me, those eyes locked in another direction.

I half lunged in her direction and attempted to spit out any utterance remotely resembling the English language. "Mia?" I finally stammered. "Is that you?"

I blushed right then and there because there must have been twenty other students within earshot, all of whom heard me jumble my words. Since I was so focused on her, I didn't care. I wondered what it would feel like to kiss her right then and there. Luckily, I didn't act on my urges.

She studied my face for a moment. "Scott? How are you? That's your name, right?"

I pulled off to the side, away from the foot traffic of our fellow Lobos, and she followed. "I'm good. Listen," I said, and paused to catch my breath, "I had a tremendous time with you the other night and really would like the opportunity to take you out on a date."

The chemistry between us was extraordinary. We could have walked off campus and into the desert at that moment and it would have felt natural. She grasped my hand in hers and smiled, "I'd like that."

--

That winter, we fell in love hard. I took Mia to a coffee shop just south of campus for our first date, and we sat there for six wonderful hours and closed the place down. It was a magical evening.

Soon, social life activities faded into the abyss as the two of us became one. Mia and I spent hours upon hours in the company of each other's arms, dreaming about the life we'd build together.

In part because she resided in the area, Mia spent most of her time on the south side of the University of New Mexico's campus. I would typically pick her up from the Center of Arts building where half her classes were. The building stands out in my memory for two reasons. Firstly, it had the perfectly rectangle overhang with white pillars that remained shaded throughout the course of the day, which I loved because they kept me cool during the first and last months of the school year, when temperatures would reach scorching highs. Secondly, the resonating sounds coming from within echoed throughout the expansive entryway, creating a backdrop that added to the building's unique charm. It is not an exaggeration to claim that the shadow cast by the overhang extended nearly as far as the next building to the north, the recently constructed student union building. The extent of the shade varied by the time of day, of course, but it provided significant coverage. Luckily, it was winter when I met Mia so I wouldn't need the shelter. It can get chilly in the high desert in the "R" months.

After class one day on a brisk, early February afternoon, I picked Mia up in my Subaru Forester on the sidewalk southwest of the multi-use Johnson Field. I knew something was up with her, and I was instantly nervous. It was a tell-tale sign that this young woman in the front seat meant a great deal to me. I truly cared for her. Everything up to that point in my life was unstable, but Mia was my rock steady.

The strain subsided when she spoke. "Scott, I want you to meet my family."

"I'd love to, Mia," I answered quickly. What a relief. I thought she was going to tell me she was transferring.

She smiled and removed her hood. It was a chilly day in New Mexico, the high hovering around fifty degrees, and she was wearing a heavy jacket.

"Tell me about them," I smiled. "I need to know what I'm walking into. You've only told me basic information."

"Well, there's my dad, Ramon," she said. "Very stereotypical Mexican muchacho. He hides his feelings, but he's a great man and would lay down his life for any one of us. He speaks English very well."

"And your mom?" I asked.

"I think I told you, but her name is Adriana," she explained, "and she's very shy but loves being a mother to her four daughters. She prefers to speak Spanish."

"Ana, Maria Elena, and Luisa?" I asked. "Are those your sisters' names?"

Mia smiled. "That's right. Ana is an extremely independent beauty shop owner over in Santa Fe. Maria Elena is a freshman at West Mesa High School, and Luisa is only eight. My *madre y padre* named her after the man who brought them to New Mexico. She has some social issues, but they think she's autistic."

"I can't wait to meet them all."

--

In our entire courtship, I don't believe it got any more scary for me than the day I met the De Leons. I vividly recall the five-mile commute from the university to the West Mesa neighborhood in which she grew up. This was but ten weeks after Mia and I met, and she held my hand as I drove my Forester west on Interstate 40.

I sincerely hoped that her parents didn't believe we were rushing things. My feelings for their daughter were authentic, and I was determined not to risk our relationship by forging a bad first impression. I had two preliminary fears before I met the family. First, perhaps the De Leons would not approve of Mia dating a white man. Secondly, her sisters were so tight-knit and none of them had ever brought anyone home before. While this was an entirely new experience for me, it was also unprecedented in their little world.

"Are you nervous?" Mia asked me.

"Of course," I said. "It's all I've been thinking about all week!"

"They're nice people, Scott. You have nothing to worry about."

I recall the instant my Subaru slid onto their street and I laid my eyes on the De Leon home for the first time. Initially, a twenty-foot pinon pine, characterized by its distinct horizontal branching, blocked the view of their modest abode. Once we walked past the tree, I noticed the tan, Pueblo style home with a blue panel on the bottom and a few windows facing the street. I knew Mia's family were of the working class, so it was exactly as I pictured—a humble dwelling. It was similar in size to the home in Minnesota I grew up in.

Ramon De Leon opened the metal door, and there was a loud screech to greet me along with his firm handshake. A young girl of about eight—presumably Luisa—wrapped herself in Mia's arms and laughed. She had pigtails and held a shiny paperback book in her arms.

"Hello," the burly man with a thick accent called out. "I am Ramon."

"It's a pleasure to meet you, sir," I cleared my throat. "Scott Sharpe."

"I know," he replied. "Welcome."

"And I am Luisa!" exclaimed the little girl. "I'm Mia's *hermana*. That means 'sister' in *Ingles*."

"He knows what it means, *niñita*." Mia smiled.

"Your *madre* is making her world-famous tamales," Ramon boasted.

"*Mama* doesn't speak *Ingles* very good," Luisa added, and tugged at Mia's dress. "Did you tell him? Did you? Did you?"

"Yes, *niñita*." My girlfriend laughed. "He knows. He knows."

Just then, another youthful smile appeared through the front door. "I am Maria Elena," the figure said. She was several inches shorter than her sister in college, but Maria Elena had a rounder face and hair even curlier than Mia's.

I stepped inside their home and was introduced to Adriana. Mia noticed her older sister had not arrived, so she inquired, "Where is Ana?"

"*Tu hermana.*" Adriana laughed. "Coming from, uh, Santa Fe."

"*Papa* called her a hippie yesterday!" Luisa shouted. "So funny!"

Ramon wore a nervous smile and skillfully deflected Luisa's accusation. "*Cómo esta la escuela?*" he asked Mia.

"Dad, can we speak *Ingles* tonight?" his daughter pleaded. "Scott isn't fluent in *Español*."

The patriarch nodded. "I will translate for you, *mi cariño*. Besides, my English is getting better."

Once we were seated at the dinner table, after a prayer of grace, Adriana said, "*Hablame de ti.*"

Mia translated, "She wants you to tell us about yourself."

"Yeah!" Luisa screamed. "Tell us, Scott!"

"Well, there's not much to know. I'm an economics major. I'm from Minnesota. I like sports."

"What kind of sports do you like?" Ramon interrupted.

"Football and basketball, mostly," I answered. "But I do like to watch other sports, too."

"Do you go to Lobos games?" my girlfriend's dad asked.

"Absolutely," I answered. "I have the student ticket package."

"Were you at the, uh, UNLV game?" Ramon asked. Despite being labelled a "quiet guy" by his daughter, Ramon certainly had a knack for engaging in lively conversations about sports. Perhaps it had something to do with the fact that there was at long last another male in his home.

"Yes!" I nearly exclaimed, but then tempered my tone, "Yes, I was there."

"You be good to my daughter, and we'll go to a game together." He wagged his finger at me and chuckled awkwardly. "Check this out." Ramon whipped out his billfold and opened a secondary compartment. In it lay a faded yellow Post-it note and written on the paper was a message from a younger Mia that read, "Thanks for protecting us, Papa. I love you. Love, Mia."

"That's neat," I said. "How old was she when she wrote that?"

"What do you think, Mia?" he asked her. "Seven?"

"That sounds about right."

Ramon rose from the table, presumably heading to the bathroom, and Mia and I quickly exchanged glances when he left the room. Her expression seemed to affirm me, as if to say, "He loves you!"

"The tamales are great, Mrs. De Leon," I said to Adriana. She nodded in my direction, expressing gratitude.

"Why do you call *futbol* 'soccer', Scott?" Luisa laughed at me. I have to say, she was tremendously bright for being just eight.

There was a knock at the front door then, and in walked Ana. Mia's older sister had finally arrived from Santa Fe. She was tall and slim, and her tightly fitting clothes stuck to her body like a magnetic refrigerator door. The De Leons poked fun of her because she was a self-described "socialist". Politically, Ramon and Adriana were moderate, and Mia preferred to stay out of current events, though I know for certain she didn't vote for Obama in the election the month prior. I was liberal in those days. I bought into the whole media hype of Obama and "change". It's not that John McCain was a superior option; rather, we simply lacked strong candidates at the time.

Mentioning Obama, Ana entered and immediately celebrated his triumph. "Two weeks into Obama's presidency and I still haven't heard a word from *either* of you?" She gestured toward Ramon, who had just reentered the room, and Adriana when speaking. "I went to Washington for the parade, for God's sake. Yeah, that went well, too. Thanks for asking." I may have been judging, but I think she was trembling as she spoke.

Ramon pointed his finger right back at his oldest daughter. "You do *not* take the Lord's name in vain in my home. It's a commandment." Adriana folded her arms, aligning her stance with her husband.

I decided to break the ice. "You must be Ana. I'm Scott. Nice to meet you." I walked over to her and extended my arm. She had long frizzy hair like Mia's, but her arms were full of tattoos. I could only make out one, the famous Che Guevara portrait everyone knows.

"You too, Scott," she huffed as she gripped my hand too firmly. "Mia has said a lot about you."

"All good things," Mia interjected.

"Mostly, yeah, but some not so good," Ana replied. She finally let go of my fingers and crossed her arms, revealing her discomfort in my presence.

"That's kind of disrespectful, Ana." Mia was visibly irritated.

"He hasn't earned any of my respect yet." Without an apparent reason, Ana chose to target her sister's new boyfriend. A part of me wondered how Mia would react. Would she defend me, or would she have her sister's back?

She chose the former. I was glad. "Knock it off, Ana. I'm warning you."

"I'll say this once and once only." Ana's smile faded a bit as she shifted her attention back to me. "You *better* be good to my sister. I mean it, Scott." The last sentiment came off as a threat. The previous brevity from Mia regarding Ana now made sense. My girlfriend had little to share about her sister, and I surmised that, following this recent interaction, there would not be anything positive to say at all.

What a fitting introduction.

Chapter 13

The first thing I noticed when I woke up on Saturday morning was a bright white light. The pain was unbearable. My head pounded, my body ached, and my eyes adjusted to the sight. The beacon came from across the parking garage in the form of a warm white colored headlight of a Toyota Tacoma. It was parking for the day. I retrieved my cell phone from my pocket, with just ten percent of battery remaining, only to be informed it was six o'clock in the morning. I breathed a sigh of relief when I observed the absence of new text messages. The consolation was temporary, however, as I realized in the top right corner of the screen that I was in SOS mode. That meant once I reentered civilization, the floodgates would open.

As fate would have it, I was right. A few moments later I stumbled outside to twelve notifications. All were from Mia. She called me. She texted me. She sent me an email. The last ding came at just past one in the morning, with a text message that read only my first name followed by more than a few question marks.

I sprinted inside the hospital. I knew Mia would be so mad at me. I'm not sure if I had ever screwed up like this. I drank into excess, and I abandoned the two people who needed me at the most inopportune time. Sweat ran up and down my body as I pushed open the door to Room 121. Inside, Mia and Marcos were sleeping soundly.

Thank God, I thought to myself. I had left them at five the night before, so it had been thirteen hours since my little rendezvous commenced. I started doing the math. Mia's latest text message had been sent around one in the morning, so there was an eight-hour gap in which I was unaccounted for. I plotted out my next lie. I was so hungover by that point that it took me five minutes on that couch to concoct my scheme. I roleplayed the conversation in my head but eventually fell back into a hangover-induced slumber.

--

My shoulder felt the tap first. I'm not sure if it was the first place on my body Mia touched me, but it was the straw that broke the sleepy camel's back.

My wife's beautiful face appeared. She was pissed. I remembered what happened the night before and sprung right into action with my lie. "Mia, I didn't hear you up. How are you?"

"Where the *hell* have you been, Scott?" she whispered these words, but that was only so our newborn son wouldn't wake. Mia crossed her arms to express her anger.

"I fell asleep on the couch in the lobby." This was all I came up with in my hungover daze.

"No, you didn't."

Now I crossed my arms. "How do you know that?"

"I walked down to the lobby and asked late last night," she replied.

"Who did you talk to?"

"The security guard," Mia explained. "His name was Harris, I think."

Clarkston had left after all. I could have waltzed back into the hospital last night and gone to bed in this room! I realized there was no way I could have rationalized this in my drunken brain.

"Well, I was there," I stuttered. "Check the tape."

"Try again, Scott. You didn't come back."

"I don't have to listen to this," I complained. "I'm telling you the truth and that's that!"

"Keep your voice down," she demanded. "You'll wake Marcos."

"Mia, I didn't do anything wrong."

"I *never* said anything about doing anything wrong," Mia said. "I am just saying you didn't come back to this room."

"You have to believe me," I pleaded. "I did."

"Scott," Mia took a deep breath. "You are lying. I know you are because I woke up at one and you were gone. So, what? You mean to tell me you came back between the hours of one and now? I was awake until eleven-thirty, you have to remember."

"That's when I came back," I lied through my teeth.

"Okay, suppose that is true," Mia said. "What were you doing before then?"

I flinched. In the heat of the moment, I recoiled just long enough for Mia to notice. It was a weak move, but I was determined to avoid the truth. She pounced, "Have you been drinking?"

"Uh—I have not."

Mia caught me before my next move. "Come over here," she whispered. "I want to smell your breath."

"Why?" My sense of desperation came over me, so I panicked. I wish I had popped one of those Altoids in the car. "So you can feel validated about what *you* think? Nice try."

"Come over here," she repeated coldly.

I said a quick prayer to myself as I inched closer to her. *I promise I'll get sober if you get me out of this one, God,* I said to myself. But it was a prayer I said to myself all too many times. Mia immediately smelled the booze on my breath.

"You lied." The chair reclined and Mia stared blankly at me. It was almost as if she was looking ten feet behind me for someone else. She finally shook her head, grasping the magnitude of the moment, and said, "I need some space."

"Mia—"

"Get out of here. Now. I'll be home tonight." My wife's cold voice sent a shiver down my spine.

I shrugged my shoulders, gathered my belongings, and left the hospital without so much as kissing Marcos goodbye.

--

After bidding adieu to my Uber driver and stepping inside our home, I paced around the halls. What else could I do? I had mishandled the birth of our son, come close to getting arrested, and then got caught.

I'll be home tonight. Mia's words rang in my head, so I started to do the math. It was nine o'clock in the morning. Could I get hammered quickly? What does tonight mean? Seven in the evening? Eight?

At the very least, I had seven hours. I swiftly made my way to the liquor cabinet, where I discovered an unopened bottle of Maker's Mark, courtesy of a recent gift basket from my in-laws. I flung open the rigid top at the speed of light.

I must have drowned half of that fifth in ten minutes, because my world began to spin. I plopped on our giant basement sofa and flipped on the television. It was late in the morning on Saturday, so there wasn't much on unless you wanted to view third round coverage of the PGA Tour's Genesis Invitational. I turned on Netflix and soon found myself in the throes of a mystery. I kicked my feet back, looked around, exhaled, and threw back another pull of Maker's Mark. *Life is good*, I drunkenly thought.

Around lunchtime, I wanted a bologna sandwich. On my way to the kitchen, I peered outside the front door. I wished I still smoked in that moment, because the nicotine rush of a cigarette would be the cherry on top of this afternoon. The chair out front would be perfect, I told myself. Through the trees thinned by a Colorado winter, I noticed a Lincoln Continental parked adjacent to our house. I thought that to be an odd coincidence, since I nearly angrily rammed into one around the same spot the other day. Never the matter, as nothing could bring me down from my high.

I could not get enough of the euphoric feeling. Although I'd been familiar with the feeling of being drunk for years, it never seemed to satisfy. By one in the afternoon I had drank the entire fifth. My sober conscience and drunken head battled one another, like the angel and devil on the shoulder. The devil spoke out, that Mia would be home in a few hours, and we could get a few more drinks in. The angel informed me I could have a nap and shower and be a decent enough husband by the time she and the boys got home.

The *boys*. Crap, I thought. Was I supposed to pick up Francisco? I couldn't remember if Mia had asked me to before she kicked me out of the hospital. I picked up my phone and noticed no new notifications. If I really needed to pick up Francisco from Marty and Lara's, wouldn't she have mentioned it? I stood up and fell back to the ground. I slammed my head on the coffee table hard. I shot back up and felt the drip of blood down my forehead slowly. My head pulsated, worse than before, and I looked to the heavens and cursed. Staring into the bathroom mirror, I saw the substantial gash. No doubt it would be something else to have to explain to Mia when she got home. I was in deep trouble.

The only way out of this conundrum seemed to be to say a prayer and hope Mia and the boys would get home by the time I was in bed. It was highly unlikely, but for the second time in twenty-four hours, I prayed. *I promise I'll be sober tomorrow if you get me out of this one, God.* I remembered Francisco again, and rapidly dialed Marty's phone number.

He answered on the second click. "Hey, Scott. Congratulations!"

"Thanks," I dismissed his flattering greeting. "Say, did Mia say who was picking up Frankie?"

"No," Marty said. "Are you not with her? What's going on?"

"It's nothing, Marty. I was just wondering what she said."

"She didn't say anything to me at all." I shook my head. At the very least, Marty was now suspicious of whatever the heck was going on between Mia and me.

"You okay, Scott?" He knew something was up.

"I'm good. Very happy. We have a second boy!"

"Right," Marty answered. "Well listen, just let me know when you guys want to pick up Francisco. He and Wyatt are having a blast!"

"Thanks, Marty."

"Goodbye now."

The clocked ticked away, and I was beginning to feel hungover again. It had been a few hours since my last drink and my fingers were shaking. Glancing at the clock on my phone, it read four in the afternoon, and I had zero new notifications. Mia had always insisted on sharing our locations using the iPhone app Find My Friends. For the first time, I found myself wishing I had hers.

I nervously took a few pulls of the Kirkland vodka bottle from our Christmas party last year. I preferred the taste of whiskey to the clear liquor, but these were desperate times. I did the math in my head and realized I had about seventeen drinks in seven hours. My heart was racing; I didn't know when Mia would be getting home, and it was driving me nuts.

The devil on my shoulder told me to call her. *Do it*, he whispered. *You're already in trouble.* How much worse could today get?

I picked up my iPhone and gave in to the temptation. Mia didn't answer. My heart sank again. I ran back to the Kirkland bottle and took another long swig. The burning sensation down my throat killed me. I realized at that moment I had drunk ten times as much alcohol as water today, and so I ran upstairs to get a glass of water. My head thumped as my foot extended to each step. I nearly passed out once my toes hit the hardwood of the main floor. I strutted over to the hideous purple velvet couch I was hoping would not make the move to the north with us. The feng shui would be spot on with Minnesota's professional football team, the Vikings, sharing the color. I thought of their purple jerseys and the new state of the art US Bank Stadium, who they'd sign at quarterback, and slowly fell into an early evening drunken slumber.

--

Just like that morning, Mia's bony index finger roused me once more. My head pulsated, and immediately I remembered that I left the Kirkland vodka bottle out in the open. *That was downstairs*, I assured myself, *somewhere Mia rarely goes.* I glanced at the kitchen clock. It was five-thirty, ninety minutes since my last drink.

Holding a napping Marcos in her arms she whispered, "You didn't pick up Francisco?"

"No. I, I talked to Marty and—"

"Don't start," Mia snapped back. "I grabbed him, you fool."

My oldest son sprinted into the room. "Daddy! Daddy!" he shouted. "Hi!"

The pain in me grew exponentially. It's not that I wasn't eagerly excited to see my son, but my brain couldn't take another moment of the thumping. My temples pulsed. My back ached. "Hi, buddy," I stammered. "Did you have fun with Wyatt?"

"Yeah," he answered, and walked right up to me and gave me a sloppy kiss. He stepped back a second, squeezed his nostrils with his thumb and index finger, and yelled, "Yucky! Daddy stinks."

Mia shot a glare at me, as if to yell at me once more. When Francisco was just out of range, I whispered, "What do you think? I'm hungover."

"Hungover or still drunk?" Mia was at her wits end.

Dinner was somber, as both my wife and I grasped the weight of the impending conversation. In the ten years we've known each other, I don't believe Mia has ever been more upset with me. I blabbed a bit and comprehended my gibberish halfway through the meal. Besides, there was still a giant gash the size of a quarter on my forehead. There is no way she didn't know I was still borderline drunk.

For the first time that day, I was right. Mia confronted me once she put Marcos and Francisco down for bed. I was done.

"How drunk are you exactly?" She placed her hands on her hips and her normally sweet brown eyes grew furious.

"Mia, I don't know what you expect me to say—"

"Tell me the truth for once, Scott." Hearing her call me by my first name and not *mi marido* or another pet name really threw me off. Mia almost always used sweet names for me and had done so since 2008. To me this was the greatest indicator she was pissed.

"Yes," I answered.

"Yes, what?"

"I'm drunk." I figured she would extend me grace if I heeded to her advice to tell the truth.

She didn't. "I want you out."

"Out where?" I threw my hands in the air in what felt like slow motion.

"Scott, not only were you drinking at the hospital last night, after our son was born," Mia said, "but you decided to come home today and drink."

"How do you know I drank?" I demanded to know, failing to remember I told her moments earlier. "How do you know I'm not hungover from last night?"

Mia turned around, opened the pantry door, and brought out the Kirkland Costco vodka bottle. I gulped. She must have seen me passed out and grabbed the bottle while I lay asleep on the hearth room couch. In the gravest of tones, she reiterated, "I want you *out*." The last word was further emphasized by the same bony index finger that had woken me up twice that day out of my stupor.

Chapter 14

Mia wept in the front seat on the drive back to campus.

"That's not how that was supposed to go," she cried out. "Ana is really messed up, Scott."

"Messed up how?" I asked.

"She drinks," Mia responded. "A lot. Not like a college kid, either."

I didn't know what to think or how to respond to my girlfriend. I was a twenty-one-year-old kid who drank a ton, too. I shrugged my shoulders. "She'll grow out of it."

"That's ignorant, Scott." Mia crossed her arms angrily in the front seat.

"Why?"

"She's an alcoholic," Mia said with absolute certainty.

"Come on, she's like, what? Twenty-four?" I questioned her.

"Her age doesn't matter. Let me tell you a story." As we approached the parking garage, Mia shuffled her body a bit to get comfortable. *This must be some story*, I thought. She continued, "I know it's odd to think now, but Ana used to be a real sweetie. She was the kind of girl who would ask the most innocent questions and expect the most innocent answers. She thought she was a princess and would tell me I'd be a princess once I'd get older. When she was fifteen and I was ten, things just started to change. She wasn't the sweetheart we all knew her to be. I think, looking back on it, that my parents probably thought she was just going through puberty. But it was so much more than that. She started to drink. She would disobey my parents. She started dating this real sleazebag white guy named Ronnie. Ronnie brought her to parties, and she would come back wasted. Since we shared a room at the time and a bed, I remember her coming into bed with me and I could just smell the booze. It was awful. It was gross."

"I have a question, Mia," I started, "and I don't mean to sound like a jerk, but what is your point? She's a moody teenager?"

"Maybe if you'd shut up and let me finish the story," Mia said, "you would feel how I do."

"Fine."

"Anyway," she cleared her throat, "Ana was in deep with this group of people. They were pressuring her to do drugs and stuff. Ronnie was pressuring her into having sex, and she would say no. There was one party where he cornered her in his family's hot tub and wouldn't take no for an answer. She jumped out of the hot tub, naked, and ran back into the house. Everyone saw her completely in the nude. Because she stood up for herself, everyone saw her naked. It wasn't fair. People in school made fun of her for years after that because, because—"

Mia stopped and teared up. It was clear from her ambience she hated retelling this story. I placed my hand on hers. She continued, "Because she stood up for herself. It pushed her into drinking, and she hasn't really stopped."

"I'm sure glad there weren't cellphones back then."

"It's more than that, Scott," Mia said back. "When you're fifteen and impressionable and wanting to be popular and you are the naked one at the party, no one wants to be friends."

"That makes sense." I still was not entirely sure of Mia's point of telling the story, but I understood the gist of it.

"Everyone started calling her a slut, a whore. Every bad name you can think of," Mia explained, "and it's all because she stood up for herself. Ronnie dumped her. Her friends didn't want anything to do with her."

I had my reservations. If everyone's worst moments when they were fifteen were broadcast to the public, we'd all drink like Ana. I had this sudden realization that my relationship with Mia is the only reason I cared about Ana. I thought about my mother, a real, mean drunk, and how badly she had hurt us. Mom, who stood barely five feet tall, packed violent fury in her alcohol-soaked binges. I was supposed to feel bad now because some other crazy lady stumbled drunkenly in front of classmates in the nude. Try empathizing with that when your own mother tells you she wishes you were dead. Not a chance, Mia.

I did what every young man in love does. I lied to her. "I'm sorry. You're right."

Mia laid her head into my chest and said, "I'm so glad you understand."

But I didn't. I was just a naïve college kid. Little did I know someday I would suffer from the same demons that imprisoned Ana.

--

Alcoholism had a stronghold on the De Leon family. Ramon's father was a drunk, as was his father before him. He often wondered why he hadn't inherited the gene himself. As they reached a mature age, Ramon spoke with each of his four daughters, calmly explaining the importance of being diligent about the potential dangers of alcohol given their family's ugly history.

They all reacted differently to the warning. Mia brushed him off. That's what teenage girls do. Maria Elena told her father she didn't want to drink in college. When she did, Ramon told her it was all right and to do so wisely; she heeded to his advice. Luisa had only just recently begun attending college, and she was still having fun. It was simply too early to tell with their youngest.

Right off the bat, Ramon knew Ana had the gene. It was obvious. Within weeks of her first drink, he noticed the lying. The lies were small at first, but they grew. She lied about what she had for breakfast, and she lied about her marks in school.

When Ana was eighteen and a couple months away from her high school graduation, Ramon and Adriana sat her down. Without explicitly mentioning her excessive drinking, they asked her if she was truly ready for college. She had been accepted into Texas Tech University, which was a five-hour drive east from Albuquerque. Her parents worried she would flunk out of school, that she lacked the preparation needed for higher education. Ana shrugged them aside. She saw the freedom in college and grabbed hold of it.

After one semester in Lubbock, Ana was booted from the university. She failed four of five classes and drank her way through the days. Her roommate, a young woman she'd never met before from El Paso but who shared Hispanic heritage with her, hated her due to her inability to stay sober and go to class. Ana was as ruthless as Doc Holliday in the region the outlaw once terrorized.

"I want to be a beauty shop owner anyways, *papa*," Ana told Ramon. "Why do I need a college degree?"

Ana's aspiration to own a beauty parlor was a dream that Ramon wholeheartedly wished to encourage. In fact, there was nothing he desired more than to see his eldest daughter succeed. However, the patriarch found himself disappointed by the way Ana misrepresented her journey. Initially expressing her intent to study at Texas Tech, Ana was now entangled in a web of falsehoods regarding the path in which she had taken to reach her dream. It was incredibly frustrating.

After she flunked out by way of a letter sent to her parents, Ana moved back into their West Mesa home. They didn't speak for days. It was January, and a bit chilly as it gets in New Mexico, and Ana spent most of her time in the room she shared with Mia.

Secretly, Ana was drinking. She started boozing late enough in the evening to the point that Ramon and Adriana wouldn't notice. Mia saw, though. She heard twisted caps popping off at midnight and the crack of corked bottles of wine. She knew her big sister was suffering.

After many years of substance abuse, Ana finally opened her own beauty salon. Mia was a senior in high school and had seen her older sister drink for a long time. Ana had begged Ramon for a loan for years, and he finally gave in. He saw the bags under her eyes, the red veins in her sclera. He felt for his oldest daughter, for he knew, like Mia did, that Ana was hurting.

Of course, Ramon's decision to gift her the money would eventually come back to haunt him. His income at the shop had plateaued in the 2000s after the construction of a rather large Albertsons grocery store across the street. Big corporations were figuratively bulldozing smaller, more family-oriented businesses like Ramon's. Also, the use of cash began to fade a bit as credit cards largely took over the bulk of monetary transactions. Often, customers were filling up their gas and leaving without entering the store. Ramon was the one taking the hit. Still, Ana was his daughter, and she had a dream. Their oldest had drawn up a legitimate business plan and they were happy with her idea. The sole condition attached to their support of Ana's parlor was her sobriety. She promised to oblige.

Twelve days into the construction of De Leon's Salon in Santa Fe, New Mexico, Ana relapsed hard. Her newfound freedom in her early-to-mid-twenties was, like her semester at Texas Tech, a recipe for disaster. As a result of her week-long bender, she missed many important meetings with the construction crew. They became agitated with her, and several of them even threatened to quit the project. Adriana made the sixty-mile trek one morning when Ana wasn't responding to calls on the new cell phone she had purchased. She found her daughter in the apartment she had just leased, passed out and reeking of booze. Ana and her parents' agreement lasted just three weeks, and Adriana became the new construction contact for De Leon's. She spent weekends up in Santa Fe to both keep an eye on her daughter and to make sure Ramon's loan wasn't blown.

De Leon's opened in 2007, when Ana was just shy of twenty-four years old. Adriana was the reason the plan went swimmingly. Her eldest daughter would pull herself together for a day or two before succumbing to yet another relapse, throwing her mother into an emotional whirlwind. It was at this point that Ramon and Adriana realized the parlor was a bad idea that could never be redeemed.

--

Despite becoming American citizens, the late 2000s were strenuous for Ramon and Adriana De Leon. Life had become a little less rambunctious because only two of their girls remained in their home. Mia was growing up and had a serious boyfriend, Scott, a white man they loved. He was sweet and good to their daughter, and that's all that mattered to them. Ana was a different story. Yes, she had opened De Leon's beauty salon up in Santa Fe, and sure, she looked successful on paper. Her parents knew deep down her success hinged on her sobriety. To be frank, she stunk at sobriety. She had tried going cold turkey several times and had failed just as many.

Adriana wept at the thought of losing Ana. Her oldest child's drinking consumed her in a very different way than Ramon, who tried his best to be the protector. Conversely, Adriana couldn't help but feel like Ana was slipping through her fingers. Every conversation, she knew her daughter was drifting further away with the perpetual boozing and the persistent lies. Oh, the lies.

Ramon had kept in semi-regular contact with Luis Alvarez, the man who decades earlier had inadvertently brought the family to New Mexico. Luis, who still lived in Arizona, had a son, Alexander, who was two years sober in 2008 when Ramon first brought up Ana's dirty little secret.

Luis, always known by the De Leons to be a man of high virtue, hopped in his car from Phoenix that same night and jetted off east to talk.

Ramon would never forget the way Luis' Lincoln Town Car headlights shined through their living room door. Adriana, who was knitting a quilt in the area lit by the beacon, gasped. She thought it was a police car coming to tell them Ana was dead. You can't blame the mother of an alcoholic for always thinking the worst.

Luis and Adriana engaged in a lengthy embrace, not the kind that could be misconstrued as pervy, but the type that says, "I'm here for you as a friend and I understand." After all, that's what Adriana wanted, to be affirmed Ana would be all right. Besides, she had proved her faithfulness to Ramon time and time again.

"My friend." Ramon grabbed Luis' hand firmly and shook it with intensity. Luis knew the intensity of the moment deserved a hug and so he wrapped his arms strongly around his friend. Ramon tried his hardest not to burst into tears. Standing next to him, Adriana's efforts didn't last.

"There are three things that happen to alcoholics," Luis said in Spanish, placing his right index finger over the triad on his left which he planned to use to demonstrate. "They either get sober, go to jail, or die. That's it."

To Adriana, Luis shone like the headlights of his Lincoln Town Car. She believed every word he said. It felt like a gut punch to hear death being discussed in relation to her daughter.

Ramon asked Luis how he knew all this. Because, he said, he had gone through all this with Alexander in prior years. Adriana, who was still processing that Luis believed there was a thirty-three point three percent chance her daughter would succumb to death by way of alcoholism, changed the subject abruptly, asking their friend if he would like to stay for the night. Luis said that would be fine, but he needed to get home the next day.

"You've come all this way," Ramon said, "just to tell us she might die?" He was right in a way. Phoenix to Albuquerque is a six-hour drive and most of it filled with sharp and elevated turns. Northerners like Scott Sharpe who drove through the plains would grip the steering wheel tightly out of fear. Depending on which route he took, Luis would've had to drive through Tonto National Forest, which is full of elevation changes and elk, or Flagstaff, which is full of elevation changes and elk.

"I came as a friend," Luis said. "To hear that your daughter may die from this disease is tough to stomach. I couldn't say it on the phone."

Ramon and Adriana appreciated the candor, even if it stung. "What do we do?" Adriana asked. "What was your role in Alexander's journey?"

"This is going to hurt to hear," Luis said. "You can't do anything."

The De Leons let out a synchronized gasp. "What?"

"Again, why I'm here. This is difficult to hear over the phone. I'll be the shoulder for you to cry on when it gets tough. You can do it. I know this is horrible. I have been there before. There will be a moment soon where she will choose her path among the three."

They spoke for another hour or two, and then Luis used Ana and Mia's old room to lay his head for the night.

Ana's life continued to tumble. Less than a year after it opened, De Leon's in Santa Fe closed. Ana had not been making payments to the building she was renting from, and she was finally convinced to sell all her property.

And yet, she continued to drink. The disease seemed hell-bent on claiming its next victim.

Chapter 15

Being kicked out of the house really sucks. The part that sucks the most about being kicked out of the house isn't leaving your wife and your two sons; it's the part where you must suddenly decide where you're going to sleep that night. That part really sucks.

I don't have any ride-or-die friends in Denver. Mia thinks we have this whole place at our fingertips, but we don't. If I were in Minneapolis, I'd have fifteen good folks who would take me in. Strong geographical connection is key to making this part about being kicked out suck less.

As I packed a quick overnight bag and swiped some cash, it occurred to me I probably shouldn't be driving in the Acura. Drinks from hours earlier would show up on a breathalyzer if I were to get pulled over. So, I decided to walk. This was, by all accounts, the first wise decision I made all day.

It was a brisk late February Denver evening, so I grabbed my North Face jacket and headed to the outside world. I checked the weather app on my phone and was informed of the twenty-six-degree air temperature.

I walked about a mile from our neighborhood to the nearest points of interest in town. I saw the flashing sign of the Red Roof Inn behind the Costco, which is coinciden-tally where I bought the bottle of booze that became the nail in my coffin. I had a few hundred dollars in cash, and so I strolled up to the motel to get a room. It was nearly nine at that point, and I was growing sleepier by the minute. I snagged a room key from the manager and lay on the stiff bed of Room 17. The headache surged through my cranium like a vicious strike of lightning.

And yet, I couldn't sleep. My whole body ached, and I felt anxious. The anxiousness I felt caused my brain to swirl with numbers. To be precise, the mathematical odds of Costco still being open. My phone informed me they closed at nine, and it was eight fifty-five.

When people say they make the most athletic of achievements when they're up against the clock, or the throes of danger, they are not lying. In the five minutes between checking my phone and Costco shutting down shop for the day, I managed to run a block to the store, display my identification to the greeter who always believe they are way more important than they actually are, locate the generic Kirkland bottle of vodka, pay for said vodka at the register that was at least fifty yards away from the liquor, and head out the doors as the overhead announcer yelled over the intercom, "Attention, shoppers! We are now closed for the day." It was a miracle.

I fist pumped my way the entire block back to the Red Roof Inn, almost losing control of the cylindrical, narrow-necked bottle on no less than two occasions. *Maybe this motel has a movie playing tonight,* I wondered. *Then we'll have ourselves a jolly old winter night!*

Then I realized as I approached the motel: I had forgotten a chaser! How was I supposed to chase this liquor? With water? I walked back up to the office I bought the room in fifteen minutes earlier and asked the manager on duty, "Do you know where I can get a pop?"

Dave, as his nametag read, snickered. "A *pop*? You mean a soda?"

"Oh, you're one of those people," I snapped back at the guy. After all, a boatload of Coloradans say pop.

"Well, we can't all be right about everything," Dave said. "In fact, when I was boy I thought giants were real. That's because my Aunt Berta used to say that—"

"Is there a vending machine?" I interrupted.

"Wow," Dave replied. "Fine then. Yes, it's around the corner."

"Sorry buddy, I'm on a time crunch."

I got out of the office quicker than you can say "Dave". I was faster than, say, a man trying to get hammered from a Costco bottle of vodka five minutes before the store closes.

In possession of a twelve-ounce can of Sprite, I sank into the flimsy double bed provided to me by the Red Roof Inn. In keeping with the tradition of other mattresses in mediocre hotels, I found myself collapsing into the center. Boy, was I fortunate that Mia wasn't with me. She harbored a particular disdain for these types of beds. My thoughts shifted back to Mia and the trouble I was in. If only I could've stayed sober, then I'd be at home in my giant California king-sized bed.

I really did screw up. I longed for my girl and missed my boys. How could I cope with this guilt? I remembered the liquid Costco courage beside me and swiped the bottle. I took a hefty swig, then another, and another, and another, and another. I nearly vomited and then laughed when I noticed I hadn't used a chaser.

Gunsmoke was on television, and it reminded me of my mother. I remember the 1990s when my mom would sit on her disgusting velvet couch, smoke copious amounts of Marlboro reds, and drink Johnnie Walker whiskey. That odor still fills my nostrils to this day. I can't get it out of my head. She'd kill me if she saw me drinking vodka. She'd call me a sissy.

I still resent her. She had a marriage, three kids, and everything was good in Minnesota. Then it hit me like a ton of bricks. My wife kicked me out. My "marriage" was good. Had I become my mother?

--

The phone rang in the morning loudly, too loudly, so loud I believed the sound to be a part of the dream I was sucked into. Reality set in, and as is tradition, my temples throbbed. I eyed a Papa John's pizza box out of the corner of my vision, and the Costco liquor bottle lay on its side. It looked like I had drunk half of the handle. I did the math quickly—that was twenty shots of vodka.

I groaned when I saw it was Mia calling. "Hello?" I muttered. The clock on the left side of the bed read eight thirty-two. It was hours later than I normally rose. I had forgotten to plug my phone in the night before, and the battery read five percent.

"Scott?" Like the night prior, Mia was all business.

"Yes?"

"How are you?" I got the sense my wife was feeling a bit guilty about kicking me out. In the six years we had been married, she had never even once requested that I sleep on the sofa. Perhaps she was calling to say she overreacted and was sorry.

"I'm fine, Mia," I lied. "More importantly, how are you?"

"I'm not good," she admitted. "I need you to hear the words I am saying, okay?"

"Okay."

"I love you, Scott," Mia sighed, "but your drinking is harming our *familia*." She oftentimes used words in her native language when she was nervous. I normally thought it was cute, but in this case I was afraid of what she would say next. The initial thoughts of her guilt faded away with the memory of the last forty-eight hours. "I even knew from the moment you answered my phone call right now that you drank last night. Maybe even this morning, too."

She was right, and I did not even try to deny it. "I want to come home, Mia," I said. "I love you, too."

"Love isn't enough," she said. "I know you love us, but you're sick. I'm not going to enable this behavior any longer."

"What are you saying?"

"I'm saying that I am not going to stand by and wait for you to be the man I need you to be." It sounded so rehearsed. I knew Mia well enough to know her nervous tics. She hated prepared speeches. She loathed the anticipation of such talks. Suddenly I realized this was one of those situations. I had become the bad guy that required the speech.

"Mia, I'm not drunk."

"Stop the lying, Scott." Her stern voice persisted.

"What now?"

"I think I'm going to take the boys to stay with my parents for a while."

"In New Mexico?" I shouted.

"Yes." Again, there was no hesitation or Spanish in her voice. She was dead serious.

"Mia. Why?"

"You need help, Scott," she calmly explained. "I can't help you with this one. Goodbye, *mi marido*."

"Mia, wait—" My iPhone clicked off. She hung up on me. In retaliation my shaky right thumb smashed the green phone icon on the bottom left of the home screen. "Recents" popped up with the name Mia Sharpe, and I pushed it with anger. The phone read "calling mobile..." as it rang once, twice, three times. My marriage flashed before my hungover, reddened eyes. About fifteen seconds after I dialed, which seems like an eternity in phone world, she answered.

"What?" She sighed afterward to emphasize her impatience. I could picture her in her sweatpants, her right hand palming the phone and her left placed on her hip. I teased her a lot for that maneuver. Boy, did I miss her.

"I miss you." It was an incredibly dumb and ill-timed thing to say, but it was the only thought passing through my mind.

"I miss you too, Scott, but that doesn't mean—"

I couldn't take the lecture again. "Let me come home, Mia."

"You can go home in thirty minutes if you want for all I care," she said. "I am packing for myself and the boys."

"That's not what I mean," I pleaded. "I mean you, me, the boys all home together."

"Scott," she said. "Let me repeat this: *you are sick.* I am going to New Mexico to be with my parents for a bit."

"What are you going to say to them?" I demanded to know. "Are you going to trash me?"

"Of course not," Mia said. "That's not who I am. I'll tell them we need a quick getaway. I'll lie for you, Scott."

"I need you to."

"What does that mean?" she huffed. "Your drinking does not mean I'll lie for you. That's my decision. I don't want to be that couple for the kids. You get your head on straight."

"So what?" I asked. "You'll go to New Mexico for, what, a week?"

"About."

"Then what?" I shouted.

"I'll come home," she said. "But I need to think about whether I want you in the house with me."

My heart stopped. "What are you talking about, Mia? Divorce?"

"That's not what I said. I need time to think."

"Think about what?"

"About whether I want my sons to grow up with an alcoholic father!" That jab by Mia stung a bit.

"An alco-what?" I hated hearing that. Immediately, my mother entered my mind. *She* was an alcoholic, not me. "Mia, do you realize how *stupid* that comment is? You know my mother was a real alcoholic, not me."

"What do you call what you're doing then, Scott?"

"Call *what*?" I was infuriated.

Mia took a deep breath and responded, "The lies. The drinking. The showing up late and sleeping in late on workdays, not workdays. Not helping with Frankie. Always using the 'work' excuse. Drinking a glass of wine with dinner, with our child there at the table. The whiskey bottle I found on your side of the closet last week. Going to the gala a few weeks ago and getting hammered to the point of you passing out in the front seat while I was driving us home. Going to the casino and getting drunk enough to call a cab home and have to have me drive you to your car the next morning. What do you call that, Scott? Is it an accident? Surely, it's no fault of your own. What kind of man, what kind of father, willingly does those things? It's not your fault, Scott, that's not what I'm saying. But to call it anything other than what it is—a problem—is not fair to me. Or your children, for that matter."

"Well—" *Did Mia just give me the answer I was looking for? Am I sick?* Of course, my first instinct was to remember "it's not your fault, Scott." That's what I was taught as a boy. "It sounds like I need to do some thinking."

"Please do, Scott," she said.

"What if I came down to New Mexico with you?" I asked.

"Don't." Mia's cold voice persisted. If I did not know any better, it sounded as if she was speaking with a lawyer present.

"I won't."

In a lifetime full of them, letting Mia and the boys drive to New Mexico by themselves would turn out to be my worst mistake.

Chapter 16

The Rio Grande splits Albuquerque in two. The east side is more populated, has more amenities, and is home to the Sandia Mountains. The jagged peaks of the range are so tall and well-defined they can be seen from almost any point of the city. "Sandia" is Spanish for watermelon, which is a reference to the chain's reddish hue at sunset. Conversely, the west side is home to a few residential areas that expand out a few miles, but otherwise there are almost no points of interest or elevated areas of note. The zoos, skyscrapers, and golf clubs are nearly all on the eastern portion of town.

Ramon De Leon was quite fond of the Rio Grande, as it distinctly delineated the west and east sides of Albuquerque. He found the river, even in its near proximity to the city, to be the most peaceful place in all of New Mexico. In fact, when he was stressed out, he was known by Adriana to either speak to Father Pedro or to venture to the only body of water in the city. Adriana would call it his "run to the Rio". Even though the river was oftentimes an unappealing shade of copper, he would run his bare feet along the slimy rocks and shallow waters of the shore. The sensation of his submerged feet pressing up against the uneven edges caused no agony. Ramon liked to look at the clumps of dusty mesquite trees and the tall, stiff yellow reeds and imagine he was somewhere further north. Perhaps he was in

Glacier National Park in Montana, where the grass was greener and the harrowing past of Mexico was a thousand miles away, or the Black Hills of South Dakota staring over the iconic granite formations. Ramon felt that, even though he lived less than a mile from the water, the Rio Grande represented a whole different world than West Mesa. Water, no matter its appearance, gave off the impression of an oasis that Ramon so longed for.

He would oftentimes bring a book along, typically a paperback written by his countryman Carlos Fuentes, and laugh at the old times he had in his homeland. He understood clearly the past was the past and he could never return to Mexico. Not now that he and Adriana had children and their roots were set, at least. Perhaps they could have gone as two adults, but crossing the border meant risking the safety of his girls. Those days, Ramon was often reminded of the famous saying, "You are only as happy as your least happy child." Ana's spirits were not high in the late 2000s, and by default neither were Ramon's. He found his sanctuary in the water during that time.

Oftentimes, he would hike a great distance along the river. He'd get in his GMC, drive an hour north, find a trailhead parking lot to dock his truck, and eventually divert from the series of dirt paths that separated civilization from the raw, rigid great outdoors. Ramon always sought to be in a place he could whip out his old *bastón*, a walking stick his father gifted to him back in Mexico, and trudge along with the snakes and scorpions like they were friends and not competing organisms of the same ecosystem. On one occasion, the man made it as far north as the famous Rio Grande Gorge Bridge, only to be disappointed as he was greeted by over a dozen tourists snapping pictures on their cameras. Ramon would be hypocritical in his attitude toward the gawking sightseers, as he often brought along his old Polaroid camera from Mexico.

Spotting wildlife was another cause for a trip to the river. Ramon had a book, *Wildlife of the Rio Grande*, he kept at home. His oldest daughter Ana had given it to him for Christmas in the mid-1990s, when she was eight or nine years old. He read the hardcover religiously, studying its pictures and descriptions of hundreds of species. Sandhill cranes migrated to New Mexico in the winter, and Ramon displayed his enthusiasm regarding their November arrival on more than one occasion at the De Leon dinner table.

One day when Maria Elena was nine years old, she came home and announced her third grade teacher had given her students the assignment of producing a booklet about a certain species. Ramon pleaded with her to select the sandhill crane as her subject. After many days of back and forth, Maria Elena finally gave into his request. If you were to ask Maria Elena to summarize the project in hindsight, she'd tell you her father completed the entire thing. Ramon became so obsessed he began working on the task without his third daughter.

When it came time to present the assignment to her class, Maria Elena broke down in tears. She knew next to nothing about sandhill cranes. Her teacher asked if she had finished the project, and she admitted her father, standing in the back of the classroom, beaming seconds earlier, had done the whole activity by himself.

Maria Elena's teacher gave her a second shot, and Ramon backed off. She chose to highlight the African elephant, the reason being African elephants stay near their parents for years. It was a bit tongue-in-cheek humor and directed at Ramon, who shed a tear or two when she presented to the class. In response, Maria Elena's father took her to the ABQ BioPark Zoo in town to show her a real elephant. Jointly they met Dumbo, the resident animal, and the picture the three took together still hangs in Maria Elena's present day room in Dallas.

In spite of that ordeal, Ramon loved the animals of the Rio Grande, and the animals of the Rio Grande loved Ramon. He could hurl a slice of Wonder Bread twenty feet into the river and be uncertain about which creature would swoop down, or swim up, to claim it. The magic never ended on the Rio.

--

On a blustery wintry day in the late 2000s, a few months after Ana opened her shop in Santa Fe, Ramon took Luisa to the Rio Grande. Luisa inherited her daddy's height and frizzy hair, yet at barely over four feet tall, she was an inquisitive eight-year-old full with curiosity and awe. She carried around a Hello Kitty backpack, stocked with a pen and paper, ready to navigate situations where communication would become a challenge. She was living proof that autistic children clearly are as smart or smarter than the lot of them.

"*Papa*, why is the Rio Grande so red?" she asked.

Ramon did not know the answer, so he improvised. "It's red because it has been touched by *Dios*." He later came to know the reason the river turns a reddish color is because minerals like iron dissipate into the water from rocks over time.

Luisa scratched her hair and fidgeted with her ponytail. "What animals live in the river?"

"It's not so much about what lives in the river," Ramon explained. Again, he didn't really know the answer. "That is a simple enough answer. Fish live in the river. It's who lives *by* the river."

"Oh." Luisa pulled out her notebook and began scribbling notes. "Who lives near the river?"

"Mammals."

"What's a ma-ma-mammal, Daddy?"

"A mammal lives on the land," Ramon said. "Like you and me, *niñita*."

"But we don't live here."

"Ah, but we do live *near* here, don't we?"

"Not really," Luisa said. "It's not even close to the neighborhood we live in, Daddy." She shook her eight-year-old head. "Not even close."

Ramon's mustache curled into a graceful arc as he smiled. Luisa did not yet fully grasp the size of the world. To her, Albuquerque was the beginning, middle, and end. Because they had just become legal citizens, the De Leons had not traveled anywhere outside Bernalillo County.

Luisa hung her head. You could see she wasn't impressed and had more questions. "What do you think about here, Daddy?"

Ramon wouldn't dare tell her the truth about Ana. He and Adriana had agreed they would never speak to their children about her alcoholism, that it would be Ana's truth to share. They also had vowed they would never utter a word about Bart Thompson, Sr. either. Luisa was far too young to learn about any of this.

"I just like the river." It was the truth, for it was Ramon's refuge.

Trying to emulate her father, Luisa dipped her painted-on hot pink toenails into the mucky brown water of the Rio. "Ew," she scowled. "That is *so* yucky, *papa*." She then opened her Hello Kitty backpack and snatched the notebook and scribbled a few words and a drawing on a blank sheet with her hunter green Gelly Roll pen—she emphasized to her parents that hunter green was *not* a boy color—that resembled a differently shaded Rio Grande. Luisa tapped the back of her Gelly Roll onto the spiral edges of her wide ruled journal. She found the sound oddly satisfying, like a housefly vigorously rubbing its wings.

As it happens once every hour or so, a kayaker made their way past. Ramon was a little disappointed that his time with his youngest girl had been tainted a bit by the sight of an outsider. However, he couldn't hog the Rio. Luisa rubbed her head. "Why would anyone ever want to come here?"

Ramon chuckled. This is what the river was all about for him. He understood the waters weren't aqua blue like they were on Cracker Lake or on the Gulf Shores of Florida. He knew many didn't dare go near it. But that's the exact reason why he and not so many others made it their haven. There was peace, solitude, even serenity on the river. He knew it, and the passerby on the kayak who gave him a slight nod with his cap knew it too.

Besides, on the Rio Grande every child is pure and innocent like his youngest and not an alcoholic like his oldest.

Chapter 17

The first day sober is the hardest. If they tell you otherwise, they're wrong.

After the depressing conversation with Mia, and an excruciating twenty-minute internal dialogue, I made a vow to myself I would give sobriety a shot. Plentiful Internet research told me the first try will likely not be the last. Having read that, I felt a giant weight released from my shoulders. Just give it a go and let's see what happens, I convinced myself. If you screw up, you just get right back on the wagon. No harm, no foul.

So, I decided in a smelly old Red Roof Inn room on a crappy Sunday morning to stop drinking. To kickstart that process, I symbolically poured the last bit of the Costco vodka down the drain of the stained, cracked porcelain sink. I hopped in the shower, ready to commence my newest trial. The piping hot water hitting my cracked skin felt good, like it was washing the drunk out of me. It was the type of shower head that only pushed out scalding or freezing water. I chuckled to myself because I knew Mia would even still regard the temperature as too chilly for her. I suddenly remembered Mia. I had to get her back. Today I would get one step closer to holding her in my arms again.

The Red Roof Inn was void of outstanding coffee and I didn't fancy walking a block, so I utilized the Keurig wannabe in my room. My fingers shook as I ripped open the container of dry coffee beans. The seconds faded away as I sat on the edge of the bed waiting for my caffeine. The tiny apparatus beeped twice and I extended my arm to pick up the Styrofoam cup.

I took my sweet time packing my clothes. I checked out of the Red Roof Inn around noon and walked across the street and ate two gigantic, greasy tacos at Torchy's. They sure hit the spot and lifted my spirits as my hangover cooled off. I walked right past the Costco and did not stop until I made my way up my tree laden driveway at two o'clock on the dot. I walked into the mud room and turned left into the bathroom. The sink still had water droplets in it, so I knew Mia and the kids had only recently departed. I engaged in another internal debate on whether to follow them down south, but my brain swiftly dismissed the idea.

Every time my body urged me to descend to the basement bar, I had to use physical restraint. My temples throbbed—I'm not sure if this was the pressure to drink or overcoming what I had hoped would be my final hangover—and I could feel my wrist pulsating at an incredible level. My muscles ached like I had just shoveled a long driveway in the aftermath of a Minnesota blizzard in January.

I made another cup of coffee and turned on the television. It was just a distraction, really. I wanted no part of anything other than to get through the shakes. There was no denying it; I was experiencing withdrawal. I had passed the point of hangover and now my body just shivered. Whereas on a normal day, I'd throw back a drink or two to level myself out, I didn't today. As the clock approached four o'clock in the afternoon, I began to feel like I was being watched. I stood up and walked about the house. As I walked up the basement stairs, I rolled my eyes at the Scottish poster we hung years ago. It read, "Lang may yer lum reek," which translates to "May you have a long and healthy life." Sharpe is a name of Scottish origin, though I had never been. Interestingly enough, neither Mia nor I have ever visited the countries where our ancestries hold the strongest roots. Because Mia's parents had been illegal immigrants when they first lived in America, she had never been able to go back and see their homeland.

Regarding Mia, she and the kids were likely in Trinidad by now, around ten miles north of the New Mexico border in Colorado. The drive down Interstate 25 between Denver and Albuquerque is gorgeous, almost like one of those fantasy calendars come to life. Mesas, tall buttes, green and brown mountain ranges, and tumbleweeds are the main attractions, and I love it all. The high desert of the Rocky Mountains transforms into the speckled Sangre de Cristo Mountains and finally into the southwestern tablelands once you make it to Santa Fe.

Too bad I didn't listen to Mia and swap Find My Friends locations. Then I'd know their actual whereabouts instead of speculating.

--

I was bored and shaky, so I flipped on Netflix. There was some new documentary or movie about *Mister Rogers' Neighborhood* and Mia had talked about watching it. The thought of the show brought me back to childhood, my superficially simple yet intricately complex youth. I remember an incident in that brick home that terrifies me to my core even today. My brothers and I were sitting in the living room watching Fred Rogers prattle on with the delivery man, Mr. McFeely, when I heard two loud consecutive bangs just outside our house. Dad yelled at us to retreat to the unfinished basement, which doubled as a place of safety in the case of emergencies and storms. He threw on his ball-cap, grabbed a baseball bat from the coat closet, and sprinted outside to investigate. The three of us boys heard blaring voices through the pipes. Minutes later Dad joined us in the basement and told us the loud noises were nothing to worry about and that we were safe to come upstairs now. Simon, Spencer, and I were all very confused, but we listened to our hero anyway. If he told us all was well then all was well.

That evening after dinner my parents told us to march outside and play "night games" in the dense forest. We would indulge in games with neighbors of capture the flag, hide-and-seek, and sardines. Truly, when I look back at my childhood, night games were a profoundly positive experience. We knocked on the doors of the Simpson and Gaines family homes, and the eight of us kids ventured out into the warm Minnesota summer night. It was healthy for us kids to play outside together, unmistakably, but it was also an excuse for Mom and Dad to get together with the other four parents and drink and smoke cigars. As the illuminated orange sky transformed into a dreary black, the neighbors were engaging in a game of hide-and-seek. I was one of the seven hiders. Part of the area in which we were to hide lay on my parents' property, and so I knew it would be a good while before someone found me in the storm window. My brothers knew of the secret spot, of course, but it was our compadre Alana Gaines who was the seeker so she wouldn't be privy to the location.

So, as soon as the hiders were dismissed, I bolted to that storm window. Sweat beads flew down my forehead as I dashed as quickly as my brand-new Sketchers would allow. I hopped the three feet to the bottom and thudded against the mound of dirt that lay between me and the earth. A few moments later, I heard more footsteps. I hoped they didn't belong to Alana, for if they did she certainly hadn't waited for the proper amount of time. Luckily, they didn't, as Spencer leapt in and smacked his own kicks against the hard dirt.

"Sh!" I called out to my brother next to me. I don't think he initially saw me, and we were lucky he hadn't fallen on top of me.

Spencer laughed and whispered back, "How did you make it here first? I thought I took the shortcut."

"I guess I'm just a bit quicker in my Sketchers than you are in your Jordans." I chuckled. "Man, I forgot how gross it is down here."

"I must have barely missed you," he said.

"That's true. If Simon were to come down here, we'd be screwed. At least one of us is losing our head."

"He's not coming here," Spencer said. "I saw him headed for the freaking tall grass."

"Thank the Lord."

Spencer laughed again, and we prayed Alana wouldn't find us. My hands fumbled around in the soil as I sat up against the brick. I felt something strange between my right ring and pinky fingers. I dismissed it at first, believing to be a worm, but I remember thinking it felt too hard to be a worm. Besides, it didn't move at all when I touched it. I fumbled it around in my fingers and I knew it was cylindrical. It was about two inches long from top to bottom. One end felt almost metallic, and the rest of the tubelike object had straight line ridges running up it. In my hand I held a shotgun shell.

Dad hunted pheasants in Madelia, a town about ninety minutes southwest of where we lived, with a shotgun, but even I knew at eleven years of age that the shell is only exposed after it has been shot. A chill ran down my bent spine as I then realized someone had blasted a shotgun on our property. Then I remembered earlier in the day when I heard the loud explosion outside. Stiffness seeped through every muscle in my body as the truth registered. Mom was shooting a gun no more than twenty feet from all three of her sons.

It was at that moment I heard the leaves rustle a few yards away. Someone was nearing the storm window in which Spencer and I lay. Panic coursed its way through my bones and I tried to be silent. Then the head of Alana Gaines popped up. "I found you! I found you!"

I never told Spencer about the shell.

--

I made a pizza for dinner, Jack's pepperoni and sausage. All factors considered it was delicious. The grease, meat, and mozzarella cheese provided a delectable combination. I couldn't think long about the food though. My family was probably somewhere in between Springer and Las Vegas, New Mexico, without me.

The protein in the pizza helped me a bit with the shakes. I knew I was irritable at this point. I'd pondered going to pick up cigarettes no less than ten times in the preceding hours. We had a porch for a reason. Why not call all my friends and have a party? It would be a boozeless party, I assured myself. Then I realized how dumb that sounded, to have a party without at least beer. I knew in my heart I could do this, though, that I could kick the alcohol and get Mia back. Oh, Mia. I wanted to kiss her like we used to, to show her what she meant to me, to get her one dozen Calla lilies and listen to that voice of hers as she cried out, "Aw. You're the sweetest, Scott." I wanted her to leave a dark red lipstick mark on my cheek that required extensive effort to wash off.

I wanted to pick up Francisco and play the airplane game he loved, to kiss the top of his head and tell him how much Daddy loves him. I wanted to tell him so many times he'd say, "I know, Daddy." I wanted to play a game of hide-and-seek with him, watching as he covered his face with his hands. I wanted to see him peek through them to cheat right before he said, "Here I go, Daddy!"

I wanted to hold Marcos. I had done it just once in the hospital, and it wasn't enough. I wanted to tell him about all the baseball games we'd go to, all the bratwursts we'd make for dinner and television we would watch because Mommy was out of town or gone for the evening. I wanted him to look up at me and know me. It killed me that he was a few days old and had no idea who I was.

That last thought triggered me a bit. I knew how difficult it was to travel with a newborn baby—we had done so with Francisco when he was a month old—and yet Mia still decided to drive 400 miles to New Mexico anyway. She decided her trials were more impactful than the kid having an immediate relationship with his father. I tried to make sense of that, but I just couldn't.

Suddenly, my phone lit up. It was a two-word text from Bart Thompson, a full sentence. The words *I'm calling* appeared. The phone rang a moment later, and my boss' name flashed across the blurry screen. The "slide to answer" button, next to the green phone icon, sparkled. I picked it up. "Hello?"

"You are in big trouble, Sharpe."

I gulped. "What are you talking about, Bart?"

"He told you this would happen." Bart Thompson's voice was stern.

"Who's 'he'?" I shouted.

"Keith Stephens."

I was utterly confused. "Keith? What did he tell me?"

"He told you what would happen if you didn't pay."

"What are you talking about? I paid."

"Scott, just how hammered were you?" Bart asked. "You borrowed ten thousand, not eight."

I wasn't quite sure how to respond. "Let's say you're right. You've known about this for months and are just telling me this now?"

"Unlike you, Sharpe," Bart said over the phone, "I prefer to play the long game. We knew and decided not to take advantage until today."

"What does that mean?"

Bart explained, "I did, uh, let's call it research."

"Research on who? What?" I asked.

"Research to nail you. Today, we took advantage. This is about more than the two thousand you took."

"Nail me for what? Took advantage of what? What is about more than two grand?" I was so confused. What was this maniac saying? "Are you with the Satriones?"

"I will call back in a few minutes with this number: 303-555-1982. Talk soon. If you try to trace, you will regret it." The line went silent. I hopped up from the couch and immediately began pacing. My knees buckled, my head burned with an intensity so great from skepticism and withdrawal. What in the world was Bart Thompson talking about? Had I borrowed ten grand and not eight like I believed? I was drunk that night at the casino. I guess it could have happened. I sudddenly remembered the family history and the mailed finger and the threats from Keith and Joey Satrione.

My thoughts were interrupted by the number flashing across my iPhone: 303-555-1982. Maybe from Denver, Colorado, it said. I answered the call within three seconds.

"Bart?" I cried out.

"Maybe," he answered. "Are you tracing this call?"

"No." I don't know if Bart knew or not, but cops could play this conversation off my phone records. I couldn't believe this moron ran the national sales department of a large corporation and oversaw millions of dollars and still didn't know the power of the authorities.

"You never paid your full debt to the Satriones."

"I sure did," I said. "I paid the eight thousand that I borrowed."

"You idiot," Bart sighed. "Keith Stephens told me he lent you ten thousand."

"Then why am I talking to you about this?"

"Oh, come on, Sharpe," Bart replied. "A first grader could deduce why. You know."

"So, you're in it."

"If you think I'm a big enough fool to answer that—"

"So, why haven't you cut off a finger of mine yet?" I asked.

"Like I said, we did our research." Bart paused for a moment, presumably to build up the tension. "You may have noticed us around town." In that instant, the recollection of the parked Lincoln Continental came rushing back to me. I had noticed it during two recent inebriated episodes; once on my way home from work, and once from my living room the afternoon before.

"That was—that was you in the Lincoln?"

"Not me, technically speaking," he laughed over the phone. "But yes, *us*."

My world was spinning. I thought perhaps my mind was playing tricks on me. I was in withdrawal, after all. But no, I glanced at my phone and realized Bart Thompson speaking to me from a burner phone with a Denver area code was no dream.

"That's stalking," I said. "I'll go to the police over this."

"Stalking is the least of your worries."

"Why do you say that? All this over two thousand dollars?"

"He warned you, Sharpe." A momentary silence ensued after his statement, indicating to me that he was grappling with an object located away from the phone. Two distinguishable voices played over the speaker then. One of them was obviously me.

"I'll take ten g's," I said over the recorder.

"Now we're talking. With ten percent interest. That means you owe eleven thousand. You in?" Keith Stephen's low-pitched tone was a dead giveaway, even secondhand.

"Yes," I said back to him on the tape.

"Now I'm not messing around, Sharpe. You know who I'm with?"

There was a pause in the action before I responded. "Yes."

"The boss doesn't take kindly to people being late on their payments. You catch my drift, Sharpe?" I remembered the tall man in the glasses he was referring to.

"Yes," I said on tape for the third time.

"You better have my money next Saturday," he whispered. "I'm not kidding. Put in on my desk at Westco in a manila envelope and label it 'Sharpe'."

In the present, Bart Thompson smashed the stop button on the recorder and said, "See? You didn't follow our advice."

"Okay, I must have misunderstood. I thought I took eight thousand." I knew I was in deep crap. Though he couldn't see me, I straightened my shoulders and puffed out my chest, recognizing that confidence plays a huge role in situations like these.

"All right, you son of a bitch. What do you want?"

"Nothing," he said. "We have what we want."

"What do you mean?"

"I mean," Bart said, "we took the two thousand in a different way."

"What do you mean?" I gasped.

"Hey Mia, do you want to come say hi to your husband?" Bart's pitch was high, as if to mock me into submission.

"You're bluffing."

My heart shattered into a million pieces when I heard Mia's voice on the phone, "Do what he wants, Scott. He's serious and he has the kids."

"Mia, I love you," I called out, my voice cracking as if I were a scared prepubescent boy.

"Listen to him. The kids are here."

"Don't you dare hurt her, Bart. Or the kids. I'll kill you if you do!" My fingers were so sweaty that the phone began slipping in my hand and I nearly dropped it. I could hardly breathe, and my heart was beating rapidly. My shoulder and neck muscles tensed up into a ball increasing in size by the millisecond. The worst-case scenario of my existence had come to fruition.

When you're in that second of time your life changes, everything goes dark. Your central vision is obscured by a blackened area. The only reason you aren't fainting is because your wife and children's lives are suddenly on the line and you would do anything to prolong them. There is a Mount Rushmore of sorts when it comes to memorable, nerve-wracking moments of my life: First, the moment my fingers nestled that shotgun shell in the storm window of my crazy mother's house; secondly, that time I was thirteen and nearly fell off a twenty foot cliff into the Minnesota River; third, the instant I spotted Mia when the church doors swung open on our wedding day and I saw her in her white dress for the first time; and lastly, this one, when Mia began speaking into a phone, turning a simple two thousand dollar mistake into a life-or-death situation.

"I may just hurt her, Scott," Bart said. "We need something from you that means a lot, and maybe we'll return them."

"What do you need that 'means a lot'?"

"Oh, *you know*," Bart imitated my Minnesotan accent, and then rattled off slowly, "A finger, a few toes, a stab wound of some sort. Something that will make it hurt, like you hurt the Satriones."

"You're crazy."

"Boy, *you* made this crazy when you didn't pay back your debts." A moment elapsed, and I could tell the phone was switching hands. "I told you, punk." It was Keith Stephens, that evil loan shark.

"Look, Keith," I tried to reason with him because Bart had no intention of doing so. "I'll pay you back. I'll come to the casino and pay you back right now. Just let my wife and kids go."

Keith erupted into laughter, slowly and carefreely, his howls resonating over the telephone. "No can do. You screwed with us, and now we're going to screw with your wife."

"If you touch her—"

"But she's so pretty, you see?" Bart interrupted. "And so young, too. Can't believe a woman like this has given birth twice. She's a knockout." Over the course of the argument, I noticed a shift in his tone. The man was beyond sinister. Before today, he was just an annoying boss but now he had risen to frightening sociopath.

I balled my left fist in fury. Nobody talked to Mia like that ever. "Bart, you son of a bitch, listen to me—"

"And such a pretty name, too," he said. "Mia Sharpe."

"I will kill you, Bart. If you think I'm joking, you better just—"

"Of course," he ignored me. "It hasn't always been Mia Sharpe, has it?"

Again, my heart fragmented into countless bits. He knew. Somehow before their interrogation, he figured out her maiden name. Bart put two and two together and realized Mia's father was the one who killed his. *That* is what he meant when he said the kidnapping was about more than the two thousand I was into the mob for.

I remained silent, and Bart continued talking, "Of course, we all now know that she was born in New Mexico. 1990, was it? The daughter of immigrants." I heard Marcos cry in the back, and Mia, whose voice was scratchy, informed the kidnappers he was probably hungry. Keith shouted in the back, "What do I do, boss?"

I heard Bart faintly say, "Give him the bottle, you dumbass. He's a baby, not a Martian." Then he placed the phone back up to his ear. "Now where were we?"

"Don't you touch her, you prick."

"Oh, right," Bart continued. "I was about to make the great reveal." Then he said the words I'd been dreading to hear for years, "This whore's father murdered my father. He took something from me, so I'm going to take something from him."

Chapter 18

Despite the lows of Ana's alcoholism, not every day was a challenge for Ramon De Leon. His daughter Mia had brought home a nice white boy, Scott Sharpe, and things between the two seemed serious. Every time Mia would come home from college she'd talk exponentially more about the boy she was dating than the classes she was taking or the friends she was making. She was thriving in college, yet in comparison to the man she met those accomplishments seemed insignificant to Mia.

A few months after they began dating, Ramon and Adriana had a short but firm conversation regarding their support of Mia and Scott's relationship.

Adriana said to him in Spanish, "She's in love, isn't she?"

Also speaking his native tongue, Ramon responded, "She sure is. Our little girl has found her man."

"How do you feel knowing he is white?" Adriana asked.

He shrugged his shoulders. "As long as she's happy, I'm happy."

"That's good, Ramon. You are a good man." She moved across the couch and nuzzled into her husband's shoulder. He planted his left arm around her side and held her close. He kissed her on the top of her hand and rubbed the fabric of her blouse as they lay together.

"We've been through a lot, haven't we dear?" he asked.

"We certainly have, but we're better for it."

Considering the magnitude of his worst mistake years earlier, Ramon was proud of her answer. "That's what makes me believe we're doing great, is that we have a good marriage. And even though Ana is going through the toughest days of her life, it has made me understand that it's not our fault."

Adriana lifted her head and arched her furrowed eyebrows. "It sounds like you've been talking to Luis Alvarez again, with all that preaching."

Ramon smiled. She was right, in part. "What do you think of Scott?"

"I like him," she replied. "He's really good to her, even if he is a little shy."

"You married a shy man."

Adriana laughed. "You know, you should get to know the boy more."

"Yes."

"I'm serious," she said. "You should."

"Yes, I should." Ramon was uncomfortable. After all, this was the boyfriend of his little angel they were talking about. She may be grown up now, but he still imagined her as the tiny girl in pigtails who liked to read and play pretend cook with him. He wanted to protect her with his whole being.

"I'm serious." She swatted Ramon. "He said he likes to go to UNM basketball games. Why don't you take him up on it?"

"I don't know."

"I do," Adriana said. "He said he had the student package."

The quiet man raised his eyebrows halfway to his hair. "You want me to sit with the students? I'm almost fifty, Adriana."

"No, no." She threw her hands up in surrender. "I mean that to say you two have something in common." She rummaged through the stack of newspapers the De Leons had forgotten to throw away, searching for the day's edition of the *Albuquerque Journal*. Adriana found it, and in her excitement she repeatedly prodded her index finger into the paper, causing an indent. "They're playing Utah on Tuesday! Buy tickets and take the boy." She shoved her cellphone in Ramon's right palm. She had teased him relentlessly because he didn't own one. Ramon reminded her after twenty-odd years of marriage that he was a simple man who hated technology. Besides, she knew where he was all the time: home, Allsup's, or the Rio Grande.

So, the timid man called up his daughter's new boyfriend. His heart pounded with unrelenting anxiousness. Seven miles east, on the third ring, Scott answered on his brand-new Samsung Gleam.

"Hello?" he called out.

"*Hola*," Ramon said back. "I mean, 'hello'. It's Ramon." Knowing Scott's inexperience with his native tongue, he decided to stick with English.

Scott was confused but unintimated. He had thought he made an impeccable first impression on the De Leons, especially considering how inappropriate their oldest daughter Ana had acted towards him. He also knew this wasn't a call to inform him of danger regarding Mia, for he had walked her to class thirty minutes earlier. She was safe. What could he possibly be calling about?

"Hello, Ramon."

"What are you doing Tuesday night?" He got right to the point.

Scott, seated in the library, opened his backpack and grabbed the folded, partially crumpled New Mexico basketball schedule he had printed off months earlier. He saw a game listed on Tuesday, March 3rd, a home date against the Utah Utes. "I'm going to the basketball game," he said. "Utah."

"Oh, okay." From behind him, Adriana nudged Ramon, who had lowered the phone in defeat. She whispered to her husband in Spanish, "Ask him *now*."

Ramon obliged, placing the cellphone back up to his ear. "Do you want to go to the game with me? I got tickets."

"Oh, sure," Scott said, in that Minnesotan drawl of his. "I don't mean to be awkward, Mr. De Leon, but is Mia invited too? Or Mrs. De Leon?"

"No," Ramon said. "It'll be just us two *hombres*." He smacked his head lightly twice in embarrassment. Adriana laughed behind him, though not loud enough for their daughter's boyfriend to hear.

"Just us. Great. That sounds like, um, fun," Scott said. "Should we meet there?"

"No," Ramon declared. "I will pick you up."

"Okay."

"Yes. We will get a hot dog at six o'clock."

"Great," Scott stammered. "I know a good place."

"Great."

"Thanks, Mr. De Leon."

"You can call me 'Ramon', Steve," the man said back.

Scott opted not to correct him, having just been corrected himself. He chose to obey the implied hierarchy of daughter's boyfriend beneath daughter's father. "Thanks, uh, Ramon."

"See you Tuesday, son." Ramon threw his head back, ashamed of his verbiage. Why did he have to call him son?

Scott scratched his head across town. "Do you have my address?"

"I can, uh, get it from Mia," Ramon said.

"Uh, okay," Scott said. "Sounds like a plan." They both hung up and reflected on their bizarre phone conversation.

Ramon fell flat on his brown cattle leather rocking chair. "Ay, ay, ay. That was so awkward."

Adriana was laughing hysterically, bouncing about the room. She mimicked her husband playfully, "Call me 'Ramon', *Steve*! Ha!" Her ribs hurt from laughing and yet, watching her husband invite their daughter's boyfriend to a basketball game was just so painfully amusing she couldn't stop. "You couldn't ask the boy for his address? You are such a man, Ramon!"

He called Mia next. "Hello, sweetheart."

"*Hola, papa*," she answered. Rest assured, this call would be much less painful for both.

"Do you have Scott's address?"

"Scott's?" Mia asked. "Why?"

"I just invited him to the UNM game next Tuesday."

"Aw!" she squealed. "That is so sweet, *papa*. Did you call him?"

"I did."

"Great!" Mia said, and then paused for three agonizing seconds. She mustered up the courage to ask her father, "Why didn't you ask for his address then?"

"I don't know." Ramon had feared his second daughter would decipher her awkward father's actions.

"You are so silly," she said, and reluctantly gave her boyfriend's address.

--

Tuesday evening came, and as they discussed Ramon picked up Scott and they dined at the hot dog stand. The temperature was a cool fifty degrees, so both men were donning sweatshirts. Scott's was a black hoodie and featured the team name above the signature wolf logo, and Ramon's was colored a faded red with the old school lobo silhouette. They could not have looked more different walking from the parking lot across University Boulevard towards The Pit, the Lobo's basketball arena.

As Ramon guided his daughter's boyfriend down the stairs of Section E, Scott couldn't help but notice the considerable investment Ramon had made on the seats. Taking their places in row six, positioned directly behind the scorer's table at midcourt, the lavishness of Ramon's purchase became increasingly apparent with every step Scott took. He glanced to the right at the student section and hoped none of his friends would see him.

At least the awkwardness between the two men would subside now that the game was about to tip off.

Scott, for certain less shy than the man he sat next to, asked Ramon, "Where are you from originally?"

In a monotonous, uninterested fashion, Ramon responded, "Hermosillo, Mexico."

"Wow," Scott replied. "I've never even been to Mexico."

"I haven't been in years." The horn over the loudspeaker interrupted the final word of his sentence, and the players from both sides flooded the court in anticipation of tip off. A popular song played loudly, and the student section went wild. A chant of "Let's go, Lobos!" rang out, and the two men stood to join the majority. They clapped out of obligation.

Once they sat a few moments later, the conversation resumed. The conversation mostly resumed because Scott, not Ramon, of course, wanted it to. "Do you see your parents much in Mexico?"

"I have not in twenty-five years."

"Oh, I'm sorry to hear that," Scott offered.

"It's okay. What about your parents in Minnesota?"

"My dad, yes," Scott replied. "He's a great man and who I look up to the most. My mom, not so much."

"I am sorry to hear about your mother," Ramon offered his condolences. The University of New Mexico faithful went crazy as a Lobo slammed home a dunk, and a second later the announcer informed the crowd of the player who added the two electric points to the scoreboard.

Scott waited nervously for the applause to die down. "Yeah. Mom likes to drink." He gestured with his pinky and thumb, a foolish move considering Ramon spoke excellent English. "I'm sorry," Scott said. "I don't mean to offend with my gesture by assuming you didn't know my language."

"You could never offend me," Ramon said. "This country is too sensitive. Look at what they've done with Obama. They made him the savior of the country when there is but one, our Lord and savior Jesus Christ." It was the first time in the game he had said more than a few words to Mia's boyfriend. Of course, it had to be a political statement with a liberal university student he disagreed with.

Scott squirmed in his seat. He not only cast his vote for Obama but also contributed money, time, and effort to his 2008 campaign. "Yeah." Maybe Ramon wasn't enlightened like he because he didn't have the opportunity to go to college, thought Scott. But he did pay for these tickets, and so the student didn't acknowledge what he conceived to be pure ignorance on the part of his girlfriend's father. Now was not the time to start such a dissertation.

Ramon, on the other hand, had forgotten he even dissed the president. He changed the subject, "Team looks pretty good, huh?"

Scott nodded. "For sure."

"I am truly sorry about your mom," Ramon awkwardly changed the subject.

"Thanks."

Sensing the tension in the air, Ramon opted to shift the subject yet again, as if the atmosphere in those seats could be cut with a Smith and Wesson. "So, you like my daughter a lot, huh?"

The chair Scott occupied became a little damp after Ramon's question. He felt the foul juices of his armpits seep into the sweatshirt. Thank the Lord it was colored black. "I do. A lot a lot."

Ramon chuckled. "Oh? A lot a lot?"

"Yes."

"That's good," Ramon said. "She's a special girl, that one. Don't you mess with her."

"I don't intend to, sir," Scott replied. "I love her."

"That's good." The switch flipped, and Ramon suddenly became the more uncomfortable one.

The crowd cheered some, and then the announcer called out the name of the player who scored on the loudspeaker. Ramon and Scott were only half watching at that moment since the conversation between the two had grown in seriousness.

"If I may, sir," Scott said. "I even see a future with her."

"Will you treat her right? Take care of her?"

"Yes, sir."

"Good," Mia's father said. "Then it sounds like I have nothing to worry about."

And Ramon didn't. That is, until Scott's actions got her kidnapped nine years later. Then Ramon had something to worry about.

--

In the fall of 2012, two years after Luis Alvarez visited on a whim from Phoenix, Ana De Leon called home to her parents.

Adriana answered. "Hello?"

"*Mama*," she spoke emotionally. Adriana flagged down Ramon, who picked up the other telephone in the kitchen. Ana was now oblivious to the fact that both her parents could hear. The wonders of caller ID.

"I am coming home," she said. Her words seemed to be slurred, Ramon and Adriana later agreed. This wasn't exactly the call the couple wanted to receive, but they had hoped there was a light at the end of the tunnel.

Ana burst through the door an hour later, obviously intoxicated—which, in of itself, was alarming considering she lived sixty miles away—and shouted, "I can't do this anymore." Her father let out an enormous sigh of relief, but not so enormous that Ana could tell what was going on in her drunken haze.

"You can't do what, honey?" Adriana asked.

"I'm paranoid. I'm sick," Ana explained.

"We love you, *niñita*, and we always have." Ramon's eyes got hot. He wondered if this was "the moment" Luis had referred to.

"I need—help." Those words were all Ana's parents wanted to hear.

"We got you, baby," Ramon said. "Come home. It's time to start all over. You can do this."

Ana's breaths came quickly between long, drawn-out sobs, sounding like the engine of an old pickup truck. "I know I can, but I need help."

"We know just the friend," Adriana said, and walked over to the telephone and punched in a number. She fidgeted with the long, white, curly cord in her fingers. After a moment of silence, she said, "*Hola*, Luis. It's Adriana De Leon. Ana has come home. It's time."

Less than twelve hours later, Luis and his sober son Alexander Alvarez arrived in Albuquerque by way of their Lincoln Town Car. Luis whispered in Ramon's ear while the others hugged, "*This* is the moment I talked about a few years back, my friend. *This* is the moment where Ana has chosen her path among the three scenarios. It may not seem like it now, but you have so much to be proud of. The road is long, but she will get there."

--

That afternoon, as Alexander and Ana spoke of alcoholism and Adriana went out shopping for groceries, Ramon went down to the river to pray. He brought along his oldest friend in America.

As they worked their way through the thicket leading up to the Rio Grande, Luis began to sigh heavily. "How is *this* peaceful, my friend?" he sarcastically retorted.

Ramon shook his head and chuckled. Considering the gigantic influence Luis Alvarez had on his life, it was amusing to witness his friend's annoyance in his being tangled up in reeds and tall grass. He had such power in every aspect of his life apart from this.

"I've brought you to pray," Ramon said.

"Ramon, my friend, you know this is not a place of strength for me."

"Let me help you."

"No, Ramon." Luis was agitated and would not be convinced.

"Luis, you have helped me indescribably—"

"I said no."

Ramon smiled anyway. "Well then, you won't mind if I do." He knelt into the twisting grove of branches, unaffected by those reaching out to tempt him away from his prayer.

First and foremost, Ramon prayed for his marriage with Adriana. She was his first intention anytime he went down on bended knee. He prayed they continued to trust each other and be by each other's side day after day.

He prayed for his children. He thanked God for Luisa, his pure, innocent little girl he had not planned for but cherished every moment with. He prayed she may be guided by His presence every day. He thanked Him for Maria Elena, his college girl, the helper, and prayed that she trusted in His plans for her after school. He thanked Him for Mia, his girl who had given her heart to another man. He prayed that her upcoming wedding be the day she had hoped and planned for all her life. He thanked Him for Ana, and prayed she be protected in these early days of sobriety.

Ramon prayed for Alexander Alvarez, for his already incredible contributions to Ana and the time he would spend with her. Lastly, he prayed for Luis. To be able to have such an unrelenting friendship was a gift he treasured, and he knew that not everyone had someone like his friend.

After he was finished, Ramon said the Our Father and performed the sign of the cross. With a smile creeping onto his lips, he turned around. He could have sworn he had seen Luis' hands folded in prayer.

Chapter 19

Bart Thompson was out for blood.

"I don't know what you're talking about," I lied.

"What's not to get?" he yelled back. "Your bimbo wife, Mia De Leon, has a father named Ramon. He killed my father in New Mexico in 1995. In an Allsup's."

"Enough with the tough guy insults," I fired back. "Just tell me what you want in exchange for her."

"I'm not done talking!" Bart screamed in a psychotic, high-pitched voice that sounded a little like Mickey Mouse. "So, like I was saying, her father murdered my father. 1995. For no reason."

"Why do you suspect that?"

"Because I interrogated your wife," Bart said. "I put a gun to her pretty little head and asked her what her father did for a living. I found this all out a long time ago. I just needed her to confirm, and she did." After he finished speaking, I heard a telephone ring in the background. The sound reminded me a bit of the chime those old landlines used to have. I heard a similar tone growing up in Minnesota.

"Tell me what you want, Bart." I tried to remain calm. Since I was dealing with an insane person, I figured the best course of action would be to remain composed.

"I want something that means a lot to you," he laughed. "Then we're even."

"This is between you and I, Bart," I said. "Let Mia and the children go, and you and I can deal with this. Man-to-man."

Bart sighed deeply. He laughed again for a second, and then replied, "No. I don't like your dumb plan. See, that's the thing about winning a negotiation. I already have what's most important to you in the world!"

I pondered for a second. Then I said, "Fine. I'll give you a finger."

"I think that offer has expired."

"Why?" I shouted.

"Because it's just not quite as fun that way," Bart said. "Plus, I wouldn't see it."

"Let them go and I'll come to you."

"No," he chuckled. "I think I'll let you wait in agony for another day. This is too fun."

"I'm serious, Bart," I said. "I'll call the police."

"And I'm *serious*," he mocked me. "I'll kill your wife and sons, especially if you call the police."

Mia yelled in the background, "Cut off your freaking finger, Scott! He's serious!"

"Mia!" I shouted. "I'm coming for you."

"Ha!" Bart chortled. "You don't even know where we are. It's not hard to figure out. You've been here before. I want you and the man who killed my father here tomorrow morning at eleven o'clock. I want two thousand dollars, and I want you to be prepared to lose an appendage."

"Fine. Great. But how do I know where to go? What if I go to the wrong spot?"

"Because," he explained, "you'd be a moron not to know where I am. Your wife and kids' lives depend on it."

"And what if the police show up instead of me?" I asked.

"If the police are involved in any capacity, I will kill all three. Your wife? Dead. Your toddler? Dead. Your precious newborn baby? Dead."

"I will not call the police."

"Good boy," Bart said. "See you tomorrow morning. Eleven a.m."

He hung up and I chucked my iPhone at the basement couch. Now was not the time to panic, I told myself. I realized then the next two steps were to get my father-in-law to hustle up to Denver and for me to decipher the location of my family. Because Bart had said I was familiar with the place, there were three possibilities as to the whereabouts of Mia, Francisco, and Marcos. The first was Westco's headquarters, though I highly doubted that Bart Thompson and Keith Stephens would risk being found on any one of the company's hundred or so video cameras scattered throughout the property. The second was Jack's Burgers, but I had never been in the back of the restaurant. To get to the back room, I would need assistance from the staff. I couldn't help but feel that Bart would have instructed me to talk to someone there. The last place I could look would be Whitehawk Casino. Of course, there was a hotel room I had been in rented out by the Satriones for the purpose of loansharking and drug peddling. I could not remember for the life of me what the number of their hotel room was. Or, the more likely scenario, the Satriones bounced around the casino to avoid detection. That would be the smarter route, I figured.

More time sensitive, though, was having Ramon join me in Colorado. I sighed and realized the ramifications of what would be the second most dreadful phone call of my life, the worst coming moments prior. My family's safety was on the line, though, and so it was obvious I needed to pick up the phone. Besides, they would know sooner rather than later since they were expecting Mia and the boys within the hour.

I inhaled slowly several times before placing the call. Ramon answered on the second ring. "Hi, Scott."

"Hello, Ramon," I started. "Are you sitting down?"

There was a short pause. "Yes."

"Mia isn't making it to Albuquerque tonight," I explained. "She's in danger."

The quiet man could only muster one word. "Danger?"

"Yes. I need you to trust me."

"Okay, Scott. I will trust you."

A single tear rolled down my left cheek. This was excruciating. "Thank you, Ramon. I need you to come up here and we'll discuss everything."

"Okay. I will leave soon." I could hear my father-in-law rustling for his keys.

"Ramon, you are a great man and I'm so sorry I've put you in this situation."

"Tell me, son," he said. "What's the situation?"

"She's been kidnapped. It's my fault. The kidnappers want you up here. They called and told me this is their demand."

A five-second-long pause on the other side as Ramon processed my declaration. Then he softly spoke, "You told me you'd take care of her, Scott. You lied."

"I'm so sorry, Ramon," I cried out. "I'll explain everything when you get here. We can save her and the boys."

"The boys too?" Then there was another stoppage in conversation. "Well, let me go break the news to her mother. I'll be on the road in ten, maybe fifteen minutes."

"I'm sorry." I hung my head in shame.

"Yeah, you said that. See you soon."

--

The two logical locations were a restaurant and a casino. It was nearing nine o'clock at night by the time I showered, gulped down a mug of coffee, and devoured a dry Banquet chicken fried beef steak. I wanted a cigarette so bad to take the edge off, but I resisted. The last thing I'd want to be is the knight in shining armor that wreaked of tobacco. But boy, could I use a Marlboro Gold right about now. Why didn't I do that before my shower?

I was acutely aware of my ongoing battle with alcohol withdrawal. My mind was playing tricks on me, like bargaining for a cigarette. Even though I took a lukewarm shower, sweat beads still flew from my forehead like dangling bodies off a thousand foot cliff. I kept the TV dinner in my stomach for about twenty minutes before I puked it all out. I poured another mug of coffee just in case I had vomited up the caffeination.

The Acura started up and so too did my journey to Jack's Burgers. I didn't know a single employee of the restaurant, so I figured I'd order something quick and ask for Bart or Keith. My fingers were tingling—I'm not sure if this was nerves or alcohol withdrawal—and my temples throbbed. I strolled up to the area in which the hostess stood and said, "Table for one."

"Great," she said, and brushed her blond hair behind her ears. "Follow me." She waltzed over to the table and laid a menu on the high top.

As she was leaving I was able to muster the courage to say, "Is Bart here today? Or Keith?"

"Bart? Keith?" She looked confused as to who I was asking for. "Let me get my manager."

The manager, a bald man with a brown goatee whose biceps looked like they were about to bulge from under his shirt, appeared to be muscle and nothing else. His nametag informed me his name was Bruce. "Who are you looking for?" He spoke to me loudly enough that a nearby table of suburban moms and an elderly couple on the other side turned to look.

I sheepishly responded, "Bart. Or Keith. Keith is good, too."

His body language seemed to indicate he knew who they were. All this unnecessary commotion wasn't good for business, so he grabbed my arm slowly and lugged me to the entrance of Jack's. I had no idea what would happen, but I obliged because at the very least this confirmed he knew who I was referring to. If he didn't, he'd just say, "who?" and walk away. I took this as a positive sign, even though he was twice my size and could pummel me into nonexistence.

"Did you bring a jacket?" Bruce asked as we stepped outside. It was late February and around thirty-five degrees outside, so the question was valid.

"No. Just the sweatshirt. Why?" I asked.

As soon as the words escaped my mouth, the bald manager pushed me off the rug and nudged me outside in the direction of the parking lot. "Get out," he whispered, "and don't come back."

"What—what do you mean?" I asked. But it was too late. Bruce had slammed the door behind him and returned to the restaurant. At least he had the decency to ask if I had left a jacket behind, I guess. I walked back to the Acura, clicked the unlock button, scooted in the driver's seat, and punched in the GPS directions to Whitehawk Casino. A twenty-three minute drive, the phone alerted me.

The ride over to the Native American gaming palace was dominated by intrusive thoughts. I worried so much for the safety of my family. I wanted so badly to pick up the phone and dial the Denver area code burner Bart had used, but I knew that would only anger him. It occurred to me again in that moment how poor of a father I had been in the genesis of Marcos' life. I had held him exactly once, and he was four days old. Or was he born three days earlier? The twenty-four-hour periods began to blend. Like the sensation in my fingers, I found myself questioning whether this was a manifestation of nervousness or my body reacting to the absence of alcohol. Sobriety is tough. Not nearly as strenuous, though, as your family being held hostage in an unknown location by a deranged lunatic.

--

The Arapaho tribe opened up Whitehawk Casino in 1997 in the hopes that suburban Denverites would come to gamble in flocks. Luckily for the Arapaho, they did. It was an instant success, and it's not hard to comprehend exactly why. Whitehawk has a fifty thousand square foot gaming floor and is home to over two thousand slots and all the usual suspects of a casino. There are blackjack, poker, and roulette tables at every corner. There is a hotel equipped with three hundred rooms; rumor has it if you are lucky enough to get a spot on the top floor you can see the Denver skyline to the east. Once in a blue moon, a big-time act like Garth Brooks comes and sells out the eight thousand seat amphitheater. The front entrance has four towering pillars beneath the tan, brown exterior. There is a golf course on the southern side of the property, one that has hosted a few junior events and is highly regarded by those who under-stand the game. It has everything you'd want in a casino and more. The Arapaho were happy to have the business of Whitehawk.

And yet, horrifying things happen there. The Satrione family operates on the property; I had seen it myself when I begged Keith for a loan. Drunkenly, yes, but I know for sure we hadn't left the building. As I sauntered through the front entrance, lit up with an embossed neon sign, I remem-bered the lost hotel room number. I still wasn't entirely sure this was the place my family was being held. It was the most logical, perhaps, because Bart had told me over the phone that I was familiar with the location. The manager at Jack's had given me the heebie jeebies and kicked me out, but he had never flat out denied the whereabouts of Bart Thomp-son and Keith Stephens. So, I was on my own.

I noticed the jarring amount of security cameras as soon as I entered the place. Like a cartoon, a lightbulb suddenly shot over my brain. What if one of those tiny devices had captured me on my way upstairs with Keith? I tried to remember details, any details, about that night that would stick out to me. I recalled the dealer, the tall Native American woman, but her name slipped my mind. I decided to walk to the section of blackjack tables at Whitehawk and see if I could recognize her. She might be able to tell me what days she worked last year when I was here. Or was it the year before? I couldn't recall.

Scanning the floor, I noticed there was only one woman of above average height. I sighed as it was obvious she wasn't the woman I was searching for. How else was I going to decipher what day of the loan? As that thought crossed my mind, I eyed the television above one of the tables. If I remembered correctly, this was exactly where I sat that night. What was I watching? Was it a sporting event? Was it basketball? I think the weather was cold when we came last year, or the year before, whenever it was. That would have made it basketball season.

Wait a second. I remember a basketball game *was* on. Who was it? The University of Colorado? The Denver Nuggets? Was it just a nationally televised game between two random opponents? I peered up at the television set in the present and noticed the Los Angeles Lakers were playing. I got an intense feeling of overwhelming déjà vu. Were the Lakers playing? Who was their opponent? It had to have been the Nuggets, right? Why else would they be showing a game? I ditched that internal suggestion. Sporting events from out of town are shown every day at a place like Whitehawk Casino.

Then it suddenly dawned on me. My mind went blank, and I shut my eyes. I rubbed my temples, trying to retrieve whatever data was stored in my brain from the last visit. I pulled out my phone and punched in "Nuggets vs. Lakers" on Google, and a million results populated. They play at least twice every season, so that doesn't help. Then I recalled a man. He was incredibly annoying. He was wearing a jersey or a uniform. Nuggets, I think. He was yelling about how some rookie on the team would be a star. He sang, too. If I was able to remember the player's name, I could determine his rookie season. Then, I could figure when he played the Los Angeles Lakers. So, I pulled up the search engine again and typed "recent Denver Nuggets draft picks". I ran down a list and was stumped.

But what was the man singing? Was it a military anthem? A national anthem? Then, I experienced a once in a lifetime moment that can only be described as luck, or divine intervention, smacking me right in the face. The anthem was *Canadian*. The man had made some off-color comment about how he liked the player in spite of his home country.

From that point on, the Google search was easy. Three seconds of typing and two seconds of scrolling determined the Canadian player in question was Jamal Murray. His Wikipedia page informed me he was drafted seventh by the Nuggets in the 2016 NBA Draft. I was also told that his rookie season wrapped up in April of 2017, so the game had to have taken place between the tipoff in October 2016 and then. I went to the search engine once more and typed in "Denver Nuggets 2016-17 schedule". It brought me to a list of their games from the season but without the results listed. According to their official schedule, they played the Lakers thrice, so that gave me three chances. The first possible date was January the seventeenth. The second was January thirty-first and the third the thirteenth of March. My memory of the night being chilly and brisk didn't eliminate any of these possibilities. Denver can be cold in January, and Denver can also be cold in March.

In the last moment of that evening that can only be described as luck, I remembered twiddling my thumbs as I waited that fateful evening in 2017 for the tall blackjack dealer to bring me to the Westco suite to retrieve my wallet. In the time she was gone—looking for a key or verifying my identity, I don't recall—I remembered having a throbbing headache and realizing that the Nuggets won the game and smiling in my haze. The Jamal Murray superfan from earlier in the evening would be ecstatic.

Did they win all three of the games? My finger scrolled through their 2016-17 season results from the top, so the website would show the most recent games. On March thirteenth, the Nuggets hammered the Lakers by a score of 129 to 101. So, that night could be a possibility. I flipped my thumb up on the screen to show more results, and lo and behold the score showed up for the January thirty-first battle: Los Angeles Lakers 120, Denver Nuggets 116.

I was down to just two dates left, the seventeenth of January and the thirteenth of March. If the Nuggets lost in one of the two, I knew I had the right time frame. I scrolled my finger another inch down the phone screen and read the third result, from the first game against the Lakers that season: Denver Nuggets 127, Los Angeles Lakers 121.

My heart sank as I realized I couldn't pinpoint the precise date I was here. Faced now with two distinct prospects, I felt utterly powerless. How was I going to find Mia and the boys now? I wanted to call the cops, but I knew better.

After a minute or two of sulking, I had an idea. I waltzed up to the hotel lobby and asked to see a room. Any room, I said, for I did not care about the size, number of beds, or if the window had a skyline view. The manager, whose nametag read Chayton, said that was fine and he checked the database for currently vacant rooms. We chatted as we made our way over to the elevator.

"Just curious," Chayton, a tall man of over six feet, said. He had dark brown eyes and if I were to make an estimation, I would say he was in his late thirties. Under his name in smaller print read "Lakota". This must have been the tribe in which he belonged to. "Why do you need to see a room? It's past ten at night and I typically do not allow visitors in beyond normal hours."

"I am planning a business trip here soon," I lied. "Besides, is there a such thing as 'normal hours' at a casino? This place is open twenty-four seven, right?"

"Fair enough. A business trip?" Chayton's right eyebrow arched. "I am sure the manager will be happy to accommodate. What kind of business is it you run?"

This time I told the truth. Well, almost the whole truth. "I am a regional sales manager at a corporation here in town. We love to gamble."

"That's great," the man, who had a long ponytail, responded. "You have come to the right place then. Well, here we are." He placed the room key up to the door, and a flash of green allowed us to enter Room 117.

Chayton tried to sell the room. "Over here we have a mini bar with complimentary water and soda. You have two double beds, but we can obviously get you a larger bed if that is what you prefer."

"Yeah, this is nice," I said, placing my hands on my hips. "This will do just fine. Hey, can I ask for a favor?"

"Of course. Anything."

"Can I call this room?" I asked.

"Call this room?" Chayton laughed. "That's your favor? Of course you may."

I whipped out my iPhone, slid my right thumb up to leave the lock screen, and pushed the green icon in the bottom left. I dialed the number listed on the telephone in the room, turned the volume on my cellphone down, and waited. A few seconds later, a familiar ring could be heard in the room. Just as I suspected, it was the same tone and pattern of the ring I heard earlier in the day. It was the old landline sound. I smiled in my sober state. Mia and the boys were close.

--

"Got what you need?" Chayton asked me in Room 117.

"Not quite." I grinned. "But we're getting there." Of course, he had no idea what I really meant.

"Oh. Do you need anything else in the room?"

"No, I'm good," I said. "Thank you, Chayton."

We walked back to the lobby and I bid adieu to the helpful man. I shook his hand and let him know I would be in contact regarding the business trip I was planning. I felt bad for lying to the guy. He stuck out his neck for me and in return I fudged the truth. Desperate times call for desperate measures, I suppose.

Whether I was at Whitehawk Casino on January seventeenth or March thirteenth of 2017 remained the biggest piece to this unsolved puzzle. If I could definitively say I was here on one date or the other, I could ask to see the security tapes. It was unlikely they'd show me unless I explained the nature of the emergency. Bart had told me twice if the police were involved, he would kill my entire family. I thought about that, though. Could the cops get a warrant into every hotel room based on my word alone? I hadn't recorded the conversation on the phone this afternoon, and there was no concrete evidence. The best course of action was to figure this out by myself.

As I sat companionless, more than twenty-four hours sober for the first time in a long while, I thought of a different way to solve the mystery of the two dates. Mia and I had a shared calendar on our iPhones. If I were to revisit the times in question, there might be a clue hidden within. I pulled out my phone for what seemed like the millionth time today and flung down my thumb on the screen for a solid ten seconds. Remember, this was a year ago we're talking about, so it took a while to scroll through all our events, meaningless or not. When I came to March thirteenth, 2017, there was nothing written on the day. I chalked that up to my tendency to be less of a planner than my wife. Flinging my finger up to January only took a few seconds. I saw an event listed on January seventeenth at six o'clock in the evening: *Scott and Mia date night*. Whatever we did that night unwillingly became one of the best dates with Mia I ever had. My amazing wife came through for me again. I took a loan from the mob on March thirteenth.

Chapter 20

Ramon stepped on the pedal of his rusted-out 2005 blue GMC Sierra and exited northbound on Interstate 25. He replayed his son-in-law's words again and again in his head. Mia had been kidnapped. The boys were taken, too. He had trusted Scott Sharpe with their lives, and Scott Sharpe had failed him. This felt like a death march. Ramon still didn't really understand his role, either. Why did the hostage takers want to see him? Why was he an integral part in rescuing Scott's family? It didn't make a lot of sense. Unless this had something to do with what happened twenty-odd years ago on that fateful day in the Allsup's.

Adriana flipped out, of course. Her husband held her in his arms and physically restrained her after he debriefed her of Scott's dreadful call. She was even more upset Ramon told her he needed to go to Colorado without her. He had to remind Adriana that she still had three girls in New Mexico who would need her now more than ever. Adriana eventually understood the sentiment, that the girls could not stand to lose both of their parents if the worst-case scenario were to occur. She was, like any sane person would be, scared by the words "kidnapped", "danger", and "safety". She also knew that Ramon would lay his life down for any of his girls and that he was going to do what he was going to do. It angered her that Mia lived in another state and that she could not save her. She felt like an abject failure as a mother. She was also beyond frustrated at Scott for involving Mia in whatever this was. Ramon had made the mistake of telling his wife that Scott mentioned it was solely his fault Mia and the boys were kidnapped in the first place. Now his wife *really* was upset at their son-in-law. The two usually were on good terms with Scott and believed him to be a kind man but this was a mistake from which he may never regain their trust. The sentiment would be especially true if the incident took the lives of Mia and the boys.

Adriana kissed Ramon and told him to "get their little girl at all costs." He knew what that meant. The only weapon he had to his name was the 9mm, now legally registered to him, which he'd used to shoot Bart Thompson, Sr. He had used it just once, during that fatal episode in the late 1990s. He realized this would be the only gun between he and Scott. Ramon sorted out as much ammunition as he could and threw on his beloved, trusty white cowboy hat, packed the 9mm in the GMC, and took off north.

His righthand man at the Allsup's, Felix, coincidentally sharing a name with the man Ramon entrusted his store to back in Hermosillo a lifetime ago, assured the boss all would be well. Ramon trusted Felix, for he was a hardworking Mexican immigrant cut from the same grain as he. If anyone would deserve the store someday, it would be Felix.

Radiance from the heavens faded, and Ramon couldn't see the Rio Grande to his west as he left town, and it made him anxious. He had long considered the river to be his friend, and the angry black sky of the New Mexico night made it impossible for him to latch on to his companion. The further he drifted from the water, the less safe he felt. A cold, uneasy feeling came over him as he meandered out of the outskirts of his comfort zone. The Sandia Mountains disappeared from the south in the last glimmer of light. It had been a few years since Ramon had driven up to Colorado. Christmas 2015, he figured, was the last time he and Adriana had hopped into the same GMC and navigated up the same interstate. It was Frankie's first Christmas, Ramon remembered. He longed for future holidays with his family.

The man then had a crazy thought, that the first time he'd ever meet his second grandson would be in the process of a kidnapping. Though Marcos had only been born a handful of days earlier, Ramon and Adriana were anxiously awaiting the call to come meet the newborn. When Mia phoned and said she was coming to New Mexico with both boys, they were elated. Ramon did wonder in the back of his head if there was trouble though since Scott wasn't coming. When he asked her why he wasn't joining, she simply said, "Work." The De Leons were unaware of Scott's imminent promotion within Westco.

Ramon crossed into Colorado and stopped to fill up on gas in Pueblo at a Loaf 'N Jug. There were two hours left in the drive and the man had become a little sleepy, his eyelids heavy with fatigue. He entered the convenience store and purchased a hot cup of black coffee to remain alert. The caffeination would last until he made it to Thornton and then he hoped he could get some shuteye. He pulled out six quarters to pay for the drink and noticed something peculiar: the front attendant's name was Bart. Ramon didn't fail to recognize the irony of the circumstance. Little did he know.

Around the time he passed through Colorado Springs, just before midnight, snow began to fall. Albuquerque gets a winter storm here and there, but the precipitation typically melts within a few days. In the thirty-plus years he had lived there, he could remember one blizzard of note. In late December of 2006, there was a ten-inch storm that was unlike anything he'd ever seen. He remembered the call he received from Luis Alvarez, an offer to come back to Phoenix. He laughed and wondered how the friend he admired so much would behave in a conundrum like this.

The thick white flakes cascading out of the sky captured Ramon's attention and in a strange way made the drive seem shorter. He could almost see each individual particle make its way onto his windshield, only to see them be smashed into the crevice between the glass and the hood of the truck by the wipers.

Campus lights from the United States Air Force Academy flashed to the left, and beyond them Ramon could make out the tall peaks of the eastern edge of the Rocky Mountains. They were a little greener up here, and he appreciated the color, even if he couldn't see them because it was midnight. He figured the peaks were covered in snow anyway.

The mountains prompted Ramon's thoughts of Montana and Glacier National Park again. He told himself he wanted to make it there before his days on Earth came to an end. Not that he was old, but Ramon thought about death a lot. Because of his age, he understood he could drop at any moment and never get back up. He was well into his late fifties now, and the distinguished wrinkles shone on his face like a weathered version of his younger self.

Ramon's dream of heading north into Montana had a lot to do with the abundant, thriving greenery of the north, to be certain, but it also offered an even greater buffer from Mexico. He had not ventured to the homeland since he made his escape to America, as it had been well over thirty years since he took Adriana by the hand and headed to the free land. He didn't know who left, who stayed, or even who was alive. Neither he nor Adriana had any way of retaining contact with the important individuals of their former life.

This somber realization didn't make Ramon sad. Far from it, actually; it made him proud of the family he and Adriana created and the life they started in a place far safer than home. He had come over the border illegally but made amends with God. He had kissed another woman twenty some years earlier but admitted his wrongdoing and repaired his relationship with his wife. He tried his hardest, whenever he hurt a soul, to be a good man. When Ramon looked back on his life, he realized that's all he could ever have wanted—to be a good man.

He wasn't ignorant to what could happen in Colorado. This February cruise down Interstate 25 may very well be the last ride he'd ever take. The lingering hugs he had come to love from Luisa might never come again. The hour-long phone conversations he'd have with Ana and Mia could be done and over with. His kiss with Adriana hours earlier could have been the final one. He realized what a good man does is offer his life for someone he loves.

Ramon De Leon was aware of the reality that he may have to give his life for Mia and her sons. And he would gladly do it.

Chapter 21

I trodded over to the front desk at Whitehawk Casino. I had confirmed March thirteenth was the day I had made my way into the hotel room then occupied by the Satrione mob. Now all I had to do was figure out the number of the room they rented. Perhaps my wife and sons were in the room, and we could begin the negotiation process.

As I made my way, I glanced at a clock on the side of one of the four stone pillars near the entrance. It read ten-thirty. Ramon would be arriving in a few hours, so I had to act quick.

"Excuse me?" I said to the woman at the front desk. "I have a question."

Sporting a gray cowboy hat and a trendy, sparkled bolo tie, she looked a lot taller than her five-foot stature. She looked up from behind the desk and replied, "Shoot."

"I need to have a look at your security camera for last March thirteenth."

"I'm sorry, sir, I cannot authorize that kind of access," the woman said calmly. "Who exactly are you with?"

"I'm investigating."

Her eyes lit up and her eyebrows arched. "Like a crime? Are you a detective, mister?"

"No," I said. "Well, sort of, but not really."

"Oh," she replied. "Sorry, I've been reading a lot of the *Longmire* series. I got excited. I started a few months ago and I'm already on *Junkyard Dogs*. It's the reason I wanted to work for the casino."

"You know *Longmire* takes place in Wyoming, right? It's not Colorado."

"Actually, it's the *Longmire* book series," she corrected me. "And besides, some of the show was filmed in New Mexico. They're mysteries in the west, anywho."

I realized then and there she was not going to help me. "May I speak to your manager, please?"

A few seconds later, Chayton materialized right before my eyes. I nearly gasped.

"Sir?" he called to me. "What can I do for you? I told you that the rooms are closed, right?" He smiled warmly.

"May I talk to you for a second?" I asked. He nodded and shooed the woman in the bolo tie behind the saloon doors.

When she was out of sight I said, "I need one more favor, Chayton. I need to see security tapes for the night of March thirteenth, 2017."

"Excuse me?" He suddenly appeared a bit more guarded than when we met an hour ago.

"Please," I begged. "I can't explain why, but it's very important I do." Chayton glanced around a bit and spoke no words back to me. I repeated, "Please. I need to know something important."

"My late father—my *neisonoo*, as The People call him— once told me, 'If we wonder often, the gift of knowledge will come.'" He gazed past my silhouette, as if he was once again coming to terms with the fact that his father had passed away.

"I don't mean to be a jerk, but people's lives are at stake. Someone is missing."

"Every single white person cringes when one of their own is gone," Chayton spoke, "and yet, we The People go missing every day."

"My wife isn't even white," I corrected him. "Her family is from Mexico."

Chayton's face flushed with color. "Your wife is missing?"

I nodded. "The police don't know, and I swear to you if you tell them—"

"You think I will speak to or trust the white man's justice system? Not a chance. I never have, and I never will." The man placed his hands on his sides. "I need a cigarette." He pulled out of his jacket pocket a container of blue Pall Malls and started tapping the pack. I noticed the absence of a wedding ring on his fourth finger but observed a lighter skin tone where one had been worn in the past. He turned behind him and said, "Ariel, come watch the desk, please." The young woman who helped me before pushed back through the saloon doors and replaced Chayton as he walked around the counter towards me.

"Follow me." He motioned toward an exit situated in a nook of the casino floor, marked by an illuminated red sign over the doorway. I followed him and he pushed open the blue door.

We stood outside in a contained space no more than six by eight feet. Before us lay a concrete pad, and it was enclosed by a sturdy brick wall. It resembled a small jail cell. Only about eight feet up was there any sort of opening, and above it you could see the scattered stars of the crisp February night.

I began hyperventilating outside as soon as our shoes tapped the concrete. A familiar feeling shot through my body. Suddenly, I was a twelve-year-old in the rolling hills of Minnesota. I was playing hide-and-seek with the Simpsons', Gaines', and my two brothers; I was among those searching for a place to hide. This designated smoking area outside the Whitehawk Casino in Colorado felt reminiscent of the storm window I stowed away in silence. Suddenly, my body tensed up and slowly rose from the ground. The distance from my feet to the ground increased as the seconds passed. After a minute, I peered over the brick wall and caught a glimpse of the eastern side of the mountain range. I rose to the heights of the sheltering, majestic peaks, and sprung up higher and higher until the lights of Whitehawk Casino were only a tiny dot on the landscape, and that speck appeared as though it was about to be smushed by the rigid bumps of the Rocky Mountain range. I gasped for air, but I couldn't breathe. A soprano voice whispered to me as I stood thousands of feet in the sky, "One up." I reached my summit, and suddenly I descended quicker than I rose. My lower lip flapped, and a bizarre tingle ran through my body. The snow on the tips of the mountains and the gleaming of the Denver lights became clearer and clearer by the millisecond. As I approached the brick wall my speed decreased and my lips retained their shape. Like Winnie the Pooh in his dream, I slowly returned to my Earthly body and felt the ground shake for a moment. A familiar voice called out to me. I wobbled my face back and forth and, simultaneously using my right thumb and index finger, pinched myself. The voice uttered something else to me.

"Yo." It was Chayton, puffing away at his Pall Mall. "You have not said a word in a minute or two. Just spacing out. I was worried about you, man."

"It was nothing," I lied.

"Sure, man." He laughed and then coughed. "You look like you're on peyote or something."

"Can we talk about my missing wife and children, please?"

"Whoa, man," Chayton gasped. "Your kids are gone, too?"

I nodded. It sounded so crazy, and yet I was completely relaxed in his presence. "That's right."

Chayton tapped his pack of Pall Malls and offered me one. "Here. Sounds like you could use one."

"I'm okay, Chayton," I insisted. "I quit a while back and don't want to start back up yet. Thank you, man."

He nodded. "So what do the security tapes have to do with your missing family?" the man asked.

"I can't say much," I said. "It could get me in a lot of trouble."

Chayton looked over at me in amazement. "You do realize I am going to have to watch you watch the tapes? How will I know what exactly to look for? If we work together, we can find what you are looking for twice as fast."

The man had a point. His presence in the last few minutes had served as nothing more than a distraction. I had nearly forgotten that mere moments earlier I had found myself in a suspended state over this place. The question loomed in my brain: was this an illusion born from the throes of alcohol withdrawal? Had I seen a vision? Chayton was in on whatever scheme I was hatching to get my family back. He had to cover for me somehow. Plus, he was sane, and I was hallucinating.

I took a deep breath, aware now of the ramifications of getting another human being involved. "Yes, I do. Let's do it."

Chayton stamped out his cigarette with the sole of his left boot and clapped his hands together. It was obvious he was happy to be my newfound sidekick. "Let's do it!" he howled.

"Sh!" I replied. "We don't want to draw any unwanted attention to ourselves."

He paused a moment and whispered, "Yay."

I smiled. "Now you've got it."

--

I chuckled to myself as Chayton and I strolled through the casino to the office where the security tapes lay. If this entire saga were an action movie, this would be the scene where "How You Like Me Now?" by The Heavy plays in the background as the two of us slowly saunter to the beat of the drum in the song. In his first brilliant move of the mission, my compadre lied to the security officer about the nature of our visit to the top-secret, heavily guarded camera room. The area was no bigger than a janitor's closet, and yet at least two dozen screens comprised the entirety of one of the walls.

My jaw dropped open. "So we're supposed to find and follow me on any of these, what, twenty-five screens?" I said.

Chayton grinned. "No one said this would be easy, friend."

My suddenly calm exterior faded away. "I'm never going to see them again. We can't just go knocking on doors. How are we supposed to find me on this crazy, God forsaken system?"

Chayton laid his hand on my shoulder. His tranquil presence brought a serene calmness to me. He looked over at me and said, "Are you a man of God?"

"I am," I said. "Well, not as good as I used to be. And Mia, well, she's always loved God the way she loves me."

"That stuff does not matter," the man moved his arm off me. "Are you Christian?"

"Catholic."

"Pray an Our Father with me." He motioned for me to sit next to him in a chair of a similar kind to the one that lay in my Westco office. And so, in the presence of a total stranger, on a pitch black, cold February evening at the Whitehawk Casino in Colorado, I prayed. In a surprising twist of events, following the completion of the prayer, Chayton offered up a few words to God, "Heavenly Father, we know your will is out of our hands, but please deliver to us—" He opened his eyes and glanced at me. He wanted me to fill in the blanks.

"Mia, Francisco, and Marcos."

"Deliver to us Mia, Francisco, and Marcos," he continued, "and please let them be safe. Amen."

"Amen." To say I was surprised was the understatement of my messed-up day. I had judged Chayton to be nothing more than an employee of the casino who had a limited outlook on life, a fellow whose smoke breaks were something of a nicotine-inhaling haven from his otherwise ordinary existence. I could not be more wrong.

"I judged you, Chayton," I said. "I took you to be a sucker who showed me a room and now I know that isn't the truth."

He smiled back at me. "Do not worry, my friend. I judged you as a self-righteous white boy, anyway. We will find them now!" He boomed the words of the last sentence and flipped himself 180 degrees in the desk chair he sat to face the litany of screens before our eyes. His fiery brown eyeballs glared at me for a second as she said, "Remember, if I get caught doing this you have coerced me into doing it. Do you have a gun?" He flashed a broad smile, revealing a lot of his bright teeth. I liked this guy.

"Let's do it," I said. I had no doubt in my mind that I could trust this man.

"March the thirteenth, 2017," my friend hummed as he pushed a few buttons and typed in a password. The computer system prompted him to place his thumbprint on the small screen next to the keyboard, and he complied.

I gulped. "Chayton, how much trouble will this get you in?"

"A lot," he smiled, "fired at the very least. Perhaps prosecuted by tribal law, too. That is, if they can justify jurisdiction in this place. We're technically off the rez."

"Then why are you helping me?"

"Your wife and children have gone missing," Chayton said without explanation, almost as if it were a prerecorded response. I could sense there was more to it than that, but for now we were on a time crunch and I couldn't afford to waste precious seconds. It was eleven o'clock and Ramon was slated to arrive within ninety minutes. The drive to my home alone was twenty minutes. That meant Chayton and I had about one hour, give or take, to solve this mystery.

A certain lingering conundrum loomed in my head. I could not unravel the significance of the high-pitched whisper in the sky. "One up," the presence murmured. "One up" was a golf term, as far as I was concerned. It meant you were one hole ahead of your opponent in a match. I am not an avid golfer, though, so I don't see the relevance. Otherwise, it could mean something to the effect of having an advantage over someone, like when someone one ups your story. I thought extensively as Chayton searched deep into the archives. It could mean nothing. I was, after all, twenty-four hours sober and in a state of light sweating. This was nerve wracking stuff and I decided at that moment not to dwell on the mysterious two-word phrase uttered in the clouds. It could be nothing more than a slight hallucination. The retrieval of my wife and two sons was rightly taking precedence.

Again, my mind drifted as Chayton drummed away on those keys. I couldn't believe I put Mia and the boys in danger. Is this the kind of man I'm destined to become? I refused to believe this was the best version of myself. I was acutely, painfully, aware this would be a turning point in my life. I would care less about the rigors of work, and I would be a more present, understanding father and husband. I owed these things to my family.

Chayton remarked in a peculiar singsong way, "March thirteenth. I've got it!" My heart sank. This could be a red herring in finding my family, but I knew I had to at least be at peace with the fact that I gave it my best shot. I still was not even a hundred percent sure that they were at White-hawk. Westco, though a heinous choice, still loomed as an option. If I deduced they weren't hidden at Whitehawk, Ramon and I would visit my office in the early hours of the morning.

"Do you know what time you were brought up to the room?"

"How long are NBA games? Two and a half hours or so?" I asked.

"That is right," Chayton replied. "What time did the game start?"

I scratched my head because the answer to that question eluded me. "They usually start at seven, right?"

The man with the ponytail nodded. "I would guess so."

"That would put us between seven o'clock and nine-thirty." I massaged my temples with my index fingers. Doing math while sober is difficult, I decided. "Meaning I took out the loan then."

"Great." He smiled. "That is an excellent starting point." He clicked a button on the right side of the screen and hit the word "seven" in a scroll down menu. "Now, the loan. Did you take it out on the floor? Or go to a room?"

"A room."

"Where did you inquire about the loan?" Chayton asked.

"On the floor," I responded. "Let's look by the blackjack table at seven."

We scanned the floor for any sign of me but came up empty. I sighed in relief as I noticed Keith crouched at a high-top blackjack table visible on the left side of the screen.

He sported a blue blazer and gave off the appearance of a man who was there strictly to give loans and not gamble.

"Can you fast forward thirty minutes?" I asked.

Chayton held down the fast forward button and, lo and behold, I materialized on the left side next to Keith. There were three other men at the table: Dave, from the tech department at Westco, some guy I can't recall, and the truck driver named Raymond who wouldn't stop talking. I giggled when I saw him especially. Out of all the people to put a name to from that night, the repulsive trucker is the fellow I remember. I'll bet he's halfway to San Antone.

I was chatting with Dave on the tape. I remember asking him to borrow some cash. He told me no, and I watched as my eyes met Keith's. Though he was sitting, I noticed he wasn't involved in the card game. He just sat there looking for people to prey upon. What a sleazebag. A twenty second exchange with Keith resulted in him pulling my dress shirt and guiding me away from the view of the camera. My eyes shuffled around the litany of screens; I was confused as to where to look next.

"Check out number six." Chayton pointed at one of the monitors.

A chill ran up my spine as I saw Keith and I walking together. Anyone over the age of ten would know I was drunk. Once my face came into full view, I was embarrassed by the grin I had on the screen. Chayton could tell something was up.

"Nineteen," he instructed me to gaze upon a screen that showed the two of us walking down the long, narrow, dimly lit hallway into the sparkling gold elevator. My heart thumped. I was about to find out the room number the Satriones conducted business.

Chayton swiftly pointed his wrinkly second digit in the direction of screen twenty-two. I was babbling nonsense to Keith for a second—you could see the disinterest in his wandering eyes—and then the bright elevator opened. He pushed a button to send us off to our destination.

"What floor is that?" I asked.

Whitehawk's most resourceful employee paused the footage and propped his left index finger on his temple while his thumb rested underneath his chin, as if he were pointing to the heavens. "It's the third floor."

He clicked a button on the master computer that was labelled "Hallway Floor 1-3", and a flash of blue lit up all twenty-four screens. My retinas were shocked by this change. Thankfully, the seizure inducing brightness lasted only half a second as each monitor displayed a picture of a hallway. Time stamps read seven forty-three p.m. and a few televisions displayed human movement. The third duo I examined was unquestionably Keith Stephens and me. He walked while I cowered behind him in fear.

As Chayton and I sat in the dark room, our eyes fixed on the grainy footage, there was a rap on the door. We both gasped. Before we had time to react accordingly, a man with a gun entered the room.

Chapter 22

I jumped back in my seat. *Of course* this would happen the moment we were about to discover which room Keith Stephens and I entered on March 13th, 2017.

Chayton and I never discussed an escape plan. We didn't plan for an armed man to enter the room no larger than my master closet with a Smith and Wesson pistol at his hip.

I raised my hands in surrender. Chayton shook his head. After all, the gun never left the man's holster in our three second surprise. He didn't show an ounce of vulnerability.

Trying to come up with an excuse for my reaction quickly, I threw up my hands. "You got me," I said. The man's face reflected a mask of confusion. I stuttered, "You remember the scene from *Breaking Bad*?"

He glared at me. My poor attempt at humor fell flat. "I don't watch television." He turned to my right and grumbled, "Chayton. What are *you* doing in here?" The thought now entered my mind that this was a new security guard reporting for duty, and he was referring, of course, to the puzzling idea that a casino hotel front desk night manager would require a look at the two dozen cameras.

That hypothesis was confirmed by Chayton. "Hello, Walker." My new friend had one skill he withheld in our early conversations: he excelled in the art of spontaneous improvisation. "This is Mr. Jones. Mr. Jones, this is our midnight on-duty security officer."

"Mr. Jones?" Walker laughed. "Like the song?"

Chayton gave off a stern stare to the officer. "So, you do not watch television. But you listen to music?" he said, referring to the *Breaking Bad* reference a minute earlier.

Walker rolled his eyes. He too was Native American, but he had short, combed-back black hair and appeared to be a little younger than me. On the side of his cheek, I noticed a lump indicating the presence of dipping tobacco in his mouth. His tribal name—Lakota, like Chayton—was displayed on his name tag. "Anyway, I still don't have an answer. Why are you two in here?"

"Mr. Jones here lost his wallet in one of the rooms. We can't remember which one it was."

The security guard crossed his arms. "Why not check his reservation? It will say which room it was."

My heart pounded relentlessly. Had we been caught? I lay numb, strapped to the chair, my fingers damp with perspiration. All Walker needed to do is look at the date. He'd ask why I just recently noticed my wallet was gone even though my visit was eleven months ago.

Luckily, Chayton was willing to double down on his lie. "He was here with his company, so his name was not listed on the reservation."

Don't look at the date. Don't look at the date. I knew we were screwed if Walker did his due diligence. Instead, he sighed and turned around to face the door. He glanced back for a moment and said, "Make it quick. I don't like having Ariel up there by herself at the desk."

Chayton smiled. "Is that because she challenges your intelligence?"

"No."

"Remember who the manager is here."

Walker scowled and slammed the door shut. Chayton chuckled a bit and said, "I knew that would get that jerk out of here faster."

"I was about to puke from that dip." I laughed.

"Now where were we?"

"Third floor hallways," I said.

"Ah," Chayton said, as if he didn't remember. He pressed a few buttons and Keith Stephens and I resumed walking down the hallway before turning at a door. We obviously couldn't read the number on the door, but Chayton knew the Whitehawk Casino Hotel like the back of his hand.

"316," he declared.

"Room 316?"

"That's right."

"Let's go check it out." I smiled.

--

This could all be for naught, for the Satriones likely changed rooms in the last eleven months. Nevertheless, I was proud of the work I had done over the course of the day. I kept thinking about Mia and the boys and praying they were not injured. What I had been exposed to today paled in comparison to what they had endured.

About twenty feet from Room 316, there was a nook in the hallway about four feet long that protruded out. I could conceivably hide in it in case Keith Stephens or the scary tall guy were to answer the door. They wouldn't recognize Chayton, so he volunteered to knock on the door with a "question" about the neighbors. He informed me it was a very regular occurrence, as the night manager at a casino hotel, to thump on someone's door in the late hours of the night.

Chayton asked me on the way upstairs to give detailed descriptions of both Keith and the terrifying guard. He could see a few of Keith's features on the screen, but I warned him he likely wouldn't be there. If he was on loan-sharking duty, he may be on the casino floor.

I concealed myself behind the interfering wall. I watched as my new friend rapped on the door three times in succession. He sat there, hands out in the open, fiddling with the lower half of his red and green argyle tie. After about thirty seconds the door swung open, and an older gentleman answered. He had icy white hair, thick framed black glasses, and his tan, brown corduroy pants were pulled up to his belly button. I would guess this man was nearing eighty, if he wasn't there already.

Immediately I had a sinking feeling in my stomach. At first glance, the old man didn't look like a threat. I froze as I heard Chayton utter the words, "Good evening, sir. I am Chayton, and I work here at the hotel."

The man massaged his eyes like a drowsy infant. "Do you have any idea what time it is? My wife and I are sleeping."

"I am sorry, sir," Chayton said. "I just had a quick question about your neighbors."

"Which neighbors?"

The night manager pointed down the hallway at no room in particular. I thought that was a smart move, to keep the "neighbors" vague.

The old man didn't seem to want to be investigated. He desired to return to his slumber. "What about them?" he shouted.

"Is it just the two of you here?"

"What is this?" the old man's face morphed into a beet red color, further accentuating his sugar-colored hair. "An interrogation or something? I see your friend over there in the corner."

I froze. Chayton began to panic a bit, too. He picked up the improvisation just a bit. "No, sir. We are looking for someone. Just wanted to make sure he was not in your room."

"No, it's just Darlene and me. Are you the cleaners?"

"Cleaners?" Chayton said. "No, we're not the cleaners."

He rubbed his eyeballs again and shouted, "Good night!" He slammed the door with as much might as an eighty-year-old could slam anything.

I motioned to Chayton to walk down the east side of the hallway so my presence wouldn't be known in case the old guy decided to look out his keyhole.

"What do you think?" he said. "Are we buying it?"

"I don't know," I replied. "You tell me. You were the one that was up close and personal with him."

"There was no way to tell if anyone else was in that room. It was too dark."

I balled up my toes and looked at the ugly black-and-white checkered hallway carpet. We hadn't found Mia and the kids, and I sighed. "One weird thing, though. Why would the cleaners come this late at night?"

Chayton just shrugged. "I have no idea."

"Why would he be wearing corduroy pants at this hour?"

He shook his head. "No clue."

"Thanks for your help, Chayton," I said. "Honestly, you did a lot for me. I appreciate you." I extended my right mitt for a handshake, and he brushed me off.

"What? Are you giving up?" The man backed away from me and angrily folded his arms into his sport coat. I shrugged my shoulders. "What can I do, Chayton? I don't know where they are."

"What about a name under the reservation?" he proposed.

"I don't know anyone other than Keith's name."

"So, let's check." He hurried to the elevator.

I followed him and said as he pushed the down button, "What time is it? I must be home when my father-in-law gets here."

"Twelve-twenty."

"I appreciate your enthusiasm, but I have to go, Chayton—"

"Just have a look at the reservation list," he interrupted.

"Fine. Why does this matter to you so much?" I asked. "You've done your part." The elevator doors fastened shut and initiated our descent of two floors.

Chayton hung his head and spoke, "Because, well," he gulped. "Because I've been in your situation."

My cheeks grew hot with anger. I yelled, "What do you mean, you've been in my situation? Your wife and kids were kidnapped?"

He lifted his index finger and shooshed me. "You know you cannot be loud in this place if the captors are nearby. What if they have a bug in the elevators?"

I took a step back and rose my hands to the heavens. "Explain yourself then."

The elevator doors shot open and revealed to us the casino floor. Chayton and I trudged back to where Ariel, reading her *Longmire* mystery, sat. We passed her and shoved open the saloon doors before us, hung a left, and walked into the office.

He left the door ajar and sat in one of the two leather chairs. He motioned for me to sit in the one furthest from the door. Displayed on the wall was a poster of an ace of spades card that read: "*The smarter you play, the luckier you'll be.*" I failed to comprehend the irony of my situation. Chayton took a deep breath and spoke in a hushed tone, "Over two years ago on the reservation my wife and son went to see a movie, *The Revenant*. I laugh because that movie was way too inappropriate for my son. As it turns out, it would be his last one." Chayton's fingers twitched and he stuttered on the next sentence, "They made it out of the movie but not home. On the way back to our house, they were struck by an oncoming vehicle. It turns out the man was drunk. He admitted to the tribal police he had been in a bar drinking all day. He doesn't even remember striking them. He is fine, and my wife and son are dead. He went to prison for three months. Three months. This is why

I am helping you, to get back at the type of person I never had a chance to."

As I took in Chayton's horror story, I suddenly realized why he was helping me. This was personal. He wanted to assist me in this situation, as he had no control over what happened to his own wife and son. I wanted to ask more questions, to gain more clarity. I knew I couldn't.

He had his hands buried in his face, horrified he had to retell the story once more. I offered a hand on his shoulder, and he brushed me off. "We should really go look at that reservation list now."

"Chayton, I am so sorry—"

"Do not feel sorry for me," he pleaded, wiping a tear from his right cheek. "Let's not make your family the next horror story." He stood up and composed himself.

"All right," I smiled. "Let's see that logbook."

The man sat back down and said, "Good. I was hoping you would say that. That's why I took us into this room, for the book is right there." He pointed to the reservation log, and I laughed.

"We should skip the first floor," Chayton opined.

"Why?"

"Because," he explained, "they are single beds in small rooms. They are what we call 'gambler rooms'. They are just for sleeping and not big enough to house underground gambling operations. Or criminals."

"Good point."

Over the course of the next ten minutes, Chayton and I looked at all the guests on floors two through six. Aware of the time, I quickly scanned the list of names: Adrian Rivers, Paul Caston, Dolly Frazier, Scott Parker, Elmer Hooper,

Bruce Jackson, and Edith Nomantz were among those on the log. I found the name Bruce Jackson to be familiar, but I wasn't sure why. Perhaps it was because the guest shared a first name with the manager at Jack's. What an odd coincidence. Was the bald man involved? Maybe Scott Parker had some sort of significance, like Bart Thompson was begging me to find out he'd booked a room under my name. That would make a whole lot of sense, come to think of it. I pulled out my phone and snapped a picture of the guestbook. I'd study any significance when I returned home.

"I have to go, Chayton."

"Now," he replied. "I will give you that handshake." The honorable man reached his arm out, and I reciprocated. His grip was tight.

"Thank you for everything," I said. "I will not forget your generosity."

I heard Chayton mutter as I walked out the door, "Go get those pricks."

--

The Acura felt especially warm even though the outside temperature hovered around freezing. As I pulled out of the parking lot, I gazed upon the exterior of the Whitehawk Casino and promised Mia, Francisco, and Marcos I'd be back for them in the morning. I said a quick prayer, both offering up serenity and vowing to try my best to continue to abstain from alcohol. I knew that my ignorance and drunkenness had led them to their unimaginable pickle. I'd be a better man without substances.

I thought about my father-in-law and the trust he bestowed in me. I knew Ramon would be upset when he saw me. I shattered his conviction in me. I wanted to earn his belief in me once more. He was a good man, and I should have followed his example.

On my way home, I felt a weird pull as I drove down the interstate. Uncharacteristically, I chugged along in the right lane. Normally I hovered around ten miles per hour over the speed limit, but tonight I was cautious in obeying the laws of the road. I couldn't afford one more slip up.

Up. There was that word again of the mysterious phrase, *One up.* What did it mean when the calm voice in the sky uttered that phrase to me? I froze when it occurred to me. One floor above Room 316 would be Room 416. I wasn't entirely sure the layout of Whitehawk Casino heeded the pattern. But who was staying in Room 416?

As I pulled off the highway at the next exit, my heartbeat accelerated and my temples thumped. I suddenly couldn't control my hands on the leather steering wheel as sweat poured from my fingers. I swiftly hung a right at the exit light and was nearly a struck by a law abiding Suburban. So much for obeying the rules of the road. Luckily for me, the man operating the SUV was paying attention and swerved out of the way to avoid a collision. Then, he proceeded to follow traffic. As I rolled up in the right lane next to him, I could make out his middle finger sticking high in my direction. I waved at him and mouthed the words "I'm sorry". His whole demeanor changed, and he smiled. What was up with that? Denver drivers aren't the friendliest, but in my eight years here I've never witnessed anything like that before.

A Conoco station appeared on my right, and I flashed my turn signal to alert the other vehicles. I pulled into the gas station parking lot and discovered a vacant spot. Three seconds after I parked, I whipped out my iPhone and pushed the colorful "Photos" button in the top right corner of my home screen. I opened the most recent image I snapped, the list of guests at the hotel attached to the White-hawk Casino.

My eyes shifted down the logbook page I'd taken a picture of. When I came across Room 416's occupant, I gasped loudly.

The name written next to the room number was Bruce Jackson.

Chapter 23

Glancing to the east of Interstate 25, Ramon could see the new construction builds of Castle Rock, Colorado. As the cosmic night in the middle of nowhere gave way to the bright living room lights of suburban, cookie cutter heaven, the stars in the sky morphed from enchanting and serene to shy and hidden. Ramon pondered progress; he had a complicated relationship with the concept. On the one hand, he was an illegal immigrant who crossed over the border and expected to steer clear of the United States government. He and Adriana had gone through the legal process to citizenship years earlier, and he felt himself becoming judgmental of those who were in the exact same spot he was thirty years ago. They also lived in a suburban area of homes. Ramon's outlook on progress was to do his best not to judge others. It was way easier said than done, of course. Nobody's perfect.

As Ramon was traveling just north of the Castle Rock city limits at twelve forty-five, thirty minutes from his destination, the man's cellphone began to buzz. His hand reached into the center console, and the front screen of the flip phone informed him the caller was Scott Sharpe. He flicked open the mobile device and smashed the "Answer" button.

"Ramon," Scott called out.

"Hi." How else was he supposed to talk to the man who had put him in the worst situation of his life?

"I know where they are, Mia and the boys." Scott sounded confident, like he had nine years ago at The Pit when he told Ramon he loved his daughter and saw a future with her.

"Where are they?" Ramon asked.

"They're at the Whitehawk Casino," Scott explained. "Come to my house first and we'll go scope it out early in the morning."

"How do you know?" Ramon was surprised for a moment, and then those feelings subsided. After all, Scott was an extremely smart man. You don't get to where he has gotten in corporate America in your early thirties without brains.

"I'll tell you when you get here," Scott said. "Where are you now?"

"Just north of Castle Rock."

"Great," Ramon's son-in-law responded. "I will see you soon."

He shut his flip phone and cracked a smile. At the behest of his wife, Ramon had purchased his first cellular device a year earlier. Admittedly, he hardly ever used the phone. If she were with him, Adriana would be yapping in his ear, "See? I told you it was a good idea!" He laughed as he registered her exactitude.

As he placed the phone in the center console of his GMC Sierra, another object came into his view. It was the black 9mm pistol he brought along. The moment of eagerness and excitement was fleeting, and reality kicked back in. He would use the gun if prompted. Ramon had only fired it once and he had been uninformed. *Not this time*, he told himself. He wouldn't be scared.

--

The last leg of the trip seemed to drag on as Ramon had second thoughts about whether to inform Scott of the weapon he intended to bring along to the casino. He figured there were dangerous people involved in the kidnapping, and he didn't want to take any chances. Scott wasn't exactly one carved out for dangerous situations, so his inexperience frightened Ramon. He was a bit of a wimp, but he had heart.

Ramon took the sudden turn that preceded the Sharpe family driveway. Their home was the first on the right. To get to the house, you must navigate up a curvy three-hundred-foot trail of faded black pavement—Scott insisted he'd retar it one day—and overhanging sycamore and English oak trees. Ramon had made it. Over four hundred miles later, he was ready to save his daughter and grandsons.

Scott was facing the television in the brightly lit living room visible from the driveway, so he couldn't hear his father-in-law's vehicle approaching. Ramon pulled out the key to his GMC, grabbed his travel bag from the backseat of the cab, and sauntered towards the front door. The pistol rested inside the suitcase, armed with ammunition and the safety engaged.

The Colorado wind whistled, and the late February chill pierced his exposed neck and fingers. He paused about twenty feet shy of the front door and looked up at the full moon that provided a picturesque backdrop to the Sharpe residence. In the near distance, he heard an elongated howl. Clamoring coyotes, he decided. Once the racket subsided, he took in a more natural sounding noise. It was past one o'clock in the morning and he was sleep deprived, but Ramon knew it was the sound of a rushing body of water. A water junkie, the man walked around the Sharpe house to investigate. He had forgotten Mia had lived so close to the creek. Ramon wanted to pray for his daughter in front of the shimmering ripples no doubt illuminated by the bright moon in the dead of night. Ramon pushed his way through thick, scaly branches and the shoulder height coniferous needles. White firs, blue spruces, and ponderosa pines sheltered him from the radiant brightness of the illuminated sky. His feet crunched on the pine straw below, which alerted a shadowy figure up ahead of his presence.

Before him stood an adult male elk, situated just above the flowing creek. The animal, about thirty feet in distance from the man, swayed its head 180 degrees to decipher his whereabouts in the thicket. His yellow brown eyes met Ramon's not three seconds later.

Ramon felt a rush of déjà vu. He had been this close to an elk years ago outside the Allsup's he owned. He had backed away from the graceful beast then and would need to do the same in the present. Just in case, he slowly reached his right hand into his backpack and clasped his fingers around the 9mm pistol. He took a step backwards, cocked the weapon, and pointed it at the beast. When his foot landed, Ramon crunched especially hard on a pile of leaflets beneath him.

The elk heard this and turned his body in the direction of the man so he could see his striking antlers, devilish eyes, and brawny frame head on. It terrified Ramon, who retreated another pace and was tripped up by the fallen branch of a towering sycamore. The wild mammal noticed the man's vulnerability and leapt forward in stride towards him.

Seeing his life flash before his eyes, Ramon De Leon, seated on the hard late winter brush, flipped the safety off the gun and fired three shots in succession at the elk. The moment seemed to last a lifetime, and the noises of the startled beast horrified the man. It was a high-pitched, throaty sound, like a last-ditch effort to save itself from its significant wounds by phoning in for help. Having been hit by the bullets, the Herculean animal dropped two feet in front of Ramon slowly and thudded against the brush.

The man exhaled a deep sigh of relief. The dying elk twitched; its eyes focused on who lay on the ground a few feet in front of him, its breaths becoming more prolonged.

Ramon trudged back towards the house. His heart sank as he recalled the day the massive elk stood in the spotlight glow in the back of the Allsup's. He remembered that the first sighting was, in fact, the day before he shot and killed Bart Thompson, Sr. Was it an omen?

Ramon's eyes shifted up to the bright sky slowly as he discerned the pattern. He sprinted up to the front door to alert Scott.

Chapter 24

I heard three sequential gunshots ring out in the near vicinity. A high-pitched yelp rang out for several seconds after the booms, and I froze. The echo of the trees behind my home sung their sad song and hordes of birds flew over the shingled roof.

What in the world was going on out there? I turned around and observed Ramon's GMC Sierra in the driveway.

Just then, my father-in-law burst through our front entry. "Hello, Scott," he said, trying to compose himself. He removed his white cowboy hat and set it on the entryway table.

"Ramon?" I said. "What was that noise outside? Did you shoot something?"

"Come see."

I followed him out through the backyard and into the tall blue spruces. After meandering through the thicket of evergreens and conifers, we came to a clearing just before the zigzagging, busy creek. Ramon gasped audibly.

"It was, it was right here—"

"What was here?" I asked.

"I shot it. An elk." Ramon threw his hands on his hips and sunk his head in defeat.

"You shot an elk?" I exclaimed in surprise. "In late February? Are you sure?"

"I swear of it." I knew he was telling the truth. In all the years I had known him, Ramon De Leon had never once told me a lie. Mia told me he had kissed another woman when drunk once twenty-five years earlier and immediately confessed his infidelity to Adriana. On another occasion, he blew off plans with his family to sit by the Rio Grande. When Adriana, Ana, and Mia found him, he admitted to bailing on the engagement to have a moment of peace in solitude at his favorite place. I believed Ramon to be an honorable, flawed human being. Just like the rest of us.

"Where's the blood trail?" I asked, looking toward the obvious area in the brush that was in fact spacious enough for a male elk to stumble into.

"Here." I saw the evidence of gore where his forefinger gestured. Drops of blood ran in a line from the point of attack up to the creek, and in the blackened gleaming wavelets of the water they disappeared.

Ramon tossed his folded arms in the air, and they furiously swept through his frizzy, dark hair. "I can't believe it, Scott. He was going to attack me."

"Are you *sure* it was an elk?" I asked. "Could it have been a deer?"

"Let me put it to you this way, son: I have only once in my life ever seen an elk. It was in New Mexico thirty years ago." He motioned to the luminous full moon in the sky and continued, "My hand to God, tonight was the second time I have ever seen one."

While I was aware that elk ordinarily don't show up often in the deep of winter, I noticed we had only traces of snow at this point. The temperature was around thirty degrees, so I supposed it was plausible the animal was in fact an elk.

"I believe you," I said. The night intensified in its angry chill, growing draftier with each passing second. "Now let's go inside."

Ramon nodded, and we made our way towards the glowing light of my home.

--

"I have a confession, Scott," Ramon, still a bit panicked by the elk incident minutes prior, said in the dark leather chair of my living room.

"Go on."

My father-in-law played with his wispy facial hair; it was a move I've never witnessed from the man before. He was displaying quite a bit of nervousness. "Remember how I said I have only seen the one elk before?"

I bobbed my head up and down. "Yes."

"This is true," he looked down at the floor, "but the last time I saw one, I killed a man the next day."

I had been waiting for this admission for years. Of course, I was familiar with all the particulars of the story but I had no intention of letting Ramon know that. This was his spiel to deliver.

"Around the time Maria Elena was born, things were settling down at the Allsup's. One day, a man with a cowboy hat walked in and he looked very sketchy. That night, I saw an elk outside of the store. Now, I backed away slowly from him and didn't shoot him like tonight—"

"I'm sorry, Ramon," I interjected, "but I need to ask: why did you bring a gun?"

"If you have to ask, son, you already know the answer." His voice was harrowing, but I knew what he meant. His daughter's life was on the line, and he was willing to do whatever it took. I admired that.

"Keen answer, Ramon."

"Anyway," he continued, "I didn't shoot the elk last time. I drove away from him, and he kept his eyes locked on me. It was terrifying, *yerno*." He sighed deeply and adjusted the shoulder of his checkered button-down shirt. "The next day the same man came back into my shop and threatened to take everything I have. He drew a gun on me, and I shot and killed him."

"Wow." I displayed an exaggerated reaction, throwing my hands in my face. Eventually, I will confess to him I was aware he killed the father of my boss. For the time being, I recognize the futility of divulging what I know.

"This is why I am nervous about seeing the elk," Ramon explained. "Because the last time I saw one, I killed a man the very next day."

"So, you're worried you'll kill tomorrow?"

He nodded. "And Scott," he paused. "I will if I must. This is my daughter—and grandsons—we're talking about."

"I know," I replied. "I'd kill for them, too."

"Good." I could sense the shakiness in his voice, and it made me a bit skittish.

Though Mia looked significantly more like her mother from my point of view, I could see a bit of her in her father. He had the same bronze skin tone, the same curly jet-black hair. Mia received her stubbornness from her father. This trait was what would help make our mission tomorrow morning successful.

Ramon continued, "So, how did you come to find out where they were?"

"The man I work for, Bart," I gulped, careful not to use his surname. If I uttered his last name, Ramon would no doubt put together the puzzle. "He told me on the phone that I knew the place they were hidden. I narrowed it down to three locations familiar to myself and the Satriones."

My father-in-law's face revealed one of confusion. Either that, or he knew who Bart was. "Who are the Satriones?"

"They are the mob syndicate that likely took Mia and the boys."

"Why would the mob want them?" he practically shouted.

I gulped. Time to be a man. "I took out a loan of ten thousand dollars and didn't pay back the full amount."

Ramon scratched his head with his fingernails. "Ay, ay, ay, Scott."

"I know."

"You really screwed up, you know," he said.

Perhaps it was in the spirit of being fully transparent, but I said in reply, "Well, there was one other thing."

"And what is that?" The tension in the room intensified.

"Bart Thompson, the kidnapper, is the son of the man you killed."

Ramon's brown eyes widened, and he let out a loud gasp. His round face turned bright red—like a ripe tomato—and his chin fell. The man's hands clenched deep into his thighs, and his thumbs turned inward. He was legitimately shocked. "How did you know?"

"I've known for a while, Ramon, that you killed a man," I admitted. "Bart told me drunkenly a few years ago while we were having a burger."

"What did he say?"

"I remember him saying some 'nobody Mexican shop owner' murdered his father. He thought it was a government conspiracy. I verified the claim on the Internet by finding a snippet from the *Albuquerque Journal* of the incident."

I could sense Ramon was attempting to remain composed. He said in reply, "That's why I'm here."

"What?"

He said, "He wants to exchange their freedom for mine."

Truth be told, I hadn't considered this a likely outcome. I thought Bart wanted to face the man responsible for his father's death and have me cut ties with a finger.

"I will make darn sure there is no swap of any kind," I said. "This is my pickle, and I'll get us out of it."

"Scott," Ramon said. "I will die for my daughter and grandsons."

"I know that, Ramon. You mentioned that."

He shook his head up and down. "Tell me about the places they might be and why you're sure you know."

I took a deep breath. "The first place is work, the Westco headquarters. I thought that would be ambitious and an unnecessary risk, so I skipped it altogether. The second place was Jack's Burgers, the restaurant I mentioned when Bart inadvertently told me you killed his dad. It's a place that has had rumored mob ties for years. I got thrown out by a manager named Bruce once I started asking questions tonight. I went to the Whitehawk Casino and asked to see a room. During the middle of Bart and I's phone conversation, I heard a distinct old ringtone. One of those nostalgic sounds. I wouldn't forget it. When I asked the manager to see the room, I asked for the phone number so I could call. As soon as the phone started ringing, I recognized the sound and knew Mia, Francisco, and Marcos were in the hotel somewhere. The next step was determining the room number, and we would get there by looking at the security tapes. I needed to find out when exactly I was there and what room the man who took me upstairs went into. I figured out the date by deducing games in which the Denver Nuggets played against the Los Angeles Lakers. I remember when I was there last year was the day in which one of those games happened. I was down to two dates, and I checked my iPhone calendar and saw Mia had marked one of the days as a date night for the two of us. Therefore, I knew it was the other day, March thirteenth. Once again, sir, your amazing daughter saved the day."

For the first time since his arrival, Ramon smiled. I knew complimenting his baby girl would tug on his heartstrings.

I continued, "Once I tracked down the exact day, I went back to the manager, Chayton. He had access to the security tapes, and we found the Satrione associate, Keith, and I walking up to a room together on video. It was Room 316. Chayton and I went and knocked on the door, and an old man answered and was adamant it was just he and his wife staying in the room. We went down to his office, checked the daily logs, and the name Bruce Jackson stuck out to me. Bruce was the name of the manager at Jack's, you see? Bruce. *Jackson*. It made sense on paper. He's in Room 416, exactly one above where the Satriones were last year." There was no point in discussing with Ramon the significance of the supernatural voice in the sky that told me to look one floor up. I don't think he would understand. That's what makes us different, I guess. He would never entertain what he perceived to be a fairy tale. I still can't explain it.

"I have a question," Ramon said.

"Shoot."

He asked, "Did you ever consider vents?"

I had no clue what he meant. "Huh?"

"Think about it," the man explained. "If the Room was 316 last time and 416 now, what kind of advantage would that give?"

I shrugged my shoulders. "What is it?"

"The vents. If they are connected by a sort of tunnel system, it's an easy chance to stow money, drugs, and weapons."

Almost instantly, I believed his theory. Every hotel room in the Whitehawk Casino could be equipped with vents positioned at the top and bottom of each wall. If they were connected via passageway, it would be very easy to switch hotel rooms but not necessarily mix up the location of the cash, drugs, and guns. Changing the room number would never draw suspicion. What this likely meant though is that there was a mole within the casino who was helping the Satriones in selecting their rooms. Someone else knew.

My brain immediately suspected Chayton. Was he leading me astray? Would he have deviously written the name "Bruce Jackson" on the paper just to throw me off so I would go to the wrong room? Perhaps I uttered the words "one up" as I hallucinated, and he heard. Maybe he altered the entire plan we had in place. He could have lied.

"You're right, Ramon," I said, acknowledging the ventilation theory. "Do you think the manager may have thrown me off by writing 'Bruce Jackson'?"

"It's possible," he replied. "I think we must consider all possibilities at this point. What was his reason for helping you?"

"He said his wife and son were hit by a drunk Native American on the reservation," I explained. "He wanted to avenge their deaths."

"And you believe it?" Ramon conveyed this not in an accusatory fashion but rather to challenge me.

"I—I think so," I stuttered. "He seemed like a good man. If he did all that just to throw me off, that's a horrible thing to do. But like you said, we have to consider every possibility right now."

"Did you verify his claim?" he asked.

"What, the crash?"

"Yes."

"I didn't," I replied. "Then again, I never got his last name so I couldn't just Google it. I don't even know his late wife's name."

Ramon continued, "I like your Bruce Jackson room number theory. It makes the most sense. If the man you spoke to was lying to us, though, we are walking into a death trap."

I pondered his pushback for a moment. If I caught Chayton off guard by recognizing the phone ringtone, he could have easily fooled me into thinking "Bruce Jackson" was a real person operating under the Satrione business.

After pausing momentarily, I said, "I'm going to think about whether I trust him or not, Ramon. This could be one of the most important decisions of my life."

"Don't mess this up again, Scott," Ramon pointed his thick index finger at me harshly. He was right; I deserved the scrutiny.

Glancing at the clock on the microwave, I noticed it was approaching two in the morning. "I'm going to bed, Ramon."

"About that time, isn't it?"

"Let's get up at eight, is that all right?" I asked.

"Sure thing, son," Ramon said, and slapped me lightly on the back. "Don't worry. We'll get them tomorrow." He grabbed his old white hat and dusted it off.

"Yes, we will," I said. "Need anything?"

"I'm good."

"Good," I said. "You know where the guest bedroom is."

"Good night." Ramon disappeared down the steps to the basement, and I retreated to the master bedroom.

We needed rest before we could unravel this mystery.

--

I lay in bed and thought of Mia. Not lost in this whole ordeal was the reality she was previously upset at me before she was kidnapped. I thought of the years I would spend making it up to her for this unbearable nightmare, and I missed her immensely. The conversations we had just before her capture were scary, but they were necessary and I was oddly excited for them to resume. I think the prospect of talking to her late at night, then holding her in my arms as she drifted off to sleep, kept me pushing on this journey. There's nothing I wouldn't do for a kiss from my wife.

The man I was now was the not the man I needed to be for her, for our children. The man I wanted to be doesn't desert his wife and newborn son to get hammered in the hospital parking lot. The man I wanted to be doesn't need to drink to stay level. The man I wanted to be needs to stay sober and be present.

I knew at the end of this chapter of my life there was only one final page. This purgatorial trial ends with me in a rehab facility, I'm sure of it, or in the program. Between my family's history and my recent oblivious behavior, there was nowhere else for me to go.

It suddenly occurred to me I needed to find a new job. A shiver ran up my back as the realization dawned on me that I didn't even know where we would live after this episode. Would it be in Minnesota? Colorado? New Mexico? I didn't have a clue. I prayed for the health and safety of my family, knowing God would provide. It's what Mia would want me to do, too.

Drifting off into sleep, I thought about Mia, Francisco, and Marcos. In a particularly hellish dream, I searched for the three of them in a hotel room at the Whitehawk Casino. Once I found Room 416, I fell into a never-ending black hole. I woke up sweating profusely.

The clock on my phone read seven twenty-four. I had fallen asleep a bit before three, so I was able to sleep a whopping four and a half hours. It wasn't a great tally, but I came to the sudden realization it was the first time in years I'd been able to sleep sober. I was proud of myself.

Dressed in his complimentary white hat and T-shirt, jeans, and cattle-branded belt buckle, Ramon was already in the kitchen fixing up a pot of coffee. If I didn't know any better, I'd say he was ready to cowboy today.

"Hello, sir," I called out to him.

"Hi, Scott," he said, followed by a prolonged and awkward silence.

I swiped two unused mugs in the right cabinet by where our Ninja coffeemaker was screaming. "How did you sleep?" I asked.

"Good. You?"

"I slept well." It was a lie and both of us knew it. My eyelids were droopy, filled to the brim with untouched accumulating yellow discharge. "I will better tonight, though."

"That's right," Ramon offered a friendly, encouraging pat on the back. I filled up our cups with hot coffee and we drank them down in a few minutes. From the pot, we refilled our coffee for a second round.

"Are you hungry?" I asked him.

"I guess," he said, and I understood the apathy. I scrambled up some eggs and sizzled some sausage on another pan, that being the only sound heard in the kitchen. The silence was eerie.

"It's show time," I said, and added, "I just realized I need to put the car seats in there. Luckily, Mia is always prepared. The extras are in the garage. Get dressed and we'll head to the casino."

Ramon glanced at his watch. It was half past eight, and we had some intel to do beforehand.

"Did you think about what I said about this Chayton?" Ramon asked. He had exchanged his white tee for a rustic blue and green plaid shirt. His black cowboy boots were sharp and lustrous and fit his Western outlaw personality well. I went a more comfortable route, sporting a red University of New Mexico Lobo quarter zip and a loose-fitting pair of black joggers meeting up with a dark pair of New Balance sneakers. Ramon wore a timeless ensemble, and I opted for comfort.

"I sure did." I smiled, having hatched a plan the night before. "Chayton worked into the late hours of the night yesterday, right?"

"Sure." I peered over my shoulder to merge lanes and saw the infant and toddler car seats I had crammed into the back of the Mazda I drove. The car itself was barely capable of fitting five humans, much less two children. We'd do our best. Mia would be proud of me for packing the car seats.

"So," I continued, "wouldn't that mean he's not working now?"

"I don't get it." My question left Ramon a little more than puzzled. I could see him twiddling his thumbs on his jeans in the passenger's seat. It was obvious to me the man was uncomfortable riding shotgun. He liked control.

"If he's not working now—and he's the mole—we could ask to see the logbook again."

"Why would we need to see the logbook again?" Ramon asked. "We already know Bruce whatever is staying in Room 416."

"Yes, but if Chayton were in on it and changed the name," I continued. "The name will be different when we ask today."

"Ah, I see. So you think if he is with the mob, he will have changed the guest log?"

"That's right."

We parked in the giant parking lot of the Whitehawk Casino. As we strolled across the lot, I motioned to Ramon the giant neon sign indicating the entrance.

"She's in there." My father-in-law stared at the huge building, mouth agape. I had already been inside the night before, so I allowed him time to process. "I mean, *they* are in there. I am sorry, Scott. Don't think I don't care deeply for your children."

"I know you do, Ramon," I replied. "Now let's go get them."

For a Monday morning at nine-thirty, Whitehawk was hopping. It was obvious as soon as we approached the sliding door entrance. There were hundreds of people inside: young frat boys on extended weekend getaways, middle-aged Denver suburbanite moms searching for a gambling fix, and the chain-smoking elderly who were likely there the night before.

Ramon noticed the bustling nature of the place as well. "Is it always so crowded?" he asked. "Sandia Casino in Albuquerque is almost never like this." My father-in-law was evidently not a fan of the gambling club. As we shuffled across the casino floor toward the hotel entrance, he held his breath to avoid the white clouds of cigarette smoke. In a sadistic way, it was hilarious.

As we neared the reception area with the swinging saloon doors in the back, I noticed a different employee was manning the desk. His nametag read Justin.

"Hello, Justin," I said. "Is Chayton working?"

"Who?"

"Chayton, the nighttime manager," I explained. "Long ponytail, late thirties maybe?"

"I'm new, and I don't work nights," he said. "Just a second."

I glanced at Ramon and we shared a skeptical stare. Shortly afterward, another man, this one with a balding head and graying hair, pushed through the batwing doors after Justin. He placed his fists on his hips when he saw us. His nametag bore the name Cal.

"Who's looking for Chayton?" he called out. Ramon and I shrugged. We were the only people within twenty feet of the desk.

Playing Cal's game, I slowly raised my hand. "We are."

"Chayton was fired this morning."

"Fired?" I gulped, suppressing the urge to scream. "What for?"

The ostentatious man frowned. "That I can't tell you, boss," he said.

Chayton's sudden dismissal threw a wrench in our plan. I glanced at Ramon, then at Cal, and asked, "Can I see the guest logbook?"

"What the hell?" Cal yelled. "First you ask for Chayton, and now you want to see the guest log?"

I nodded. "It's important."

"What is it that so is damn important?"

"I can't tell you," I said.

Ramon pulled me aside and whispered once we were out of Cal's hearing range. "Why don't we tell them? Or call the cops? They can go investigate and we'll all come out safe."

I pondered the proposal for a moment, then I returned to reality. "These are dangerous men," I murmured. "They told me not to call the cops, and I don't want to find out what happens if we do. These are the same guys who staked out my house for two thousand dollars and found out you were the one who shot Bart's father."

"You're right." Ramon putzed around a bit with his head. "No cops." I remember what he had said the night prior about exchanging his freedom for Mia and the boys. He came here this morning expecting to die.

When Bart spoke to me on the phone, he had advised me to prepare me to lose a finger. I believe the actual term he employed was "appendage". That could mean finger, arm, leg, or—gulp—something below the belt. If it was Ramon's life he was seeking, that would be greater than the sum of anything he could take from me. I decided to lose my right ring finger if given the option. I am keenly aware of my ignorance in the realm of the science behind it. I chose the right ring finger simply because my 14k gold wedding ring rests on my left hand.

We walked back over to Cal. "Please, sir, let us see the book."

"No," he pointed his index finger at us both, "and if you ask again, I'm calling the cops."

Ramon and I sulked as we left the front desk. As we passed by the janitor's closet, the small door swung open. A figure grabbed me by the quarter zip and threw me inside the small space.

Chapter 25

A blinding phone flashlight shined on me. I looked to my left and saw that Ramon too had been drug into the room. The space, which had a small mail slot about knee height level, wreaked of cigarette smoke and a faint aroma of body odor.

I braced myself for the worst. "Scott?" the voice called out. Just from one word, I recognized it was Chayton addressing me.

"Chayton," I breathed a sigh of relief. "You scared the crap out of me."

"Sorry about that," he said, and turned to Ramon. "This must be your father-in-law."

"Ramon De Leon. I have to say, that is the worst way I've ever been introduced to someone before. And I killed a man once." He laughed uncontrollably, sweat pouring from his forehead into his eyebrows. I'd never seen him so terrified. In the dark chamber, he shook Chayton's hand.

The former employee replied, "It's a pleasure to meet you, Ramon."

"We heard you were fired," I said.

The man looked at us and smiled. "They figured out what we were onto last night, Scott."

"And you've been in here?"

"Yes," he said. "Only one janitor has been in here, and I claimed to work here. He didn't speak English anyway."

"Aren't you exhausted?" I asked.

"Of course. You owe me the strongest freaking cup of coffee."

"We thought maybe you might be in on it with the Satriones—"

"Of course not," Chayton interrupted me. "I want to help your wife and sons return to you."

I gazed at Ramon. He was still processing what was happening to us. The quiet man was especially hushed in this instant.

"How did you know we were walking by?" I asked.

Chayton shined the scintillating, headache-inducing flashlight from the phone on the mail slot on the door. "I saw you through the little window."

"Boy, your knees must be killing you," I said.

"You can say that again."

All three of us tried to contain our laughter in the tiny closet. "What's next then?"

"That's what I was going to ask you," Chayton said, as he flicked on his Bic lighter that cast light upon his face. He took a long drag from his cigarette and asked, "What else did you find out?"

"I think they're in Room 416," I said, pulling out my phone to show him the photo. "It was booked last night for a Bruce Jackson."

Chayton inhaled another long puff of his Pall Mall and switched off the flashlight from his phone. I couldn't see his face. "I don't get it."

"Bruce was the name of the manager at the Jack's yesterday," I explained. "So either the Satriones are in the room or that's one hell of a coincidence."

"How do you know Bruce is involved?" It was a valid question.

"I just had this odd feeling about how he threw me out of the restaurant last night," I said. "The way he reacted when I asked for Bart, it was unnatural. He literally put me on the street."

"I get that," Chayton said.

"Plus," I admitted, "when you and I were outside last night during your cigarette break, I heard a voice say, 'one up'. So, if we were looking in Room 316, that means we'd have to look up one room. Room 416."

Ramon broke his silent streak. "You heard a voice?"

I lowered my head a bit in shame and said, "Yes." The reason I didn't mention the mysterious speaker in the sky to my father-in-law was the possibility of this exact scenario. He didn't believe me. I knew if I could get him in the car, to the casino, that it wouldn't matter anyway.

That intuition proved to be accurate. From three feet away, Ramon sighed deeply. Between the misleading statements and the overwhelming odor of smoked Pall Malls, I ascertained his desire to leave camp.

After several silent minutes, my new friend mixed up the conversation. "Do you want me to knock on the door?"

"416's door?" I asked.

"Yes. They won't recognize me like they would you two."

If it wasn't abundantly clear at this point, Chayton was our teammate. That is, unless he was the red herring in our investigation. We had to take the chance. "Sure. That would be great."

"Awesome."

The next hour consisted of peace and quiet. One of us would check our phones from time to time, but we knew the meeting was set for eleven o'clock, and there was idle time until the minute hand hit the twelve to commence the hour. My thoughts in the interim consisted of a lot of the same. My family was within reach, and now was the time for me to step up and be a man. I knew I was up to the task.

At ten-fifty, Ramon nudged me. "Is it time?" he asked.

I nodded. "Let's go get them."

My father-in-law gripped my hand and shook it rapidly. "You know," he began. "For as little hope as I had last night, I think we can do this."

A tear swelled in the corner of my eye. It was perhaps the most emotional moment I've ever seen from Ramon. I smiled and responded, "Sir, I would do anything for your daughter, including hiding in a closet for an hour."

"We're going to wreak of smoke," Ramon added, and laughed at Chayton. Once the moment passed, we stared at each other intensely.

"It's time," I said.

"Great," Chayton said. "Now cover me." He jiggled the doorknob and swung it open. The man ducked around the corner and briskly ambled to the elevator. Ramon and I peered over our shoulders. Being that Chayton was fired, he was risking prosecution with this next move.

Once inside the elevator, I pushed the button that would raise us to the fourth floor. Ramon tapped his waistline to reveal his pistol, which he removed and slid inside one of his cowboy boots. The control in the elevator with the number four illuminated to signal our arrival, and I drew in a long-lasting breath.

"Oh, no," Ramon whispered to me once we exited the elevator.

"What's wrong?"

"I forgot my cowboy hat in that closet." He smiled, as if to acknowledge its absence wasn't a big deal.

I flashed him a grin. "I've seen you cowboy out there without it, Ramon."

Chayton interjected, "You were wearing the white hat with black boots. They don't go together."

"That's true. Let's go."

My father-in-law and I hid ourselves in the small nook of the fourth floor, identical to that of the third. We gave Chayton a thumbs up as if to proceed. He rapped on the latch of Room 416, and the door swung open. I recognized the six-foot-five man with the glasses from the video footage; he was with the Satriones. "Come inside. Bring your friends."

Ramon and I appeared from behind the nook. Another prolonged breath later and I stood inside the hotel room.

Chapter 26

Room 416 appeared at first glance like many hotel rooms. On the left side two feet from the door was a large walk-in closet, opened halfway, the other fifty percent obstructed by a giant mirror. I observed Mia's white Canada Goose jacket from Nordstrom's among the litany of coats. My heart sank. I was *that* close to my wife.

To the right was a stereotypical casino hotel bathroom. There was a recently updated shower with colorful tiles, and a lone sink and lavatory of average size. There was a crusted film of yellow brown on the floor in front of the toilet. To me, this signaled whoever rented the room possessed the authority or sheer presence to decline a customary offer like daily housekeeping. Red, almost crimson, walls and unhinged, scattered marks on the carpet made the place feel like a casino gaming floor. There was a wide screen television facing the king-sized bed, and next to it laid a desk whose weathered walnut stain hadn't been updated in years. A wooden chair was pushed in. The bed had a colorful Rocky Mountain-themed comforter. A small couch lay beyond the bed with a coffee table stacked full of books, coffee cups, and empty beer cans. This observation further proved my theory that housekeeping had not been in this place in days. Across from the sofa was a conspicuous, single-wide royal blue door. I wondered if my family were behind it.

The tall man with the glasses and the sparkling black suit looked directly at me and laughed. "You made it." He glanced at his watch and added in a thick European accent of some sort, "With five minutes to spare. Bart will be pleased." He frisked all three of us, and erred failing to confirm we weren't carrying weapons in our shoes. Ramon's pistol was not found by the examiner. I breathed a sigh of relief, quiet enough that the man wouldn't hear. The inspector's massive frame sauntered over to the mysterious blue door.

He propped it open—just barely enough to where I couldn't see what lay on the other side—and in walked my jackass of a boss. Technically, Bart Thompson was still in charge of me at work, but there was no chance life would return to normalcy after this saga.

"Look who it is!" he bellowed at Ramon and me. "The liar and the murderer!"

In a shock to me, my father-in-law gritted his teeth and said, "I don't know you."

Though he played the role of kidnapper, Bart Thompson still appeared as though he was on the verge of bawling. He and the man in the glasses, put together, were at least a foot taller than Ramon and I. Bart's sad brown eyes glazed over Chayton as he called them out, "Who the hell are you?"

"I am Chayton, sir." His voice never wavered.

Bart peered over at the other tall man and delivered a single nod. In the blink of an eye, Mr. Glasses pulled out a black double action revolver and pointed it directly at Chayton's forehead. Bart continued, "And who the hell are you, Chayton?"

"Just a guy who worked here."

"Worked?" Bart scratched his head in confusion. "Okay, what is going on here?" He glanced over at me and shouted, "I didn't tell you to bring this lunatic!"

"Fine, Bart," I said. "Fine. What should he do?"

I heard the bespectacled individual whisper into Bart Thompson's ear. Bart uttered something back along the lines of, "He's just a loose end."

Bart walked over to Chayton and grabbed him by the ponytail. The former casino worker shouted in pain as he was dragged by his hair into the bathroom. Bart left the room and slammed the sliding door. "And don't you *dare* come out. Now," he glimpsed back at us and slapped his hands together, "where were we?"

Remembering that Ramon had a pistol in his cowboy boots and Mr. Glasses was also armed, the encounter began to take on the sinister aura of an approaching shootout. I gulped and made eye contact with Ramon. Sweat beads poured down his forehead like the water fountain on the casino floor. We needed a few pennies worth of luck.

"Oh, yes," Bart said to no one in particular. He paced a few steps back near the blue door. "You owe me a finger, Sharpe."

In the other room, I suddenly heard a baby wail. It was the type of cry to inform you a child is certifiably fussy. How dare this monster contain my child. I scolded Bart, "Two thousand dollars and you resort to *this*?"

He laughed. "You know it's not just the two thousand dollars." He pointed at Ramon with his fat finger. "That bastard killed my father."

"Your father *attacked* me," Ramon said. "I had no choice."

"You had a choice," Bart said. "We always have a choice. Every single moment of our miserable existence is defined by choices. You made yours."

Ramon shook his head. He didn't understand Bart's gobbledygook. "Let them go," he said.

"They'll be safe."

"Why should we believe you?" I shouted.

Protected by the man in the glasses and the dark revolver in his right hand, Bart said, "You know what I want, Sharpe."

I did. I sighed in despair, understanding now more than ever that I would resort to any method for the safety of my family. So, I thrust out my right hand and pointed to my ringless fourth finger. "So, do it."

Bart chuckled a bit and reached into his pocket. In his fingertips, he held a black Kershaw switchblade knife. He flipped the safety lever, revealing a jagged edge. My brain went numb and I swallowed violently as I remembered the blade was intended to be used on me. Bart ambled his way over and held out the blade. The Kershaw made its way dangerously close to my face, and as I fixated on its spike the background blurred into vagueness. I moved backwards when I only had a few inches left before I hit the wall.

Chayton must have known something was amiss because he shouted from the bathroom suddenly, "Let me out!"

My soon-to-be former boss motioned to his wingman, who strolled toward the facilities slowly to build up the tension. He threw open the sliding door glass and his face was met instantly by the angry fist of Chayton. Mr. Glasses was sent flying backward into the mirror on the side of the closet closest to the door. I gasped audibly, and so too did Bart.

The head of the man by the closet oozed blood. On the mirror door by the closet was a fresh indentation where his noggin had violently smashed. Though he stood right behind the corner, I could not see Chayton. My jaw hung in amazement by the power of his strike. Bart's sidekick outweighed the unathletic Chayton by at least sixty pounds. And yet, here they were, the bigger man lying on the ground and the inferior on his toes and shaking his throbbing fist.

Ramon too was in shock. He acted a lot quicker than I, as he reached down with his right hand to grip the pistol. A moment later, Bart Thompson threw his hands in the air in surrender as my father-in-law aimed the 9mm between his eyes.

"On your knees." To a certain extent I was surprised by Ramon's demand. Obviously made aware of what happened in the Allsup's a long time ago, I was keen to the idea he could remain cool under such immense pressure. Even still, he'd never shown the skills to me before, and so I was taken aback by this three-word command.

I was especially astonished Bart listened to the stocky man. "You brought a gun to a knife fight." He grinned. "We should have patted you down better."

Ramon gestured toward the other room and ordered, "Open the door."

"Okay, okay," Bart threw his mitts in the air. "I get it. I get it." From his knees, he slithered the ten feet to the barrier. He reached up with his right hand, jiggled the knob, and thrust open the door. I paced behind Ramon but gasped as I heard the man in the glasses behind us groan. He was regaining consciousness and rubbing his aching head.

Bart remained on his knees. The man was in possession of the knife, so the battle would suddenly become dangerous if Mr. Glasses drew his revolver.

Ramon uttered to me, "Hit him."

"Hit who?"

"Him!" He shouted, pointing at the threat behind us. "And take his gun."

In my thirty-two years on Earth, I had never hit anyone not named Simon or Spencer. Now was, for all intents and purposes, a good time for my first real punch. I flipped my body around and charged at the groaning man with a bare fist. My father had informed me as a child that if you extend your arm to punch someone with your thumb folded under the protection of the rest of your fingers, you will no doubt break your hand. In the three seconds between Ramon's direction and the time I made it to the man on the ground, I'm glad I remembered my father's bit of wisdom. With a closed fist and extended thumb, I aimed for Mr. Glass' nose, and I smacked him as hard as I could. His head retreated to the ground, and he rolled over ninety degrees on his side of his body. The weapon he drew lay under his right arm. My hand hurt like hell, but it was worth it.

Chayton, also obviously a novice in the art of violence, was hyperventilating in the bathroom. It said something to me that he stuck around after hitting the big man, risking his own safety in the process for the betterment of our situation. I said to him, "Help me push him over so we can grab his gun."

We rolled the burly 250-pound man another half revolution, his lower body in the closet beneath Mia's jacket, his head and chest remaining outside. His body was twisted like a contortionist, but with his free hand Chayton recovered the gun and passed it to me. Suddenly, we had them out weaponed.

I gazed at him and called out, "Chayton! Go." I pointed with the hand holding the revolver to the room's exit, and he sheepishly walked out of the room. We made eye contact as I slowly closed the door and I mouthed the words, "Thank you." He saluted me and scampered out of the room and into the hallway.

Back near the blue door, Bart was pleading. "Don't shoot me," he said. "I'm just a pawn in all of this." It was unlike him. I sensed something was off.

Ramon, clearly at the helm now of this situation, was savoring the power. "Tell me why I should not shoot you right now."

"I have a family."

My father-in-law chuckled in that monotonous way of his. "And you think Scott here doesn't have a family?"

"I'll let them go," Bart Thompson pleaded for his life. "Just don't kill me."

Weighing his options, Ramon nodded slowly. "Give us Mia and the boys and you go free."

"No questions asked?"

"No questions asked."

Bart's sorrowful eyes gave him an elongated stare before uttering, "How do I know you're not going to shoot me once I let your family go?"

"Trust me, I won't." Ramon never wavered in his confidence.

"But you killed my father," said the man with the pistol six inches from his forehead.

"I didn't kill your father," Ramon corrected him. "Your father asked to die."

"What? No, he didn't."

"He may not have asked to die specifically," Ramon explained. "But his actions that day led to his death. His actions had consequences, just like yours will too."

"But—I—you just said you'd let me go if I let your family go."

"Those consequences will not come from me," Ramon paused for a moment, and made the sign of the cross by tapping his forehead, chest, and shoulders in succession. "Those consequences will come from someone else."

"What about crossing the border illegally? Did that action have consequences?" Though he sat inches away from a man capable of ending his existence, Bart laid his cards on the table. He ended his whole beggar act. I knew something was amiss. "That's why you killed my father, isn't it? He was going to expose you! The government was in on it."

"What He and I have or have not settled is not your business, just like yours is not mine."

Bart snickered. "You don't know, do you?" He cackled eerily, like a sinister Marvel villain. A grin curved up his lips and his eyebrows furrowed. "You don't know either, Sharpe? Do you?"

"Know what?" I asked in confusion.

"There is no promotion. There never *was* a promotion."

"*What?*"

"There is no promotion," he repeated. "I made the whole thing up. I told you I needed an answer quicker than I'd led on. I knew it would drive you to fight with your wife. I knew the plan was in action when you texted me and told me the baby had been born. I *knew*. I knew she'd go away from you and take the kids. Once I figured out you were an asshole alcoholic who drank at work and took a loan from the mob, it was too easy. You were so foolish, Sharpe. I should say, *are* so foolish."

My heart sank. "Go to hell, Bart. I want my family. I'm going to tell the cops all about this. You'll go to jail for a very long time. That's where you deserve to be."

"You're going to die today," he whispered. "You boys may think you hold the cards."

"Move over, Bart. We have the weapons now."

"Oh, you're in for a treat."

"What?" I shouted. "Step aside *now*."

I moved past Ramon towards my boss. Gifting him with a swift kick in the leg, I crossed over his now crouched over body. Bart winced in pain but managed to muster the words, "The police won't believe you, Scott."

"And why not?" I remarked while fidgeting with the doorknob.

"You're in for a treat," Bart repeated.

The blue door swung open, revealing an adjoining hotel room. It had the same crimson walls as Room 416. The floors were identical, a messy pattern fit for a casino. The wide screen television mirrored 416's, as did the king-size bed that lay in front of my eyes.

The only thing missing were my wife and sons.

Chapter 27

In the wake of the family's news, the four De Leon women came together in Albuquerque. Adriana had called three of her four daughters—Ana, Maria Elena, and Luisa—and informed them of the ongoing situation with their sister, nephews, father, and brother-in-law.

To say the reactions were supportive would be an understatement. Ana swooped down from Santa Fe and picked up Luisa, a freshman at the University of New Mexico studying film. Maria Elena, in her mid-twenties and working as a bank teller in north Dallas, hopped on a plane two hours after the call to be with her mother. Within four hours of the phone conversations, all three daughters sat in the De Leon living room. They held each other tightly and went to bed shortly after.

The mood the following morning was somber, but each of the three younger women held high hopes for their endangered family members. They all had their own coping mechanisms. Ana sat on the couch next to Adriana and slowly brushed and twirled her fingers through her mother's graying hair, assuring her everything would be all right. Maria Elena cooked huevos rancheros, a fried egg and tortilla-based dish full of avocado, cheese, and steak. She often threw on an apron and became the caretaking chef when stressful situations like this arose. Luisa ferociously texted updates to her dormmates at UNM and garnered Snapchat sympathy from the boy she liked, like any eighteen-year-old girl would.

Adriana cried many tears. She was disappointed in herself, however, for not being the rock her children needed. But that thought was daft, she convinced herself, as she knew all except Luisa, who had special needs, were grown up now. Adriana knew her other three girls no longer needed their mother the way they used to.

--

After they ate lunch, Luisa asked her mother if she could go for a walk. Adriana said of course that was fine, for she was an eighteen-year-old adult and could make her own decisions. Luisa, still a little unsure of this whole thing called freedom, assured her mother she would be back within an hour. The young woman decided not to bring her cell phone along. The endorphin-producing notification sounds of Facebook and Instagram could wait. Instead, she grabbed her father's old Polaroid camera and an old, tattered, hoodless black and red University of New Mexico sweatshirt he gave her years ago. The top was still four sizes too big for her scrawny five-foot-four frame. Her long brown curly hair nearly tucked into the massive hood of the sweatshirt. She wore it when she missed her father and now clearly qualified as one of those times.

As she sauntered east on Central Avenue in the West Mesa neighborhood, enjoying the beautiful New Mexico day, Luisa considered the bright sun. She pleaded with God for a cloud or two so her Polaroids weren't obstructed by evidence of the bright beam above. No, this stroll was intentional. Nothing could prevent her from completing her mission.

A film major, Luisa had recently discovered her love for pictures both moving and still. It was her shared passion with Ramon, which is why she decided to bring his Polaroid camera along on her rendezvous. Her father once told Luisa that the magic of a photograph is better kept on print than a screen shared with millions of others. And on a day like today, while her father's health was in question, Luisa fully understood the meaning. There were no buzzes in her pocket, no Snapchats from boys on her dorm who wanted to earn sympathy points. Luisa was pretty like her mother, like her older sisters, and she knew it. Pretty, like they say, as a picture.

Off Central Avenue, just before she passed Sunset Road, Luisa turned left from the crosswalk to a dirt pathway. She knew this was the way her father took by the tan ascending columns of the illuminated Route 66 sign just shy of the elongated, steel beam bridge rail. She crossed through the thicket of deciduous trees stripped of leaves by the grip of winter's chill. The yellow grass and reeds in the foreground gave way to the red-brown waterway her father had come to love.

She stopped and snapped a panoramic photo in her mind. Maybe it was just her imagination, or her youthful age the last time she visited, but Luisa couldn't help but notice the water levels looked a little low. The question burned through her mind, and she wanted to know desperately. She wished her father was around to ask. He knew how to communicate with her better than anyone.

As Luisa walked through the reeds heading north, away from the noise of vehicles cruising on Central Avenue, she felt a wave of nostalgia come over her. She had been here before, with her father, but had never viewed it the way his creative mind had. The Rio Grande was his special place, and she felt wistful in its murky presence. All the years had gone by and she had never taken the time to tell him what he meant to her. Luisa continued walking alongside the shrinking brook for a quarter of a mile, passing the sand bar a hundred yards from the Central Avenue bridge and reaching the first bend of the river. The young woman did this intentionally, so she could not see the automobiles flying by. It would be just her and the nature of the river, like her father loved it.

With her right arm, Luisa retrieved the backpack from her left shoulder. She laid her brown Jansport on the ground and chuckled at the irony of its hue matching that of the river. Ramon would remind her of the minerals and that it wasn't necessarily grubby water.

Luisa smiled. Though Ramon was not with her physically, she felt his presence in the meandering river. His body may be over 400 miles away, but his spirit remained with her.

Abruptly, a noise echoed in the thick of the willow trees of the valley. Luisa gulped and cried out, "Hello?" Her voice reverberated through the trees, and a flight of birds flew over her head. It was a frightening scene for a young woman alone.

Out of the corner of her eye, to her left, Luisa noticed a moving animal. It was walking at a brisk pace and lay about twenty yards to the north. She could see antlers or horns of some sort, but she couldn't identify the ambling beast. Once more, Luisa wished Ramon was with her. He would know what to do, how to treat whatever mammal was headed her direction.

The beast stopped, and its head peered above the reeds. About thirty feet in front of Luisa stood a mammoth of an elk. She pulled out the Polaroid camera and snapped a photo of the mammal.

She wasn't scared.

"Where were you?" Adriana asked when her youngest daughter returned to the De Leon homestead.

The girl chuckled. "You're going to laugh at me, *mamita*."

Her mother shrugged her shoulders, waiting for an answer. "What?"

"I was at the river."

"The Rio?"

"Yes, *mama*. I didn't run though."

A grin crept across Adriana's face. "Your father, wherever he is, is smiling at you."

--

Scott's promotion was a sham. The two-thousand-dollar loan was the scapegoat. Really what Bart Thompson and the rest of the mobbed up Westco execs wanted was Ramon De Leon. By designating Scott the whipping boy, they had lured Ramon out of New Mexico and into their web.

For a man, Ramon had always been a wizard of the side-eye. A connoisseur of the peripheral, one might say. So when he noticed to his left the weaponless man with the glasses and twisted nose rise to his feet, away from Scott and Bart, Ramon took action. From the parallel room, Scott yelled out in anguish as Bart laughed. Judging by Scott's high-pitched screams, Mia and the boys were still missing. Ramon pulled out the pistol once more from his ankle and firmly spoke at the unarmed bodyguard, "Where are they?"

The big man retreated. "I don't know, man. I'm just a former college football player." The ruse was exposed when the man's once European sounding voice shifted abruptly to an American accent. Pointing in the direction of Bart Thompson, he continued, "He hired me to look tough. I ain't playing with no gun pointed at my head."

Ramon's head swiveled ninety degrees toward Bart. The evil man shouted at his hired hand, "*That's* all it takes, Darrell? A gun to the head? If I surrendered like that every time a gun was pointed at me, I'd be Napoleon freaking Bonaparte!"

"Why the accent?" Ramon asked.

"It makes me sound scarier." He removed his sunglasses to reveal himself to Ramon.

"So you're a liar."

Darrell hurled a few four-letter words at Bart and pleaded with Ramon. "Let me go! I swear this was just a job out of college."

He was shaken up, and it upset Ramon. Bart had lied about his daughter and grandson's whereabouts. How was Ramon supposed to trust him after that?

"Spare me," Darrell begged. "Please."

Ramon turned back to Darrell and sighed. The man in the glasses had a tear streaming down his cheek. He was incapable of murder, unlike Bart. Ramon chose to believe he didn't know what he was signing up for. However, he couldn't just let him go. It was at that moment he made eye contact with the frightened man. Darrell's brownish red eyes mirrored the hue of the Rio Grande, and Ramon felt a wave of compassion upon recognizing this intimate detail.

"Scott," Ramon called out to his still stunned son-in-law.

"Yes?"

"Grab me the chair." He gestured toward the wooden seat next to the television, and Scott walked it over to him.

Ramon pointed at the bathroom. "In," he demanded.

Darrell folded his hands and uttered, "Thank you. Thank you, sir, for sparing my life." He freely waltzed into the lavatory and Ramon shut the sliding door. There was an indent where the door opened, and Ramon stuck the chair inside it to intimidate Darrell. He knew it wasn't strong enough to hold the big man back from escaping.

"What time is it?" he asked Darrell through the door.

"Eleven-twenty," the scared man answered.

"You better not leave before one-thirty," Ramon said, acknowledging the man's brawn. "You got it?"

"Yes, sir. One-thirty."

"See you."

Chapter 28

I frantically searched the second room. I realized this was the same hotel suite as the one next door. To be honest, there wasn't much time to speculate. There was no sign of Mia and the kids anywhere.

"Where are they?" I yelled at Bart.

He laughed at me. "I told you you'd be in for a treat."

After a few moments of silence, my heart skipped a beat as I heard a baby scream again. The sound was coming from the bathroom. I took three big strides toward the room and rammed open the sliding door.

Hanging from the shower curtain was a string, and attached to the string was a phone. The mobile device played a recording of my children screaming at the top of their lungs on a loop. We got duped.

I snatched the cellphone and heard a commotion from the next room. A man was pleading for his life, it sounded like. Could it be Ramon?

Upon entering the main room, I noticed my father-in-law exerted control over the man who was supposed to be guarding Bart. I pressed the gun against Bart's head, and Ramon called out to me, "Scott."

"Yes?" I answered.

"Grab me the chair." He muttered some words to the man, who had taken off his sunglasses or was forced to. The next thing I knew, Mr. Glasses walked into the bathroom on his own accord. He was folding his hands to thank Ramon, and I was beyond confused.

"What time is it?" Ramon called out. I discerned that he wasn't directing his shout at me because his back faced me.

"Eleven-twenty," came the response from behind the sliding door. Deductive reasoning told me the voice must have belonged to Mr. Glasses, but his accent had changed. He suddenly sounded American.

"You better not leave before one-thirty," Ramon said. "You got it?"

"Yes, sir," said the voice.

"See you."

"What was that?" I whispered to Ramon.

He smiled. "He won't be leaving until one-thirty, didn't you—"

Interrupting my father-in-law's statement was a thump at the door. Ramon and I leapt about a foot in the air. I knew it could only be one man, so I was not surprised when I flung open the door to see Chayton perched in front of Ramon and me.

He was beaming from cheek to cheek. "I know what room they are in."

"What?" I gulped. "How do you know?"

"Give me just a second. May I borrow one of your weapons?"

I stared down at the man in the bathroom's revolver and handed it to Chayton. He strolled over to Bart, who was sitting on the ground against the blue door. Chayton raised his right hand and smashed Bart in the face. The man fell slowly, and his forehead hit the ugly flooring. He flipped on his side and lay motionless. He was unconscious.

I let up a fist pump in excitement. "I did not expect *that*!"

"Well, there's a thing or two about me you don't know," Chayton smiled.

"So how did you figure out what room they're in?"

"It was easy," Chayton explained. "I went downstairs and looked for Keith Stephens at the blackjack table. When Scott and I saw him on the security camera, I took a snapshot on my phone. I opened that picture and hit the casino floor in disguise." He pointed to his red Whitehawk Casino hat and smiled. "I recognized Keith at the table and asked him for a loan."

"You did *what*?" I shouted.

Chayton grinned, and all his teeth shone. "I asked him for a two-thousand-dollar loan. I told him I knew Bart. He took me to the room the Satriones currently hold."

Ramon and I were puzzled. "They have *three* rooms?"

Chayton nodded. "He's in Room 216. Two floors directly below this one."

Of course, I thought. "One up to Room 316," I said out loud. "There was an old couple in 316, and the Satriones could have easily used them as their patsies. Or, more likely, maybe they're a long-term stay."

"Maybe they're connected." Ramon, having previously been silent, spoke these words from the corner of the hotel room.

"You think they're involved?" Chayton asked.

The quiet man shuffled his toes a bit on the hideous patterned floor and continued, "Maybe the Satriones need someone to fill their old rooms. Wouldn't you use someone like an old couple to distract any pursuers? I would. It would make authorities think, 'oh, this is just an elderly couple,' and nothing else."

"You may be right," I said, my right index finger and thumb rubbing through the peach fuzz of my beard. "That way the Satriones could use two different vent systems and remain undetected."

"Well," Chayton paused a moment and folded his arms. I must admit, he looked goofy sporting a ponytail with a fitted hat. He continued, "That means now we can be one hundred percent certain there is a mole at Whitehawk Casino. Three hotel rooms like this cannot be just a coincidence."

"Indeed it isn't a coincidence," I said. "But that can be a mystery for another day."

"So what are we waiting for?" Ramon chimed in. "Let's go!"

I slapped my father-in-law on the back. The rush of adrenaline flew through me, and I howled like a banshee. I forcefully slammed Bart Thompson's cellphone at the ground.

Chayton opened the door, and as we left Ramon banged on the bathroom door with his fist and shouted, "One-thirty, Darrell!"

Chapter 29

I can't explain it other than the epinephrine. I remember grasping the concept of the hormone in school. Essentially, when your body faces a flight or fight situation, the adrenaline rush can sometimes negate your shortcomings.

In that moment, trudging down the hallway of the Whitehawk Casino hotel's fourth floor, I felt no fear. Growing up in Minnesota, the wintry chill wasn't the only reason I'd freeze up in circumstances such as these. I was weak, a scared little boy. With every pace next to Ramon and Chayton, my confidence grew.

My father-in-law noticed it, too. The reserved man was out of his shell, in his element of protection. He wanted more than anything to rescue his daughter and grandsons because their safety was his livelihood. I understood it as a father and a husband, and his devotion to his family was admirable. Once we made it out of this conundrum, I vowed to be better, and Ramon is a great example of who I could look up to in that way.

So focused on my rush was I that the two-minute walk to Room 216 felt like a flash. Before I knew it, Chayton was pounding his fists on the door. Part of me wondered if leaving Bart alive was a mistake. At the end of the day, my ultimate desire was the safe and joyous reunion of my family. Certain matters like Bart Thompson's involvement would eventually be revealed, and that gave me solace. I couldn't wait to see that jerk in prison where he belonged.

The third knock yielded the presence of another heavily armed man. He was tall and wore thick, black-framed sunglasses like Darrell but donned long brown hair fashioned into a mullet. His burnt sienna colored beard was long and flowing, like he was a member of ZZ Top. He wore a gleaming black suit like his compadre, but his tie resembled the same shade of blue that divided the two bedrooms of Room 416. I'm guessing the difference in hue had something to do with rank among the Satriones.

"What are *you* doing here?" Blue tie, speaking in a thick European accent, recognized Chayton immediately, having likely been a part of the loan process an hour earlier. Against his arm he grasped a sizeable firearm. Although I could not see the weapon in its entirety, from the brief glimpse I would say it was a hunting rifle.

Still riding the adrenaline high, I pushed ahead of him to the front of the line. I faced the giant, at least six inches taller than me, and noticed a distinct heavy smell of men's cologne. Where had I smelled that before? A charge of déjà vu swept over me like a seasonal haboob of the southwest. I couldn't put my finger on the odor's familiarity. Perhaps the drunken haze of a night in which I procured a loan was coming back to me. I shook my head violently. Now wasn't the time to speculate.

"*I* am here for my family," I responded, stepping in front of Chayton.

"I do not know what you are talking about." The big man propped his right arm high on the door to appear intimidating, and he was.

"I am Scott Sharpe," I talked very slowly. "You have my wife and children."

"Oh." the European smiled. "So *you* are the one I take a finger from. I see you still have all ten."

"Yes." I gulped as I realized the ramifications. I had hoped that distancing myself from Bart and Mr. Glasses would end the discussion of my losing a finger. I had been wrong.

The guard glanced around the door and into the hall-way. "Where is Bart?"

I pointed to the ceiling. "He's up in Room 416."

"So how did you know to come down here?" The European processed the information and, laying his eyes on Chayton, answered his own question. "*Oh,*" he said, the second letter dragged on at such a length that the tone resembled a valley girl.

"Now we understand each other," I coldly stated.

"Go get Bart, and then we talk."

"How can I trust you?"

"You," he pointed his massive gun at my father-in-law. "Go get him."

Ramon obeyed, and Chayton and I stepped inside. I was strapped. The revolver sat near my ankle under my sock.

A painful minute or two later, Ramon walked in along-side a hobbling Bart. I was proud of my father-in-law as he stood resistant to help my former boss. Bart's nose was twisted, looking more like the letter Z than a snout, and his already sorrowful eyes, outlined now in red, were on the verge of bursting into tears. Dried blood lined the left side of his face as a result of Chayton's blow.

Bart pointed at his attacker and muttered, "Who is this man? He needs to die."

"Over two thousand dollars and a punch?" Chayton fired back. "You'll kill me over *that*?"

"How many times must I tell you idiots?" Bart went on. "This is about more than two thousand dollars. Ramon De Leon killed my father. Murdered him. *But*, at the very least he has a reason to be here. This Indian does not." He shared a glance with the European and repeated, "This man needs to die."

"This wasn't the deal!" I yelled at the man in the blue tie. "You said you would give us my family if we got you Bart."

"No," the man waved his weapon, "I told you we would *talk*."

"What if he leaves?" I asked and turned to Chayton. "You won't say anything, will you?"

Our friend understood and nodded slowly. "Of course not," he said. "I am an employee here. Anything I say can and will get me fired."

"I don't trust him," Bart said. "Kill him."

In what seemed like a flash, the ugly bodyguard with a European accent pulled out a pistol with a silencer from his left pocket and blasted Chayton in the face. The next second pierced my brain like an arrow from a stiff Bear Legend XR. Chayton had no time to cry out in anguish, no time to defend himself from the monsters before us. I thought in that instant about how the man just wanted to help my family because he thought he couldn't protect his own. He was to be the mortally wounded victim of a single gunshot, the top half of his flailing corpse collapsing into the tiled bathroom floor and landing with a loud thud. What a tragedy.

I groaned. "*No.*" I had bent over to grab my own weapon, but it was too late. The man in the sunglasses worked far too quickly. He drew his rifle and placed the tip of the big weapon against my temple. Consider those two seconds the scariest of my life.

In my peripheral vision, I could make out Ramon's silhouette. Luckily for us, I was the only one who saw. The man in the black sunglasses didn't see, and so when Ramon smacked him in the side of his head with the pistol from behind, blood squirted out the front of his mouth in my direction. I've always had a bit of a casual relationship with blood: the scarlet matter flew from my snout in the form of a nosebleed every month, and I passed on that trait to my oldest son. Though I will say, getting blood on you from your own face is a whole lot better than having a stranger's blood shoot at you in spurts. I thought that type of perfusion was reserved for fictional Hollywood films. Plus, the muzzle of Blue Tie's rifle pushed in my cheek a bit in when he was struck. I can't blame Ramon for that, though.

The splatter blinded me for a nanosecond. When I opened my eyes, Ramon stood in front of me. The blue tie donning bodyguard had crumpled to the ground, and my father-in-law sported a surprised expression.

I saw Chayton dead on the floor, and decided in that moment I'd mourn him later. Once more, we had Bart Thompson outnumbered. Ramon told me to watch the guard's fallen body and to hit him if he regained consciousness. Then, he shoved the front of the pistol into Bart's temple and whispered, "Where are they?"

There was no answer. "I'm counting to three, but in Spanish to make it hurt a little more. I can claim defense now that your friend has killed ours." Bart appeared stoic despite his life being threatened. "*Uno*," Ramon began, and cocked his handgun. "*Dos.*"

Finally, Bart displayed some semblance of fear. "All right, all right," he said. "They're here." He gestured towards the blue door, identical to the one we had observed in Room 416 minutes earlier. "Now get that pistol of my face, *muchacho*," Bart requested of Ramon.

My sweaty palms gripped the L-shaped handle on the blue door. My mind went blank for a second as I prepared for the worst. I inhaled a deep breath and my right hand twisted to pull the lever down. The door swung back, and I saw another empty room.

I turned to Bart, gritting my teeth, and said, "This is getting old—"

Just then, I heard the muffled scream. Someone somewhere in the dark room was calling out to me. I shut the door behind me and flipped on the light. My dilated eyes adjusted. Still, Mia and the boys were not standing before me. I heard another noise coming from the bathroom. Through the sliding door and in the presence of a bare shower, panic set in. I flicked on the light switch in front of the bathroom. Then I noticed the closet behind me and proceeded to pull apart the sliding door, revealing the interior.

Lying on the ground were Mia, Francisco, and Marcos.

Chapter 30

Bright blue duct tape strapped both Mia and Francisco's mouths shut. Swaddled in a blanket in my wife's arms was our newborn son, and I teared up. They sat cross legged, Mia's hands folded and bound and Francisco's full of bruises and held together by some sort of zip tie. My wife's face presented a few scratches and cuts, and I wondered who had marked up her skin. I wanted to vomit. More than that, I wanted to kill. I have never had the murderous urge like I did in that moment. I wanted to point the revolver at Bart Thompson's pathetic, useless, child-harming face and squeeze the trigger. I wanted to for Mia, for Francisco, for Marcos. I wanted to for Chayton. Now that Bart lacked leverage, all bets were off. He kidnapped my family for my father-in-law's act of self-defense over twenty years ago and a two-thousand-dollar debt. Not exactly what I'd call an even trade. The Satriones were ruthless.

"*Mia!*" I gasped. My wife, unmistakable from her curly hair and painted on pink nails, turned away from the bright light and shielded her big brown eyes. I am sure the past twenty-four hours had been hard on her, but her face sparkled with relief when her eyeballs adjusted and she recognized me. Francisco tried to scream through the cruel duct tape barrier to no avail.

I slowly tore off the duct tape from their faces and unbound them. No words were spoken, but the three eldest among the four of us wept and exchanged kisses and hugs. Despite the senseless violence of the Satriones, this reunion was a beautiful moment.

I cradled Marcos in my arms, planting a gentle kiss on the top of his forehead. The cruelty inflicted upon he and his brother is unfathomable to me.

We walked back to the main room, holding hands and weeping.

"Ah, ah, ah." Bart Thompson stood up now in the primary suite of Room 216. The European man stood next to him and they both motioned to their hands. Even after shooting Chayton point blank in the face, these men had the gall to make demands.

Besides, how did the bodyguard regain consciousness so quickly? Had Ramon lost focus? Was he hurt, too? These thoughts ran through my mind as I once again found myself directly in the eyesight of the burly guard's rifle barrel.

"Give me a finger or give me your family." Bart's confidence was back. Out of the corner of my eyesight, Ramon lay motionless on the hotel room floor, his face turned away from us. Mia had gasped a few seconds before, and now I was catching up. I watched as Ramon's body bounced up and down rhythmically, indicating he was still breathing.

I stood there, pondering and speculating, trying to fathom what led to this moment while I was rescuing my family in the other room. Then, to Bart's left, I noticed the man in the blue tie and the now blood-stained suit. His face was gushing with blood, and he tried his darndest not to admit his pain.

I was through with their games. I wanted to leave White-hawk Casino with my family and never return. "Give me the damn knife, Bart," I said.

He stared at me with his mouth agape. He blinked his eyes slowly with surprise. I don't think he expected me to surrender the way in which I did, and I don't think he thought I would volunteer to cut it off myself. But I wanted this nightmare to be over. No longer would my family suffer because of my misdeeds. If I had to lose a finger for it, so be it. We were outnumbered once more, and the only chance we'd have at escaping this hellhole was if I left with nine fingers.

Mia began, "Scott, no. Stop—"

"Mia," I said firmly. "This ends here." I turned to Bart and repeated softly, almost to myself, "Give me the knife."

He chuckled as if he were the one who had convinced me, not the other way around. His shaking hands placed the Kershaw blade in my palm, safety on. I did a little bargaining in my brain once more, but none out loud. It was time to own up to my wrongdoings. I owed it to my wife. I owed it to my sons. I owed it to my father-in-law. I owed it to Chayton.

And so, in Room 216 of the Whitehawk Casino outside Denver, I laid down my right hand on the room's desk. I pulled back four of my fingers into a mostly made fist, leaving only my ring finger exposed. I had decided earlier that would be the digit to go if given the option. Part of the reason I forced Bart's switchblade into my hand was to select the finger I'd lose myself, but mainly I usurped the situation because I lacked control up to that point.

At that moment it sunk in that I had cost Chayton his life. It is not a desire of mine to wish this guilty burden on anyone. I went and got the man involved. I lost him his job. I severed the chain in his family line. He would never remarry, never have a chance to build another family after a drunken idiot destroyed his first. The last thought hit me like a ton of bricks. One alcoholic destroyed his first life, and another took away his chance for a second.

The culpability from this was overwhelming, really. Getting out of here alive with my family was only half the battle. I would suffer from survivor's guilt, probably for the rest of my days. I suddenly remembered the promise I made to myself earlier, that I would table my emotions regarding his death until I knew my family were safe. They weren't quite there just yet.

By chopping off the digit myself, I could seize control of the situation. I could begin to make amends with the four people I had hurt—and really, the rest of the De Leons as well—and confess my sins and move on with my life.

With my right hand balled into an almost fist, I lowered my other hand. The jagged edge grazed the peach fuzz of the metacarpal, and my stomach sank into a pit. The realization that I lay two seconds from the life sentence made my heart race. I directed my attention to the subject at hand, took a deep breath, felt my shoulders relax as they sank, and lowered the blade.

The pain was excruciating. When the Kershaw knife pierced my skin, I felt a shiver throughout my body. I had read at one point in anatomy class at the University of New Mexico years ago that when you know a certain part of you is going to experience pain, you can shift your focus to another part of your body to dull the agony. The moment the blade sank into the epidermis of my finger was unlike anything I've ever experienced. It was torture. No amount of inattention would prevent me from comprehending the loss of what used to be my right ring finger. Tears streamed down my cheeks, but I did not cry out.

When it was over, blood squirted out of me like a shaken can of pop. I nearly fainted at the sight of the gore oozing from me. It was the single most vile, disgusting thing I've ever seen in my life. Standing up abruptly, I made eye contact with Mia. She stood frozen, her eyes wide and shocked like a deer caught in headlights.

Bart Thompson threw his head back and laughed several times, while the man in the blue tie stood near the bed with his rifle pointed directly at Ramon's temple. My former boss cackled for a solid fifteen seconds, before gesturing to the entrance to Room 216. "All right, Sharpe. You did it. Good for you. You've paid your debt. Now get the hell out of this hotel room." He pulled a Ziploc bag from his pocket and said, "Put your finger in this. We'll need to get a bandage for the wound." I listened, my body trembling from the shock, my forehead dripping profusely with thousands of little sweat beads. Picking up what used to be my phalange, and gagging, I heard Francisco shout, "What is that?" before a man I had not previously seen—not Darrell from Room 416—picked him up and covered his mouth.

When did he come into the room? I had sworn it was just Bart and Mr. Blue Tie. Vomit poured out of my mouth as I placed what used to be my ring finger into the plastic bag the same man who ordered its removal handed to me. I felt myself drifting off into a haze as I swayed around the room.

I looked down at my right hand. The missing digit exposed a gruesome sight of tendon, bone, and tissue in its place. In response, I staggered around the room for a few more seconds, my balance faltering, and I collapsed to the floor. The last thing I remember seeing as I fell were Chayton's limp, grayish, dead legs.

Chapter 31

Mia slapped me in the face hard. "Wake up, Scott!" she shouted. "*Wake up!*" Ever since we met ten years earlier, I had teased Mia regarding her playful smacks. They always caused discomfort for more than a few seconds. She meant no harm, of course, but even the most relaxed love taps stung like a mischievous bee. This episode was no different.

Adjusting my eyes, I noticed we were sitting in the Acura. Gazing at my bandaged right hand, I realized we hadn't been dreaming. I did in fact lose my right ring finger. However, I turned around to look in the backseat, and both Francisco and Marcos were strapped in their seats and off somewhere between REMville and dreamland. My little family was safe.

"Where are we?" I asked.

"We're in the Whitehawk Casino parking lot, *mi marido*," she said. "*Papa* is inside."

"I'm sorry, what?" I rubbed my eyes and considered Mia. Even locked up for twenty-four hours, she was beyond beautiful. I needed to redirect my attention to her startling statement. "Did you say your dad is inside?"

"They kept him when they dragged us out," she explained. "What are we going to do?"

That statement snapped me out of my fog. Ramon was inside with three associates of the Satrione family. Not only that, he *killed* one of their fathers back in the 1990s. He wouldn't make it out alive.

"Let me think," I responded. The most logical thing to do at this point was to call the authorities. Now that Mia, Francisco, and Marcos were out of harm's way, it made sense. Not only that, but we were acquainted with the room numbers of both Satrione fronts, just in case they decided to relocate Ramon to the other room. Then I remembered: Chayton's body was inside Room 216!

"Of course. We should call the cops!" I nearly cried out. "Chayton is in Room 216. Once they find him, they will believe anything we say. Plus, they chopped off my freaking finger."

In a jiffy, I whipped out my cellphone from my bulging back pocket. I opened the lock screen and punched in the universal three-digit emergency number.

A hoarse sounding operator answered, "911, what's your emergency?"

"I'm at the Whitehawk Casino outside Denver," I said. "There's a dead body in the hotel."

"A dead body?" the woman responded. "How do you know?"

"Because I've seen it with my own eyes."

"Did you kill somebody, sir?"

"No," I said.

"I don't understand, sir."

"I saw someone get killed," I explained, "and there's someone else in there who may be in danger."

"All right, sir," she said. "Dispatch is sending a unit in your direction. They should be there in three minutes."

"Thanks."

Updating Mia on the situation, I exited the Acura and ambled toward the entrance of the Whitehawk Casino. We had jointly decided she would abide in the car instead of joining me in Room 216. I gazed down at the new reality that was my right hand. Save for the bandage on top, the juncture in which a normal ring finger presided was bare, and the throbbing hurt worse and worse every time I pulsated. This was my new reality. It was time for me to find Ramon before his new reality somehow became worse than mine.

--

A few minutes later, a Ford Crown Victoria squad car pulled up. Two officers sprung out. In a peculiar way, they reminded me of the cops in the movie *Super Troopers*. They had flat top buzz cut haircuts, sunglasses, and sported thin brown mustaches. One was white, and the other African American. Each were muscular to a certain extent, and I instantly felt a wave of hope.

I flagged them down. "We got a call for a dead body," the white cop said. His name tag read Nelson. His left leg fidgeted incessantly, and it gave me a sudden panic. "Where is it?"

"It's more than that," I nervously explained. I won't lie, it was a little bothersome he referred to a lifeless form as an "it". "There's another man who is inside who is in danger. My father-in-law."

The African American cop, named Washington, lowered his sunglasses so I could see his eyes. They were brown and piercing. Suddenly it appeared that neither of these two men seemed to mind my life-or-death struggle. "All right," he said. "Lead us to where you think he is."

The two police officers strolled into the casino as if to say one dead body and another in danger wasn't anything to pick up the pace over. Their demeanor made me feel a little uneasy on the inside.

I followed the pair, who stopped at the customer service desk in which I found Chayton the night before. My heart sank again as I remembered his untimely demise.

"We got a call," Nelson said to the desk attendant. It was the same young woman, Ariel, from the night prior, the one who had been flipping through the pages of a *Longmire* mystery.

"Room 216," I interjected.

"Sounds good," she responded without glancing up from her novel. After a few moments, she caught a glimpse of the two responding officers, sat up straight, and said, "You know what to do, don't you fine policemen?"

The duo nodded and headed for the elevator. I trudged slowly behind them. The cops didn't so much as glance in my direction. They were discussing Denver Nuggets basketball and whether they'd earn a postseason berth. Washington seemed to think they would sneak into the Western Conference playoffs, while Nelson said no, they were too young and Jokic and Murray would eventually take them to the postseason.

The ding on the second floor knocked me off my balance. I'd heard it several times that day and the one prior, but I think the intensity of the circumstances made my heart thump faster than it ever had. The cops reached into their pockets and holstered their weapons. As if on a casual hike, they marched across the second floor, past a small blue bucket with a handle on top, and made it to 216. They informed me I'd need to step aside to a point where, if someone returned fire from inside the room, I'd be in a safe spot down the hall a ways and unharmed. I appreciated that. The two made eye contact, then a simultaneous nod, and then Washington rapped on the door loudly more than once. Their poise was astounding; here they stood investigating a dead body, seconds after they were talking about something as meaningless as sports. I couldn't believe it.

No one answered the knocks. Nelson leaned up against the door with determined authority and asserted his way into the hotel room after three pushes. The nature of it was so informal.

Washington swiftly drew his gun and sprinted inside the room, shouting, "Police!" From the angle I was situated, I could not see beyond the bathroom near the entrance. I could see the tile where Chayton's feet lay however long ago that was. How extensive of a blackout had I experienced? I pulled out my phone and saw the time was two thirty-three in the afternoon. I'd have been out for an hour at least. That gave the Satrione cult enough time to sweep clean the hotel room and make it appear as if the murder never happened.

I heard a noise nearby, perhaps coming from a room behind me. Engrossed in the unfolding episode in the vanguard, I pressed ahead without pausing to cast a glance behind me.

To say I was surprised when the two cops exited the room, declaring it "Clear!", would be a lie. I half expected a bleak outcome when we had arrived on the second floor.

What I didn't expect to see was Keith Stephens nestled near the elevator corridor.

Chapter 32

I was aware of the potential ramifications. Here was my golden opportunity to chase down an accomplice of the whole ordeal. Keith was going down. I sprinted towards the man.

He didn't turn away, didn't try to run. Instead, he smiled as I approached him. "You must be out of breath, Sharpe!" he bellowed around the corner, out of the eyesight of the cops.

"What the hell is going on here?" I shouted. "Where's my father-in-law?"

He shrugged, pretending to be ignorant. "Whatever do you mean, Sharpe?"

"You know."

"I don't," he replied, "I'm just on a casual walk around Whitehawk Casino." He pushed the down button on the elevator shaft, and the beep of its readiness forced me into a decision.

"Well, whatever you're doing," I said. "You're not supposed to be here."

As the elevator door opened, Keith glared at me and uttered, "A true shame what happened to your Indian friend. He should've just let us be."

My mouth flew open agape. Unleashing a commanding fist in his direction, I connected on a punch squarely between his creepy eyes. My right hand throbbed. Considering I had lost a digit of this very hand hours ago, it appeared inexplicably foolish that I would have thrown a punch with it. The resounding echo of Keith's whimper attracted the attention of not only the police officers but also an elderly woman heading towards the elevator. She carried a walker, sported a hunchback, and wore black eyeglasses guarded by a chain. She was essentially the real-life version of Mrs. Hogenson from *The Incredibles*. As soon as the cops arrived on the scene, the lady pointed at me and shouted, "He did it! He did it! It was him and the man in chains."

I glared at her, feeling implicated. She reacted as if I had committed some heinous crime. Not only that but she seemed to have some sort of mental illness. She was imagining the presence of others when it was clearly just Keith and me in that hallway.

The law enforcement officials scowled at me. "What are you doing, son?" Nelson asked.

"This man is in on it!" I shouted. "He's involved!"

Deputy Washington scratched his balding head and subsequently ran his fingers through his wispy, black mustache. He turned to Keith, whose nose was gushing blood, and placed his hands firmly on his hips. "Sir, were you involved?" He turned to the elderly woman—perhaps a lonely figure seeking some excitement in her life—and spoke, "Ma'am, you can go now. Thanks for your help."

"Of course," she responded. "Bert and I are just down the hall in 232. Near the chained man."

The cop offered a feigned grin and said, "Thank you. We'll let you know if we require anything else from you. Have a nice day."

Nelson removed his police cap. His filthy hair was slicked back like a greaser in *The Outsiders*. He whispered something to Washington about the man in chains, presumably named Bert, and how this elderly woman was involved in some sort of sex-crazed game. Nelson pivoted back to me and stated, "You say this man is involved."

"Yes."

"But he wasn't there when the dead body we didn't find expired?" he asked.

The situation sounded crazy when spoken aloud, sure, and I figured law enforcement wasn't going to believe me. I wondered if Keith would rat me out for taking a loan. *No*, I thought, since the admission would incriminate him. He would, however, let it be known to the mob that I was a rat. In a sense, I may have signed my own death certificate.

Aside from the bruises on Mia and Francisco's bodies, I had no proof of the Satrione wrongdoings. We needed to find Chayton's body. My story sounded like a bunch of gobbledygook sans Chayton.

"No, he wasn't," I finally answered.

"Were you in on it, sir?" one of the police officers asked.

"No." Keith hung his head, portraying himself as the victim. The performance was worthy of an Academy Award.

"So you have no idea what this man is talking about?"

"No idea."

"Do you want to press charges?"

Keith held his gushing snout. "No."

The white cop shrugged his shoulders. His partner shooed Keith to the elevator and said, "You can go, sir. Go take care of that nose."

My bandaged right hand kept on palpitating. Keith Stephens walked away freely, and I wanted desperately to follow him. He deserved to be knocked out, to be waterboarded, to be tortured. He and his minions had done the same to my wife and sons.

"He is in on it," I said defeatedly once Keith disappeared into the abyss of the elevator. With my luck, I'd never see him again. I lowered my head in an acknowledgement of defeat. Only having one more option, I said, "Take me to 416. That's where this all started."

Washington shrugged his shoulders. "We're all yours until we find this dead body, I guess." Nelson delivered a little smirk to his partner, as if to say he wasn't sure I was telling the truth.

We headed to the stairwell and sprinted up to Room 416. My voice echoed as I asked Washington, "Did you find anything in the room?"

"Nothing more than some old cowboy boots," he replied. "We didn't keep them though."

Of course, I thought. *Those were Ramon's.*

The search of Room 416 proved to be as lackluster as the hunt of its twin two floors below. It had been obvious someone was in the room recently, but there was no evidence to incriminate. Ramon was nowhere to be found. Darrell had left the bathroom. What specific time had Ramon instructed him to remain in that location until? For some reason, one-thirty stuck out in my head. I cast a purposeful gaze at the time displayed on my iPhone. It was just past three, and Darrell was long gone. Ramon recognized the man's strength was more than capable enough to break down the chair barrier.

At that moment, it dawned on me we were on a cat-and-mouse sort of chase. Where could they have possibly gone?

As I scanned my brain for likely outcomes, I recalled the peculiar interaction we had earlier that day with the older couple in Room 316. The tunnel system theory would seem to concur with the hypothesis that the Satriones peddled their money, guns, and drugs through the three rooms, from top to bottom. Our earlier inspection had yielded no favorable results, but I wanted to have the cops explore every option.

I informed Nelson and Washington of my conjecture, and they seemed to believe it. God help them, they had forced their way into two hotel rooms and had zero meaningful evidence, but they wanted to give credence to my theory. I thoroughly judged these two books by their cover.

So, we trekked back down to the third room in question. In a way, I felt this was the last dance. Soon, Washington and Nelson would be quizzing me about what I saw. Surely, I did not see a dead man but a wine spill or a figment of my imagination.

The same man, with corduroy pants and sugar-colored hair, answered the door of Room 316. He bristled with displeasure the moment we made eye contact.

"Now what?" he shouted at the cops. "Damn it!"

"Sir, I'm Deputy Nelson," the cop stated, "and this is Deputy Washington." His partner raised his police cap with one hand and flashed his badge with the other.

"No, I haven't heard any of my neighbors!" the old man continued. "I told those two that yesterday."

"Two?" Deputy Washington's eyebrows furrowed, almost parallel to his thin mustache.

"Are you sure there were two and not three men here last night?" Nelson looked at me and frowned. "This man says three of them knocked on your door."

"No, I didn't," I said. "That was last night. Only Chayton and I were—"

"Yes, Chayton," the man with the icy hair interrupted. "The guy who worked with the hotel. Indian fellow. Sorry, the *Native American* fellow. I know how you young people are politically correct nowadays. That guy right there was the second. He was trying to hide over in that corner, but I knew he was there."

"Are you sure he wasn't Hispanic?" Nelson asked. "The man we're looking for is Hispanic."

"I'm positive he wasn't no Mexican. I mean, *Hispanic.*"

"You sure about that?"

"Do I have to say it again? I'm positive. I thought he was a yahoo the moment I saw him. What kind of man wears a ponytail anyway?"

I smiled. This decrepit old man may have a hand in saving Ramon's life. The two deputies gazed at each other. Mr. Corduroy had just delivered some veracity to the tale I told them.

"Has anyone else come by since then?" Washington continued the interrogation.

"Just the cleaners," the elderly gentleman explained.

"The cleaners."

"Yes, they come by every day."

"Men or women?" Nelson asked.

"Always men," he said. "I've been here a week now and it's always this burly Russian guy. I thought, what a bunch of barbarians here at Whitehawk. To have *men* as cleaners? I guess it is 2018."

"Any Hispanic men?" Washington inquired.

"Yeah, just one though. Pretty recently. He came in with some white guy."

"How recent are we talking?" Nelson asked.

"Twenty, twenty-five minutes ago," he admitted. "Darlene and I were laughing at him. It looked like he had some patches missing from his mustache. He looked scared as a kitten. It was a real knee slapper!" He let out a loud howl followed by two coughs. "It was the darndest thing. He was zip tied or something. Some odd way to clean! I thought it was one of those smut deals. I told them I ain't okay with that stuff in my room in the middle of the day. This is Denver, not Las Vegas."

"Thanks for your help, sir," Washington said. "Did you see which way the Hispanic man went?"

"No, he was with the other guy," he said. "Come to think of it, they never cleaned anything other than the vents. Shoved some cleaner in there or something. And only one guy left. He was all sweaty when he left."

"Which one left?"

"I ain't too sure about that one. I was trying to take a nap after all. I was tired, for Chrissake. Being forced out of my room like that. Darlene's down at the craps table now, I reckon. How can a man take a nap with all that ruckus going on here?"

"Can I see the vents, sir?" Nelson asked. *Finally*, I thought. We were getting to the nitty gritty of this ordeal. Ramon had to be close by.

The police motioned for me to join them in Room 316. Nelson flicked the bathroom lights on and we all shielded our eyes, needing a moment to adjust to the illumination of the brightness. However, the room itself was relatively dark. The vent in question was located on the right wall above the unmade bed. Washington hopped on the bouncy king mattress, and asked, "How do we open these?"

"I haven't the slightest idea," the old man suddenly turned witness said. "But I do know the cleaners keep a toolset in the closet."

"A toolset?" Nelson gasped.

Washington added, "Why would cleaners need a toolbox in the closet?"

The old man ran his fingers through his thin, gelled, icy hair and said, "I'm starting to think these aren't no cleaners, officers."

Some of us, me included, chuckled at that one. The old man's astounding ignorance was both baffling and entirely plausible. He was the poster boy warrior of old folks who rented a room in a hotel casino and were subsequently taken advantage of by the Colorado mob, if there was a such hero.

Deputy Nelson unlatched the front closet doors and revealed to us the aforementioned chest of tools. He gripped the kit's black rubber handle by his rough, calloused right hand. I am guessing Nelson worked some sort of manual labor gig before he became a cop. Come to think of it, Washington's hands looked weathered as well. The two were experienced, to be certain, or older than I had gathered judging by the fact they still wore sunglasses. How many wrinkles were they concealing under those black lids?

A terrifying thought seeped its way into my body, poking every nerve. Were these cops crooked? I glanced at my phone and confirmed I had punched in the three-digit emergency number to the authorities. My brain tried to wrap itself around the possibility that these men weren't who they said they were. Was Whitehawk Casino technically on the Arapaho Reservation? Doesn't that mean police officers couldn't conduct their business on these grounds?

By that point, Nelson was already standing on the king-sized bed over the old man, Deputy Washington, and me. He shined his iPhone flashlight on the vent. My spine tingled, and I suddenly felt a target on my back. Were all three of these men conspiring against me? Why had they left the room dark?

"Give me a flathead, please," Nelson called down to his partner. Washington tossed up a small screwdriver headfirst.

Nelson caught it and mumbled some cuss word under his breath at his fellow law enforcement officer.

I remembered I still had my iPhone in my left pocket, and while the rest focused their attention on the vent, I pulled it out. I had three bars of service in Room 316, so I pushed the Safari button at the bottom of my home screen and punched in a web address: Google.com. Slowly, and stealthily, I began typing in the phrase "Is Whitehawk Casino on the Arapaho Reservation?" While punching in the penultimate word, I froze when Nelson shouted, "*Aha!*" I slipped the mobile device back into the pocket of my joggers.

He slipped out in his left hand a brown paper bag, donned with the faded emblem of a local fast food restaurant, and threw it to Washington. The man squealed like a baby, "Jackpot! Jackpot!"

I stood motionless. The two cops remained invested in the loot, so I once again retrieved my phone from my pants pocket and completed the Google search. It took a second for the Safari page to display, and my heart sank. Soon the HTML loaded fully, and a result populated the page. It read, "The Whitehawk Casino in Colorado, west of Denver, although remaining loyal to its rich Arapaho culture, is not technically located within the confines of the reservation. There is no rule that says Native American casinos must be on reservation land."

Whew. I let out a huge sigh of relief. That meant at the very least my call processed and that police officers were allowed on the casino and that I was not dealing with a couple of phonies. Someone was on my side here.

As I looked back up in the direction of who I once more believed to be police officers, I noticed the flowing cash. There were hundreds upon hundreds of wrapped bills. I couldn't tell how much money lay in that bag, but I do know it was enough to cause a fuss.

They whispered words back and forth, and then excused themselves from the room. "Just for a moment," they said. The old man and I stood alone in Room 316 then, a fast food bag full of money lying a few feet from us.

The man distractedly scratched his fingernails on the back of his head, gently stroking his thin, white, stiff hair follicles. It was evident that he had no interest in engaging in small talk with me. He turned many degrees to the right, straying from eye contact with me, and tapped his right foot up and down on the checkered hotel room floor. I deduced he was still a little sore about the whole incident yesterday.

I ended the discomfort between us. "That's a whole lot of money."

"Sure is." Apparently, this geezer was only a chatterbox in front of law enforcement officials. His corduroy pants were pulled up in the vicinity of his navel, and I was unsure if this was intentional or not. I prayed it wasn't, because my testicles hurt just looking at him.

Suddenly, the entryway to the room swung ajar and the duo of deputies waltzed back in. They flipped the master lights on now that the old man didn't stand in their way. Their eyes were wide and cautious, especially Officer Washington. I realized shortly after their entrance why Washington seemed to be shocked beyond comprehension. His brown eyes locked on something behind the old man and me. I flipped around 180 degrees to catch a peek at what he was seeing. My jaw dropped as I noticed the trail of blood stemming from the coat closet in the back of the room. It reached all the way to the entrance of the bathroom.

Standing near the bed, Deputy Washington drew his pistol and paced over to the wooden coat cabinet. He jiggled the handle and the hatchway sprung open, and out popped a lifeless corpse.

Chapter 33

In the haze between unconsciousness and alert, Ramon dreamt. Of course, his vision was of the Rio Grande. Not a soul on Earth would be shocked this was the case. In the dream, he was presiding over himself in the third person. He witnessed himself sitting with his bare feet dipped in the flowing river, an old fishing rod in his right hand. Though not aware he was hallucinating, the sleeping Ramon was happy when his dream hologram reeled in a purposefully sized Gila trout. The fish looked to be a little less than a foot long and had sporadic black cheetah spots on its otherwise mostly yellow-green body. Ramon held the creature in his hand, smiling from cheek to cheek, before letting him softly back into the water. Minutes later a red shiner of above average mass fell for the lure he set into the river, and Ramon gave the fish a big smooch just before releasing him. Next to him sat a cup of freshly brewed coffee that never seemed to have a bottom as he sipped and sipped from his bright red New Mexico Lobos mug. Life seemed to be good on the Rio for Dream Ramon.

Suddenly an object came crashing down from the sky at a high velocity. It was hard to make out at first once it came to a screeching halt on top of the river, but Unconscious Ramon knew it was the cash register of his Allsup's. A gondola of tasty snacks crashed down shortly after, as did the shelf below the register where Ramon hid his gun. He saw his earthly 9mm a few feet in front of him.

Now perched behind the counter, levitating on water, Dream Ramon stood patiently, waiting for a customer to show. Across the river, he could make out a figure swimming, not floating like him, in the direction of the convenience store counter, and some sort of black object above them wading in the water. When the silhouette reached the counter, Dream Ramon gasped. The item was a jet-black cowboy hat, one he had seen twenty-plus years earlier in his shop. To say Dream Ramon was nervous to see Bart Thompson, Sr. in this fantasy suddenly turned nightmare would be a complete minimization of the trauma he experienced back then.

Bart Thompson, Sr. approached him and eulogized, just as he had in the mid-1990s, "God knows the truth, and I know the truth." The man in the cowboy hat threw his head back and laughed, declaring an identical falsity to the day he died in the physical world. It was a moment of intense déjà vu as Bart asked, "Do you know the parable of the lost sheep?"

Above Dream Ramon, Unconscious Ramon lost his marbles. He cupped his cheeks in his hands and shouted, loud enough he reckoned his doppelganger would understand him. He was wrong. Unconscious Ramon watched as Dream Ramon wrapped his fingers around the 9mm pistol, appearing as unsteady and nervous as he did the first go around. The déjà vu feeling intensified in Unconscious Ramon's soul, and he became more rattled by the millisecond.

In a moment of sheer terror, Bart, Sr. gazed up slowly—agonizingly slowly—at Unconscious Ramon and said, "One second makes all the difference in the world. I could have just as easily killed you then. God knows this is the truth, and I know the truth." The fourth wall had been broken, and sweat beads flew from Dream Ramon's temples like mucky brown water in the Rio.

Unconscious Ramon panted for a moment before letting out an exuberant cry, "You don't know that. You were the criminal. I was just His vessel. He prevents evil."

"You, Ramon, *are* evil. You're nothing more than a no-good, illegal son of a—"

"No!" the man shouted. "I paid my dues. I took my citizenship tests. I confessed." Unconscious Ramon was frazzled, jittery, and distressed beyond comprehension.

"Did you confess to murder?" Dream Bart folded his arms as the sky around the Rio Grande faded into a fiery demonic red. The devil had seeped his way into the nightmare. Ramon closed his eyes for a few seconds and prayed.

When he opened them, Dream Bart drew his weapon up to the head of Dream Ramon, whose fingers slipped off his hidden pistol. He lost his grip, and the gun plunged into the Rio and swung back and forth as it disappeared into the copper trout-laden waters.

"I did *not* murder you," Ramon pled for his life. Bart, Sr. laughed and squeezed the trigger. Dream Ramon's brains flew everywhere. It was a beyond gruesome sight, and the Rio Grande reddened as Dream Bart assumed the figure of the devil. Flames flew up in every direction and the Allsup's counter was engulfed by the piercingly bright orange inferno.

Ramon awoke dazed and confused on the checkered floor. Even in real life, his forehead erupted in droplets of sweat, and the moisture sprayed in every direction. Without moving his head, he peeped around Room 216 and noticed only one other soul was there. Bart Thompson, Jr. lay with his feet draped over the bed, bruises on his face the size of pennies and the length of toothpicks, distracted on his barely working cellphone. Scott's former boss muttered a couple words together and spoke to Siri more than once. He was unaware Ramon had regained consciousness a few feet below him, lying in a puddle of self-inflicted dampness.

Chayton's corpse no longer graced the bathroom floor of Room 216. There was a bucket of some sort near the entrance to the room, and Ramon thought he could smell the decaying body through the strong odor of Clorox bleach. He searched the room with his eyes for his white cowboy hat, and then remembered he had lost it earlier in the day. His signature item lay in that dumb, bite-sized janitor's closet Chayton had dragged them into. His toes wiggled, and he observed the absence of his black cowboy boots. They were neatly and vertically positioned against the window.

Bart's phone sang a jolly ringtone a few minutes later, and he answered the call. "Police officers? Here?" he shouted. "How do you know they're here for us?"

Ramon knew Bart's next move would be a glance toward him, so he shut his eyes. "Yeah," Bart said, "he's still unconscious."

From the ground, Ramon could hear a man screaming on the other line. Bart hung up the phone and practically lunged at him, his hands grasping Ramon firmly around his sweaty shoulders.

"Wake up!" he shouted. "We need to move you. Now!"

Ramon arose, trying ever so hard to linger his movements just a bit. "Now! Now!" Bart continued to yell. Ramon stood on his feet now, noting the pool of his own perspiration had seeped into the patterned floor. It wasn't easy to observe unless you were standing above it, he noticed.

Scott had called the chota, Ramon thought. What an extremely pleasing turn of events. He could continue to delay his actions and milk every step. Every little gesture mattered.

About fifteen seconds of impatience later, Bart snatched Ramon by the collar of his blue and green pearl snap. He brandished his revolver, placed the butt on Ramon's head, urging a hastier response time. Ramon let out a loud murmur of assent. He didn't want to move fast, but now he had no choice. If he held on long enough, the police would be there and he would be safe.

Unfortunately, Bart didn't give him a choice, lugging him like a misbehaving dog. Ramon considered his black cowboy boots near the back of the space. If he could convince Bart to at least let him collect the boots, it would buy them about fifteen seconds. All bets were off then.

"Let me at least get my boots," Ramon pleaded.

"No," Bart fired back. "We need to leave *now*."

Though not a gambler at heart, this was a casino, so Ramon wagered his odds. With the entryway ajar, he slipped intentionally. Bart's grip on Ramon's plaid shirt loosened but he maintained position over him.

"What do you think you're doing?" Bart's face was flush red with anger. With his other hand he held the bleach bucket. "I said we need to leave!" Ramon obliged, only after a brief tussle that hampered their pace by a few more seconds. The police officers had to have been rising in elevation by now.

This was getting too close for Bart's comfort, so he cocked his revolver and pulled Ramon into the hallway leading to the elevator. He struggled for a second, so he threw the gun in the bucket and proceeded down the corridor.

After a few seconds of motion, the button from the elevator on the second floor dinged, and Bart dropped the blue bleach bucket and pulled out the revolver. He placed it up to Ramon's head, where it lingered; he didn't want the man to give away their position. The two were positioned far enough away for Bart's liking. A moment later, Ramon watched in horror as Scott and two other men made their way to the room; they looked like police officers to Ramon. Scott stayed around the nook, maybe fifteen feet from the entrance, as one of the cops knocked on the door.

They were so close, practically in Ramon's grasp, and yet he could not say a word. Scott watched the duo scan the room and saw from an angle the look of disappointment on his face. The cops, one African American and one white, both with mustaches, retreated from the room. One held up an object of some sort.

Ramon wanted to scream. He attempted a soft yelp to draw attention, but not before Bart pushed him out of Scott's view. Emerging from the shadows behind the nook and beyond Scott's sight, another man materialized to lend Bart a hand in subduing Ramon. Upon duct taping Ramon's face so he could not speak, and tying his arms behind his back like they did Mia and Francisco, the aiding man dipped away and jumped into Scott's view. Hearing his footsteps fade with every second, the mysterious man had to have been in front of the hallway by the elevator. Ramon wanted badly, more than anything, to warn his son-in-law, but he couldn't.

"You must be out of breath, Sharpe!" a man yelled to Scott. Presumably, this was the man who had bound him moments earlier, but Ramon couldn't be sure since he hadn't heard his voice.

He recognized Scott's voice, "What the hell is going on here? Where's my father-in-law?"

An elderly looking woman with a walker and eyeglass cord passed by Ramon, who was being restrained by Bart. Bart lay directly behind him to avoid detection by way of the old lady. She appeared to be heading to the elevator, which could bode well for Ramon's chances of escape. The man closed his eyelids and prayed she saw him, even though she didn't look in his direction for more than a fleeting glimpse.

Some sort of altercation occurred between the mystery man and Scott. Ramon tried so hard to shriek through the duct tape binder, but no sound came out. He also couldn't tell exactly the nature of the squabble down the dimly lit hall.

The senior started yelling as others made their way to the scene. She loudly declared Scott's guilt, and offered up a pertinent piece of information, that the "man in chains" was involved as well.

Ramon attempted to rise to his feet, but Bart tackled and held him. There was some more chatter between three distinct voices. Or was it four? Ramon could not make out how many were involved. He sighed through his nose as the culpability fully shifted on Scott.

Scott pleaded with the men, "Take me to 416. That's where this all started."

Another voice responded, "We're all yours until we find this dead body, I guess." Ramon felt affirmed in a way because initially he believed the two additional men were cops, and now he had no doubt. He turned his head to see Bart, whose mouth was agape as he understood the ramifications. The lunatic began whispering to himself.

Ramon pondered his next move. He knew where Scott and the cops were headed next, but how could he get there when he was bound like this? An idea popped into his head, like when a lightbulb suddenly materializes over the head of a cartoon character. If Ramon could untie himself and get to his gun, still lying in his cowboy boots no more than a hundred feet from where he was currently situated, he'd blast Bart. The bad man deserved to die. No, that wasn't right. Ramon thought about how humans had no right to decide who lived and who died. There was only one who controlled that.

Getting out of his shackles that bound him proved to be the most substantial of Ramon's problems. Once he removed them, he would be able to save the day.

Chapter 34

A week prior to Ramon's cruel and unusual shackling, Elmer and Darlene Hooper checked into Room 316 of the Whitehawk Casino's hotel. They were an elderly couple in their eighties from Cheyenne, Wyoming who had made the two-hour drive to enjoy time as a couple in the bliss for them that was retirement. The one hundred-mile drive would take two hours because Elmer controlled the wheel. If Darlene insisted on driving—which she wouldn't, for she was afraid of driving at night due to the wildlife of the Rocky Mountain region—the journey would take ninety minutes. Elmer would argue that's why she doesn't drive anymore, because she flew down the highways like an angry bat out of hell who accumulated speeding tickets like it was going out of style. Darlene would respond and say he drove like a grandfather. Elmer would say yes, he drives like a grandfather because he *is* a grandfather. They were as happily in love now as they were when they tied the knot back in 1961.

One morning back in January, Elmer and Darlene agreed to go to the Whitehawk Casino for an extended stay. For how long they would stay, they had no idea. It had been years since they had been to Colorado, and they longed to mix up their routine and have a nice, long visit. Darlene liked to play slot machines, and Elmer liked to sleep in a king bed where he could roll over and not have to hear Darlene's incessant snoring. It was a good compromise.

When Elmer called to make the reservation, he was delighted to hear he and Darlene would be staying in Room 316. Elmer was a lifelong Christian and upon hearing the room assignment, he was reminded of his favorite verse in the Bible, John 3:16. The verse read: "For God so loved the world that he gave his one and only Son, that whoever believes in him shall not perish but have eternal life." Elmer was a true believer and took the 316 issuing as a literal sign from God that he wasn't supposed to give up the room under any circumstance. So, you can imagine his response when the Satrione connection of Whitehawk Casino suggested they switch suites. The link called him back and told him that Room 316 had a perpetual asbestos problem. This was a lie: the Satriones rented out Rooms 216 and 416 and wanted to utilize the vents to stow money, drugs, and weapons.

When Joey Satrione, a higher up in the mobster family despite his young age of thirty, heard Room 316 had already been spoken for, he was livid. Though it was below his paygrade, he personally showed up to scare away whoever the new short-term occupants were. He banged on the door loudly and laid his eyes upon the feeble old man in 316. The man, with no regard for the intruder's reputation, told Satrione to beat it. Satrione didn't take kindly to that, and when he demanded for the rooms to be swapped Elmer said he had a distant cousin that was a lawyer, and he would happily take him to court.

Satrione was infuriated, for the "fool proof" vent system was foiled. When he brought it to the attention of his uncle

Salvatore, a middle-aged chain-smoker in the Denver mafia, he told Joey to roll with it. Sal offered a solution, that "housekeepers" could enter the room every day and go undetected. It was a golden opportunity, he told Joey, as it would draw suspicion away from the family. Joey liked the idea and implemented it right away.

Being that the mobster family had a connection in the know at the casino, the Satriones possessed the capability of entering any room in the hotel at a moment's notice. Hiding all their valuables away in 316 would be a breeze. Or so they thought.

Joey Satrione wasn't stupid. He knew Elmer could identify him in a jiffy, so he sent his patsies to do the dirty work for him. The first few "cleanings" were routine: a man or two would walk in, ask Elmer or Darlene if they'd like to leave, and do their business as quickly as possible. Being that Elmer and Darlene were of an age where they no longer possessed 20/20 vision, the Satriones were only somewhat concerned with the actual cleaning. Oftentimes, they'd come in and make the bed, shove thousands in the vent, and leave within five minutes. Joey Satrione proposed bringing a woman in to make the cleaning look more natural, but that idea was quickly shot down as Sal pointed out the type of women they hung around—strippers and prostitutes— were the exact kind of women that would cause the Hoopers to start a fuss. Besides, Sal had said, it was 2018 and men could clean hotel rooms as they pleased.

By the fourth visit, the only thing out of the ordinary according to Elmer Hooper was that men were the ones cleaning his room. Darlene reminded him that it was 2018 and men could clean hotel rooms as they pleased. It would be sexist to bring it up to the hotel, she had told him. And so, the Satriones had a foolproof way to vent their cash, drugs, and guns up to 416 or down to 216 without detection, and it was all because Elmer Hooper felt shamed into not voicing his politically incorrect thoughts.

About ten days into their journey, the Hoopers were suddenly awoken by a loud banging on their door. Elmer thought it was an odd time to clean. Darlene was too busy marrying Sean Connery in a dream.

Elmer saw it was twelve-fifteen in the morning and sighed. He got out of bed, threw on his pants quickly, then his black rimmed glasses, and strolled over to the entryway. There was a man at the door, and he introduced himself: he was Chayton, an employee of the hotel. Another man stood down the hall, and he was silent. Elmer thought this was peculiar. Chayton asked him if it was just him and Darlene there, and the interrogation frustrated Elmer; he was just trying to sleep. Elmer asked if they were cleaners, and the man at the door said no, so he slammed the door shut.

The peculiarities reached their zenith on the afternoon Bart and Ramon walked in. "Housekeeping," Bart announced, and Elmer spied through the peep sight.

--

On the walk up the stairwell, Bart had laid out the rules for Ramon. Rather, Bart laid out the *rule* for Ramon.

"If you talk, you die," Bart explained.

Ramon nodded silently. He understood who held the cards here. If only he had been able to recover his gun from his boots, this would be an even fight.

For the second time in his adult life, Ramon found himself contemplating his own mortality. He detested the now likely outcome that he would perish after saving his daughter and her sons. He got the sinking feeling that his life wasn't complete and that this shouldn't be it. Adriana, the love of his life, the woman who he'd put through torture when he was a young man, was counting on him to survive. So too were his daughters, or at least the three unmarried of them. It couldn't end like this.

He wished he would've made himself known to the cops on the second floor. It may have cost him his life, sure, but at least he would've gone out on his own terms and Bart would have been captured. Instead of that result, Ramon was now bracing for his demise and Bart walking away unscathed. What a cruel, unfair world we live in.

Ramon remained as zip tied as he was confused. Who was this old man and why had Bart taken him to his room? Ramon guessed the man was part of the Satrione web of organized crime. Was he going to be killed in this room?

Any speculation he harbored regarding the elderly man's ties to the mob was effectively squashed when Bart invited the old gentleman to leave while he attended to "cleaning up the room".

"Are you the only one here?" Bart asked.

The old man replied, "Darlene is probably at a slot machine or something."

"Great," Bart grumbled. "So, will you be leaving the room now?"

"Holy Toledo. Yes, yes, I'll go down and check on Darlene."

Bart was doing his best to conceal Ramon's restraints, but the old man noticed them as he walked out of the room. As soon as Bart saw him walk away through the peephole, he turned to Ramon.

"I have to ditch this weapon we killed your buddy with here." Bart grimaced as he walked toward the vent on the floor.

Ramon lingered near the entrance in bewilderment. "Why are you telling me this?"

"Because it won't matter anyway."

Ramon gulped. "What do you mean?" Though, to be fair, he knew precisely what Bart meant.

"What?" The sociopath laughed. "You think you'd get away from here unharmed? No, siree!"

The fasteners held Ramon's arms together tightly. He looked around the room as Bart unlatched the vent, desperate to find some way to escape this situation. After Bart's final words of the exchange, the situation appeared all but lethal.

Before he opted to drop the gun into the aperture in the ground rather than the wall, Bart glanced at Ramon. "I suppose I could do this here," he calmly explained. "Besides, it'll take the old man a long time to realize it. That man is decrepit!" Bart threw his head back and roared, close enough to Ramon now that he could feel his hot, putrid breath in his nostrils.

With seamless grace, Ramon thrust his zip tied arms over the head of Bart Thompson, to the point where their faces were touching. Bart turned his head and Ramon responded by squeezing with all his might. Ramon had him trapped in a guillotine head lock and continued to compress his hands into Bart's throat, and as he did the zip ties loosened. After a few more seconds of pushing, he would cut off the man's circulation and drop him to the floor.

As Bart wheezed, he uttered the words, "You son of a bitch," and gave out a hasty breath. Ramon and his shackled hands let the man go, and he dropped and thudded on the ground. He wasn't dead, but Ramon figured he had passed out.

Ramon sighed a breath of relief, but there was still work to be done. He lifted his arms high above his head and slammed them into his legs, and the sides of the fasteners separated. His thighs were sore, but at least he was free.

With the end of the zip tie still on his left hand, he began his strut to the entryway door. A step short, he heard the voice behind him. "Where do you think you're going? We were just starting to have some fun."

Bart's hand was on his pistol, and he placed the silencer back on the end of the gun. Ramon, feeling a new sort of tingle down his back as he remained exposed, suddenly wondered why he didn't just kill the pathetic man while he had the chance.

The time to act was now. He was exposed, weaponless, so he dove into the bathroom. He had cover, if only for a second. He held with all his strength the sliding door shut as Bart Thompson approached him. The door to the bathroom wasn't completely transparent but anyone with good eyesight could make out a moving figure. Ramon tried to remain still, but he couldn't lay under the tiny sink and continue to hold the sliding door shut. If Bart really wanted to, he could have a clear shot at him. In a desperate measure, Ramon released one of his hands and shut off the light. Perhaps that would trick Bart, who wasn't able to open the door in the instant Ramon held it shut with just one hand.

In what Ramon expected to be his final moments, he closed his eyes as Bart's resistance grew, the angle in which he pulled the door significantly better than the man inside the lavatory.

Ramon thought of Adriana and again regretted his decision to leave Bart alive. Ultimately, he believed his attempt to be the good man would cost him his life. He'd never see his wife, his daughters, or his grandchildren ever again. He would never again rest by the river and appreciate the existence God gave him. Tears blurred his vision as his fingers trembled violently in the last gasp of his grip.

The highlight reel of his life played before Ramon as he lay under the sink blinded by the intensity of the moment, the competence of his left arm dwindling with every passing second. He considered letting his right arm go. His left arm remained at full strength, so if he were to release himself from the sliding door, the force in which Bart would open it might cause him to fall.

He prayed to the Lord for a brief second, begging for a chance. He let his right arm go, and as predicted the sliding door swung open with full force. Bart fell to the ground, the pistol hanging out of his hip pocket. Ramon threw a jab with his left hand, and it connected with Bart's already disfigured face.

The force of Bart's rear smacking the ground was so intense that his gun, previously hanging out of his jeans pocket, flew across the floor in the direction of the bed. He and Ramon were still punching each other on the floor, too focused on the brawl to notice the unattended weapon.

After a second of heavy breathing and separation, both men stood up simultaneously, pushing each other in opposite directions of the narrow bathroom doorway. Ramon released his fatigued right hand and unleashed a strong strike, then hit Bart right on the nose with a jab. Bart shielded his face and fell back to his knees. Lying on the floor at an awkward angle, he kicked Ramon as hard as he could in the testicles, which caused the man to fall and inhale a mouthful of hotel room carpet.

Everything throbbed in Ramon's body, so the shot to the groin wasn't necessarily the dagger. It hurt, to be certain, but he took a few measured breaths to regain his hardiness. While lying on the ground, his head facing the window, he noticed the gun. This was his opportunity. "Fool me once, shame on you; fool me twice, shame on me" was the phrase flowing through his pulses. After the labored breaths, he jabbed Bart, who huffed and puffed as he lay void of energy, a few times for good measure, and army crawled his way over toward the pistol like a war hero in a Hollywood film. He'd seen them all, from *Saving Private Ryan* and *Platoon* to *All Quiet on the Western Front* and *The Bridge on the River Kwai*. Without taking anything away from the real-life heroes, this was Ramon's own personal Normandy, his very own Vietnam.

His legs gave out halfway through the twelve-foot trek, and he turned around to see Bart recouping his brawn. His face was so overcome with blood that he was hardly recognizable. Those sad eyes lacked meaning, and his bruised over nose was twisted in several spots. He was so ugly to gaze upon that Ramon forgot to survey his own face for gore. From what he could tell, no part of his body was truly broken, but he had lost at least one tooth. Gushing from the root was a seemingly never-ending supply of blood in Ramon's mouth. He swallowed a number of times and tasted the almost metallic flavor. He gagged in response. Bart coughed up blood once, and again a few seconds later. He eyed the gun as Ramon crept to retrieve the firearm.

When Ramon reached the gun, he picked it up and noticed the absence of bullets. He turned around, still in a slithery position, and now understood why Bart had not tried to shoot him. There was nothing to shoot Ramon with. He wanted to fight to the death.

Bart slithered in Ramon's direction, assuming a posture reminiscent of someone attempting a one-kneed pushup. He groaned with every stride, the pain reaching so many parts of his body.

It occurred to Ramon he was trapped. He reached this realization once he became cognizant to the fact that Bart still had possession over the switchblade with which he demanded Scott's right ring finger be smashed into oblivion a few hours earlier.

He had to wait it out or duke it out. There wasn't any backup option. Scott and the police officers were directly one floor above them, not below, so it's not as if they could bang on the floors or cause a commotion. Instead, Ramon prayed the old man would come back.

Bart lazily swung the knife at Ramon's throat and narrowly missed his target. Ramon braced for the pain but had moved his head far back enough to where he only felt a slight breeze from the swinging blade. Bart positioned his crossed over right hand on the ground and struggled to lift it. With every ounce of power he had left, Ramon clenched his right fist and swung downward in the direction of Bart's outstretched hand that held the knife. Precision was key. If Bart moved his arm up, Ramon would cross paths with the knife. If he moved it down, his palm would not flop open, which was the plan. Luckily for him, Bart's right palm was exposed, and as a result the knife flew in the air once more. The flight path of the Kershaw resembled a jump ball in basketball, hovering upwards between the two.

The knife was pointing downwards, and the middle of the blade smacked the ground; Ramon swore he heard it make a loud sound. In another stroke of luck, the Kershaw bounced a second time and landed slightly closer to Ramon, and he snatched it.

Bart Thompson glared at him, conscious between the blood and the bruises, of the result. He looked Ramon directly in the eye and said, "What luck you have."

The man sitting opposite him couldn't help but grin. He breathed an enormous sigh of relief as he registered the importance. He had a tremendous chance now of walking out of there alive, and this was due to Bart's physical condition and now weaponless status. He would likely see Adriana again, kiss all his daughters, and fish the Rio Grande once more.

The man wouldn't make the same mistake twice. He raised the Kershaw in his shaky right hand, blood flowing out of his mouth, and before his arm would come crashing down Bart spoke in that confident tone once more. "This won't end here. I'll haunt you in my dreams. All you will ever be is a murderer. You murdered my father, and you'll murder me right here."

"I haven't made up my mind yet." Ramon's right hand remained frozen in the fighter's pose.

Bart boomed, "You *liar*!"

"I am no liar."

"If you don't kill me here, if you make that mistake again," he said, "I will kill you."

"I know."

"You're better off killing me. And if you think I'll kill you fast, think again." A shudder went down Ramon's back as he listened to the words of this psychopath. "I'll pull your fingernails off one by one. I'll cut your throat, but only a little bit so you can watch the blood trickle down your neck and go cold. I will make it hurt."

Ramon repeated, "I am no liar."

The bloodied man tilted his head to the left and a sly grin slowly crept upon his face. "I know the truth."

Ramon felt a sinking sensation in the depths of his chest. Those four words were the same uttered to him before he shot Bart Thompson, Sr. twenty-plus years earlier.

He could not take another moment of this agony. He remembered the promise he made to God, that he would not take the life of another man, and performed the sign of the cross as he realized now he couldn't keep his promise. Like a cinematic moment, Ramon felt a rush of cool wind sweep through the gloomy hotel room. He took it as a sign from God that what he was doing was okay, for he was protecting his family. He did not need to live in fear for his own life.

Something in Ramon prompted him to say, "I will give you one last chance. If you leave here and do not bother me or harm me, I will let you go."

Bart took less than a second to consider Ramon's offer. He spat on the man's face from two feet away. "I will murder you like you murdered my father," he said. "Even if you go to the police, I will come for you. Even if I am behind a cell, I will hire someone to make you suffer. You will die if I make it out of this room alive. It's you or me today, compadre."

"Then you have left me no choice." Ramon motioned to the door of the coat closet, barely large enough to fit a human inside. Bart obliged because Ramon held the knife to his throat to persuade him, and people usually listen to someone when they are holding a knife to their throat.

It was a funny thing to watch because Bart Thompson stood at least eight inches taller than Ramon De Leon. The cornered man backed into the coat closet slowly, aware he was going to die. Ramon had offered him a way out, an escape route, but the stubborn fool refused again and again. He wanted the quiet man dead because ultimately Ramon was the catalyst in his father's demise. That much could not be argued. However, his unwillingness to negotiate would prove to be his downfall.

And so, in one sturdy motion, swinging his right arm from the left rapidly, Ramon slashed the man's neck. The seconds following Bart Thompson's demise were brutal to endure for Ramon. He was conscious of the fact that he made a good decision but the result was sure to be enduring. The impact of Bart's death would not end today for Ramon. The De Leon patriarch had decided in those moments that he would turn himself in regardless of whether law enforcement claimed the act to be self-defense or not. He had to escape this wretched place first.

He tried not to investigate Bart's face once the man passed away. He couldn't help but notice the sad brown eyes looking past him at nothing. It was an image that would haunt Ramon the rest of his days. He was so frightened, both by the man who threatened to kill him and by himself, that he left the Kershaw blade in his harasser.

Bart and Ramon's excessive gore dyed the previously blue and green checkered floor a crimson hue, near the coat closet. A witness would be hard pressed to see the bloodstain near the bathroom, but anyone with decent enough vision would notice the discolored floor near the coat closet in the back. Ramon grabbed a towel from the bathroom and hastily wiped the floors of the bathroom, while a dead Bart Thompson lay fifteen feet away. Ramon swabbed his own face, too. He still had a few cuts and gashes here and there on his face, and part of his sweatshirt was torn off, but he was in pretty good shape all things considered.

On his way out of Room 316, he crossed paths with Elmer Hooper.

"Hello," Elmer said. "Am I good to go back into my room now or what?"

"You should be set," Ramon, less than five minutes removed from cutting a man's throat, feigned a smile.

Elmer grinned back at him, saying, "See you boys again tomorrow."

"I doubt it." Ramon laughed. He wanted to get away as far from Whitehawk Casino as possible.

Ramon took a step towards the elevator and heard the man calling behind him. His shoulders stiffened, but he managed to turn around. "What did you say?" he asked Elmer.

"I said, 'where's the other guy'?"

"He's, uh, gone," Ramon said.

"Oh. Well, I hope he finds another job."

Ramon smiled. Had the old man come by even three minutes earlier, both their lives may have been taken by Bart. It's all about perspective, Ramon thought.

Chapter 35

Bart Thompson, Jr.'s dead body fell onto Deputy Washington, who let out a scream akin to an eight-year-old girl. I let out an enormous sigh of relief as I realized the ramifications. Ramon had escaped! Or, at the very least, he didn't die here.

"This here your father-in-law?" Washington asked.

"No." I sighed again. "No, it's not. But I can identify him. His name is Bart Thompson, Jr."

"Is he the dead body you were talking about?"

"Believe it or not," I said, "no, he isn't."

"So we got another dead body on our hands then." Washington sighed deeply.

"Did you know about this?" Nelson glared at the tenant.

"No." The elderly man threw his hands up in surrender. "My vision ain't what it used to be. Besides, I came in herea few minutes ago and turned the lights off."

"Is it anywhere else in here?" Washington called out.

Nelson whipped his head around ninety degrees, back to the television, and began scanning the floor. "Not that I can see." He moved towards the bathroom, and practically screamed, "Look! In here, Washington."

Washington brushed up next to me in that narrow hall between the bathroom and sleeping quarters, and I felt the tickle of his dark mustache. I shuddered, and when they looked at me and informed me that it was a crime scene and I needed to leave, I was more than happy to oblige.

I glanced into the bathroom as I waltzed out and noticed the streaks of blood on the mirror and the tiled floor. What had happened in there?

--

Seated a few feet from the entrance to Room 316, I wondered where to head next. I still hadn't found Ramon, but at the very least he was free from the clutches of Bart Thompson. If he was caught in the act, they'd probably kill him. Elmer, the old man in the room with the cops, was still there, so I was guessing Ramon was hiding out or trying to find Mia.

A few more cops and a detective walked past me into the room, mumbling about "the victim" this and "the victim" that. I wanted to scream in their faces, "Don't you see who the evil man was here?"

I pondered Bart Thompson's pathetic existence. What a gloomy, lonesome life this guy lived. He climbed the suffocating corporate American ladder, only to become involved in mob shenanigans that would ultimately cost him his life. He dedicated himself to Westco and the Satriones, and in the end neither stood on the frontlines of war to defend him from the miserable death he had procured. He would give his life for them, and they didn't in return. That's the downside of working with the mob, though, that life can be one way in a moment and another in the next. At least, that's how *The Godfather* portrayed it.

Three children would grow up without a father. It's not like the kids knew any different, though. Bart was absent in moments big and small. His ex-wife hated him and took him to court to make sure those three would never have to grow up knowing their father intimately. That thought, that he could die like that and no one would grieve, forced me to yearn to live as a family man. I was ready to continue sobriety.

However, as my old therapist used to say, two things can be true at once, the second of which being I could really go for a stiff drink. I would have loved to just tip back the handle of Stranahan's whiskey and hear the glugging sound of the bottle emptying ounce by ounce. My throat would burn but it would be worth the trial. However, I knew I could not do it. I needed to be the man I could by being there for Mia, Francisco, and now Marcos.

Mia. If she hadn't already left the parking lot, she would be sitting in the Acura with the kids. I wanted to leave but knew the police might need to interview me, so I opened the door to 316. It was crowded with about six men by now, among them Deputies Washington and Nelson.

I asked them, "Can I leave? I want to go find my wife. Besides, my father-in-law is still out there."

Deputy Nelson pulled me aside into the bathroom where no one else would hear us. "Are you sure this isn't the dead body you saw?" he asked. "That we're looking for *another* one?"

"I'm positive. The other man was Chayton, a former employee. They executed him in 216." I pointed to the ground, signaling he was just below where we stood when he died.

"Chayton, huh?" Nelson fiddled with his mustache, still wearing those nineties sunglasses.

I nodded.

"Elmer!" he shouted, and about ten long seconds later the old man made us a company in the hotel room-sized bathroom. I was close enough to Nelson that I could take in every bit of his coffee and nicotine-smelling breath.

"What do you want?" Elmer shouted way too loudly for the tiny space we were positioned in.

"This Chayton fellow," Nelson continued to fondle his mustache. "You say he was Native?"

"Yes," he answered. "Like I said, he was a weirdo. An Indian with a ponytail! I ain't never seen one of those."

"You clearly don't know the history." Nelson smiled. "Did he have an employee name tag on?"

"No, I don't think so," Elmer responded.

"You have to believe me," I said. "Go check 216 again. Right by the bathroom. It's oriented the same way this room is."

"And you have to leave," Nelson said. "We've got everything we need from you at this point, sir." He motioned to Elmer, "And you. Go find Darlene at the craps table."

Elmer and I ambled behind him and through the door. "I like you," he said. "You put prepositions at the end of words. Like when you told that pig 'it's oriented the same way this room is'. You could've said 'it's oriented the same way as this room.' It sounds better."

I feigned a smile. Didn't I hear this same man tell me he "ain't never" seen an Indian with a ponytail? Wasn't that a double negative? Having fought my battles for the day and then some, I turned to him and said, "I'm from Minnesota. It's just the way I talk, I guess."

The old man laughed. "Where in Minnesota are you from? My momma was from there. She and my daddy met in Wyoming, though, and they stayed."

"Carver."

"Like Carver County?" he asked.

"Yes, but in the city. You know Carver County?"

"Course I do. That's where my momma was from," Elmer said. "It was Young or Little America or something like that."

"Ah, yes. Norwood Young America."

"So is Carver in Carver County?" he asked.

"It's in Carver County, yes," I explained, "but it's the city of Carver."

"Oh, I see. Kind of like the city of Laramie in Wyoming and Laramie County in Wyoming."

"Exactly," I said. "The city of Carver is a city in the county of Carver County."

"It's sort of funny, though." He laughed. "Laramie County is where I live, in Cheyenne. But the city of Laramie is about fifty miles west in Albany County."

"Oh."

He continued talking, "Ain't that funny, that the city of Laramie isn't in Laramie County?"

"Yes. Very funny." I felt myself growing irritable. Other than learning that the city of Laramie is in fact not located in the nearby county of Laramie County, which is a rather peculiar geographical mystery, I had no use for this conversation. Instead of continuing to curl my toes and tensing my muscles, I needed to find Ramon.

"Have a good one, Elmer," I said, and as I bounced past the man he extended out his right hand for a handshake. He smacked me unintentionally in the stomach, and I let out a quiet yelp. I shook his hand.

"Goodbye, Scott."

--

Mia and the kids hadn't moved an inch.

"Where's *papa*?" she asked, burying her hands in her face, overwhelmed by the weight of the circumstances.

"I don't know," I said. "But I know one of the guys looking for him is dead. We found the body."

"Who?"

"Bart."

Mia continued to shield her face. "My God," she said, and performed the sign of the cross.

"Can you think of anywhere your dad might go in a casino?"

"He doesn't really gamble." She half smiled. "But he would be the type of man to hide among the crowds. You know, safety in numbers."

"Brilliant," I said, and waved to Francisco and Marcos in the backseat. "I'll be right back." I kissed Mia and lingered for a second, feeling the warmth of her in that parking lot.

Sprinting under the neon sign that read "Whitehawk Casino and Hotel" for what seemed like the tenth time today, I made my way onto the casino floor. Adrenaline still must've been flowing through me, because more than a few patrons stopped what they were doing and glanced at me. I slowed my jog and began scanning the casino floor. I massaged my temples to overcome the flashing and screeches of the copious slot machines. I wondered if the Hoopers were nearby and if they had seen anything. After all, Elmer was able to tell Ramon was Hispanic from their earlier meeting.

It didn't take long to find the couple, slouched over a slot machine like each spin was a slow dance with lady luck. Darlene was in the seat, Elmer hunched over her like she was Whitehawk royalty on a quest for the high score.

"Elmer?" I yelled loud enough so he would hear me over the bellows of the machines.

He instantly recognized me and grinned. "Darlene here is up twenty dollars!" he shouted. "Been here an hour on this machine."

I didn't have the heart to tell him that, because she had an empty plate of chicken wings and a beer in front of her, twenty dollars an hour at the casino was basically a wash. But I smiled anyway. "Good for you," I said. "Say, have you seen that Hispanic cleaner you saw earlier?"

"Darndest thing." He laughed. I sensed some irony in the fact that this guy who wore a hearing aid was on a noisy casino floor and practically whispering to me. Luckily, my hearing has always been spectacular. "But I saw him by the elevator lobby a while ago."

"You sure?"

"Yes," he said. "I nodded at him, and he waved at me. Same wispy facial hair and cuts from before. Boy looked like he had been in a fight!"

"Did you see which way he was headed?"

"Nah," he offered. "I just saw him standing there."

"Thanks." I trotted over to the elevator lobby where Ramon was last seen. I searched the halls and the elevator bay. I was tempted to go talk to Ariel at the hotel service desk, but all I'd receive from her was the latest update on where she stood in the *Longmire* series.

I ambled back over to the gaming floor, overcome with irony that the Denver Nuggets were on television again, just like the night I was here over a year back. A second after I eyed the big screen, Jamal Murray of the Nuggets checked back into the basketball game. The last few minutes were loaded with irony. God loves satire, I suppose.

Ramon was nowhere to be found, and I felt my search dwindling with confidence every passing moment. Where could he be? If he had in fact killed Bart, he would either be hiding or, as Mia suspected, lying low among the crowds. It seemed more and more like Ramon was intentionally concealed. But where?

Suddenly, like a lightning bolt of realization, it struck me. The closet! I hadn't checked the janitor's closet in which Chayton kidnapped us hours earlier. I remembered the small mail slit in which Chayton saw us, and I kept my eyes peeled for it. Having walked through what seemed like a hundred doors today, the 101st turned out to be the right one.

I saw the entrance to the room with the knee-high mail slot and turned the rusty knob. Crouched inside the dark room was the silhouette of a man, a man I hoped and prayed was my father-in-law.

Ramon protected his face from the blaze of light protruding from the lobby. I fist pumped in excitement, and he lowered his hand and recognized me. He wore a smile disproportionately large for his round face. I shut the door and utilized the iPhone flashlight application, set it on a counter, and we embraced in the closet that still smelled like Chayton's Pall Malls.

Ramon pulled himself back, grasping my shoulders with his cold, calloused hands. "Son," he said.

"*Papa*," I replied. "You found your cowboy hat."

Chapter 36

Scott, Elmer Hooper, and Ramon sat in the Denver Police Department lobby. Scott and Ramon were seated next to each other, of course, and Elmer was yapping behind them with another patron about Wyoming Cowboys football. Apparently, Elmer found the only other Cowboy fan in Denver County. They were jawing back and forth about how 2018 would be a difficult year for Wyoming, as their quarterback Josh Allen had been drafted into the NFL by the Buffalo Bills. Ramon wondered if they stood a chance against his Lobos, who had finished last in the Mountain West the year earlier.

Ultimately the banter was good, as Ramon was aiming to divert his attention. He was going to have to recant the story of killing Bart Thompson and convince the police the act was self-defense. He and Scott had rehearsed answers for questions law enforcement would throw their direction.

Ramon remembered all those years ago, in the Albuquerque police department, when the cops called Bart Thompson's father the victim. He pondered whether they'd treat him the same way. He thought about the fact that he wasn't an illegal immigrant this go around and let some of his worries go out the lobby window.

A policewoman entered the room and called out, "De Leon." Ramon sprung to his feet hastily. Scott wished him luck, Ramon told him thank you, and then he scooted off. Like the Albuquerque building, Denver's corridor was dimly lit and hair-raising. The somber hall seemed to go on forever. It was like a gloomy, never-ending purgatory, he decided. Ramon imagined walking through these halls as a man with less confidence and more guilt. How were criminals not supposed to slip up in conditions like these?

As the woman guided him on what seemed like a prolonged five-minute torture walk—though it was probably only thirty seconds—they eventually settled into a room with a teeny window and a hefty white door.

The room was no more than ten by ten feet. No art decorated the walls. The room was unfurnished other than a small table and three folding chairs, two on one side and one right in front of Ramon. Seated in the pair on the opposite end were detectives. The first was a man with golden hair fashioned into a flat top and thick rimmed black glasses like Michael Douglas in *Falling Down*. He wore a short sleeve button up white shirt and looked almost cartoonish with his features. The other investigator was a redheaded woman of about forty, a spot on the ring finger of her left hand bare where diamonds used to reside. She sported a smile, even if Ramon knew it was probably fake. The divorce appeared to be recent based on the gray bags under each eye.

The policewoman who walked Ramon down the hall exited the room. The Michael Douglas lookalike cop called out to Ramon, "Sit down, De Leon. I'm Detective Andrews, and this is Detective Nichols."

Uh oh, Ramon thought. *Here we go again.*

"What brings you to Denver?" the redhead, Detective Nichols, asked.

"My son-in-law," Ramon stuttered. "He was in trouble."

"What kind of trouble?" Andrews asked. "Take it from the top."

"He owed some guys some money. Not a lot, but some."

Nichols raised her eyebrow. "What is *some*?"

"Two grand," Ramon explained. "And they took my daughter and grandsons because of it."

Nichols placed her left foot in front of her right and cradled her left hand under her chin. "This was a kidnapping, you say?"

Ramon nodded.

"And how is it that you ended up killing another person?" Andrews asked.

Ramon knew what that meant, that they had done their research on him. "So you know." He bowed his head and began to pray. "You know the answers to all the questions, apparently."

The detectives looked at each other. "Well, we know about your previous run-in with the law."

"Previous run-in?" Ramon said. "A man pointed a gun at my head and threatened to take away my store. I was exonerated of wrongdoing."

Andrews threw his hands in the air in surrender. "All right, all right," he said.

Nichols interrupted, "We just find it difficult to believe you now have killed his son and not committed any crime."

"I'm sure it looks that way," Ramon responded, "but I have done nothing wrong."

"Explain it to us." Nichols relaxed her position and glanced over at Andrews, who took a sip of his Styrofoam cup of likely burned coffee. He noticed Ramon eyeing the cup and asked, "You want some?"

"No, thank you." Ramon put his hands up and declined. He took a prolonged breath and began the lengthiest of his life's monologues. "As you officers know, Bart Thompson, Sr. came into my store a long time ago. I shot him in self-defense. Albuquerque police can corroborate that story." He inhaled again, remembering the irony of a police officer explaining to him what the word "corroborate" meant all those years ago. Ramon's English had improved exponentially in the years between. "I was acquitted of all wrongdoing. Twenty years later, his son, Bart Thompson, Jr., the deceased, aided and abetted in the kidnapping of my daughter, Mia Sharpe, and my two grandsons, Francisco and Marcos Sharpe. I was brought into the situation with a phone call from my son-in-law, Scott Sharpe. He told me I needed to leave New Mexico immediately and come up to Denver to help rescue them. I know now that Bart was luring me in because he knew that I was the one who shot the bullet that ended his father's life. He took us to a room at the Whitehawk Casino's hotel. I don't remember the number because I bounced around a lot. He forced Scott to chop off a finger, and his men killed Chayton. They bound me and handed me to Bart so he could kill me. He told me several times they used Room 316 as an avenue to keep money, drugs, and weapons inside the ducts of the vents. Look at the vents. You'll find the evidence you need. Anyway, Bart Thompson told me he was going to kill me if I didn't kill him, that he'd haunt me forever, and that I was not safe if he was alive. So I cut his throat with the knife he wanted to use on me."

"Where is that knife, Ramon?" Nichols asked. "It's okay if I call you Ramon, isn't it?"

Ramon gulped. He left the knife pierced in Bart's neck. His prints would be all over it. How would they prove Bart was the fellow who purchased the Kershaw?

"Who is to say you didn't come up to the casino by yourself, hunt down Bart, and kill him to shut him up about the debt your son-in-law owed?" she asked.

"Look, I did what I thought was right. He threatened to kill me."

Nichols and Andrews spoke in an ESP cop sort of way, and both stood and exited the room that resembled a prison cell.

A few excruciating minutes later, after what seemed like an eternity, Andrews walked back in. He adjusted the frame of his black glasses and stared at Ramon. In his gaze, there was a sense of empathy exhibited from his lizard-looking green eyes. It sure felt like he wanted to be the good cop here. "I have good news and bad news, Ramon."

"Give it to me straight," Ramon said.

"Good news is," Andrews said, abandoning conventionality, "that the blood lab results have come back on the blood from the missing body you claim is dead."

"Why is that good news?"

"Because," he glared at Ramon, obviously upset he was interrupted, "the blood type doesn't match that of our victim, Bart Thompson. There's another dead man."

Ramon knew there were two dead men before this conversation, so he wasn't sure how that was good news. He was infuriated if anything, hearing that word again. *Victim.* It bothered him to high heaven. The guy kidnapped

Ramon's daughter and grandsons and yet is labelled a victim. What a sad reality this was for Ramon to accept. "What's the bad news?" he growled.

"Bad news is that we found the weapon, and your fingerprints are all over it."

"I know. I admit to killing the man, but it was self-defense."

Andrews huffed. "Do you think the jury will believe that? They also recovered a gun registered to you in Room 216. Ballistics recovered fingerprints from you. Now why would a man bring a gun if he's the victim?"

Beads of sweat piled on Roman's forehead once more. "Self-defense."

"You're in trouble, Mr. De Leon. In fact, you're being held here on suspicion of murder. You better lawyer up."

Ramon's jaw dropped, and a second later Andrews added, "Now is when I actually have to handcuff you."

--

That evening was especially rigorous for Ramon. He lay in a chilly, unkempt cell Denver police usually reserved for the drunk or disorderly. With every passing hour the man believed his misfortune was intensifying. The thought of being sentenced to prison terrified Ramon. He trusted in God and knew He would provide, but the free will of humans had more control over this conundrum than his higher power, and that worried him.

What Ramon wouldn't give to walk along the river again. He missed his old pal. He yearned so badly to feel the reeds slip through his fingers as he approached her, to feel the smudgy sand beneath his toes after an Albuquerque rainstorm. He wanted to dip his fingers and watch them disappear in the slimy copper waterway. For the first time in his life, he had the desire to bring Scott Sharpe to his special place. Ramon hadn't processed the day's events properly, but he knew without question his son-in-law was the root cause. That all said, he admired Scott's tenacity. He came through when it mattered for his family, and Ramon would always remember that, even if others chose to ignore the heroics.

Nichols brought him a peanut butter and jelly Uncrustable and a Mott's apple juice box for dinner. Ramon realized the first bite was the first calorie he had consumed since the eggs and sausage that morning.

"Thank you," Ramon said.

It took her a moment to respond. "You're welcome."

Ramon asked how the prison cafeteria food was, and Nichols said it was okay. He knew there was recent hurt in her eyes and asked her if anything was the matter. He wanted to get on her good side before she and Andrews rushed to judgment. It would be pleasant to have someone who might go to bat for him if things hit the fan. Which, if he was being honest with himself, he expected now.

"No," she answered.

Ramon laid out his cards early with Detective Nichols. "I notice you've been through a lot," he said, motioning to her indented, ringless finger.

"Oh, that." She covered the divorce divot with her right arm and scooted her chair back. "I was unfaithful, and he chose not to forgive me."

"I was unfaithful once," Ramon admitted. "Worst mistake of my life." A pit in his stomach formed that reminded him of the agony he put Adriana through in the early 1990s.

Nichols looked down at Ramon's gold wedding ring and said, "Good for you. She was more forgiving than my ex."

"I think about how lucky I am every single day," he said, "that she decided to keep me. I don't deserve her."

"How did she forgive you?"

Ramon lifted his right index finger to the heavens. "God. And a whole lot of therapy." He smiled.

"You are beyond lucky, sir. I lost my chance forever. The worst part of all this is I see him all the time and I can't tell him—"

Ramon sensed Nichols had just realized she had crossed the line, talking to the accused like this. Nichols thought about her husband and wished she hadn't made the mistake. Like Ramon's lapse in judgment thirty years ago, she had gone to a bar and kissed someone other than her spouse. The incident was recent—nine months ago, to be exact— and she and her now ex-husband had become legally divorced in the last few days. She chalked up her bone headedness at the time to the rigors of her occupation, and the couple's struggle to navigate through the adoption process. She met the man with whom she was unfaithful five minutes before the kiss and told her husband later she was "just curious". That reasoning wasn't good enough for her husband, and he moved out the next day.

Ramon paused for a moment. "Have you prayed about it?"

"I tried. I'm no good at it."

"Prayer is about intention, not having problems answered," he argued.

Nichols could not believe what she was hearing. "It's amazing you feel this way even after they've accused you of something as horrible as murder."

"I know He'll take care of me no matter what."

"You're crazy." She swatted her forehead and rubbed her left eye. She'd been awake for eighteen hours and her shift was about to end. Nichols decided after a full night's sleep in her lonely studio apartment that she would give this prayer thing a shot.

Ramon exhaled thoughtfully and said, "God can't solve your problems, but faith in Him can give you every bit of reason to try."

"It's amazing you have that kind of belief."

"You can too," Ramon explained. "Prayer and faith alone may not get your husband to forgive you, but it gives you something to work with, something to live for. 'If you lose faith, you lose all.' I believe Eleanor Roosevelt said that."

Nichols rubbed her left index finger on the bridge of her long nose, taking in all of Ramon's words carefully. It was a lot to process, she realized, but she had a fresh sense of motivation to get through her trials. Her cellphone rang, and she answered on the second ring. Ramon was surprised there was cell service in this dungeon.

"Andrews," Nichols said, then there was a long pause. "Right now?" she asked the mysterious person on the other side of the call. Then, there was a lengthier pause. "We're on our way."

She gazed at Ramon void of emotion, and Ramon wasn't quite sure how to react to her. She cuffed him again from behind and led him down the same gloomy corridor to the same gloomy interrogation room as earlier. They entered the desolate room and were the first to arrive to whatever this was.

A few seconds later a tan, well-built man of ordinary height with balding hair that resembled an upside-down white horseshoe, with his police cap removed and in his right hand, entered the room. He eyed Nichols, then Ramon, and then Nichols once more, this time lingering for a few moments. He walked over and situated himself in the vacant seat next to the detective. Once seated, he moved the chair another foot or two further from Nichols. Ramon found this confusing, because Nichols was a relatively young, attractive woman who was recently divorced and would be considered someone men would find desirable.

Andrews came in a moment later and leaned against the plain gray wall of the windowless room. He glanced over his detectives, laughed, and then looked at Ramon.

"I'm Detective Grimes," the muscular man in the chair said, and placed his cap back over his balding head. "This is Detective Nichols and Detective Andrews, who I know you know." Ramon peered down at the table, bracing himself for the worst of news, when he saw it. On the left hand of Detective Grimes was an indent just like Detective Nichols'. Absent from his finger was a wedding ring. Ramon put all the clues together of the last hour, and Nichols' confessions made more sense. It was Grimes who she had been unfaithful to, the man she claimed to be recently divorced from but still saw frequently. Ramon felt for her in that moment. She had a moment of weakness like he did years earlier and he empathized with her set of circumstances. People are imperfect and make mistakes, but it's what they do after they make mistakes that define them.

That doesn't excuse cheating though, Ramon knew, and Detective Nichols was actively paying the price for her actions.

Grimes continued, "Detectives Nichols and Andrews, thanks for coming down. I wanted to brief you all on the new update we've received regarding this case." Ramon was so deep in thought he forgot all about the immensely important meeting taking place in front of his eyes. How could he? His freedom, his livelihood, was at stake here, and yet all he could think about was the poor battered cop across the table who didn't come out as lucky as him.

He shifted into focus once more, for Adriana's sake.

"The new update," Grimes explained, "is that we have a new witness in the investigation. A witness who, I might say, is incredibly helpful for you, Mr. De Leon."

A witness? Who was the witness? Scott's words would be tossed out, as he'd be considered biased as a family member. The only link between Scott and Ramon was the phone call the night earlier when Scott informed his father-in-law of his daughter's kidnapping. Try getting that held up in court.

Ramon nodded slowly in anticipation. "And who might that be?" he asked, shrugging his shoulders high enough that the chains clinked as he displayed his emotion.

"I'm not at liberty to say," Grimes answered.

"So now what?"

"Hell, you're free to go." Grimes extended his arm to the doorway in a dramatic way. Nichols uncuffed Ramon, and the shocked man walked in the direction of the door.

All Ramon could think to say as he inched toward his freedom was, "Thank you."

Chapter 37

In my arms lay Marcos as he slept. Francisco napped in his new "big boy bed". Situated on the other side of the couch, Mia dozed off into a whole new dream land full of possibilities. That she could sleep here in my presence again meant she was building her trust in me. My lips curved into a smile as I came to terms with this positive revelation.

I felt a sudden urge to drink. I would be a fool not to recognize a problem where there is one. I know that white knuckling isn't the long term answer. I was riding the high of saving my family the day before, so I was occupied. Being occupied is the only thing keeping me from drinking. Everyday life would prove to be incredibly difficult, and I knew I could not sustain the life I wanted *and* drink. It's just not possible. Three days of continuous sobriety was difficult enough.

Mia opened her eyes and smiled at me. It was in that moment I recalled just how beautiful she was to me, and how I would go to the ends of the Earth to protect her. In her momentary glance, I felt that ounce of trust once more. Mia's heavy eyelids begged her to return to slumber, and she gave into their request.

I sat there another hour, without an agenda until Marcos woke up. Newborns are hungry every time the little hand on the clock advances, it seems. And when he was alert, so too his mommy would be. They were, as every baby and mother are, a package deal.

Soon after, Marcos' eyelids lifted at a leisurely pace. Our eyes met, and my heart sank. I was so sorry I put this little angel of a boy in harm's way. I would never do it again.

My right hand supported his baby head and my left lay underneath the blanket keeping him warm in a cocoon of coziness, snug like a bear in its den in the blistering Rocky Mountain winter. After a minute of intense eye contact, Marcos threw his teeny noggin back and began sobbing, a distinct "glah" sound forming when his tongue lifted from the soft palate. Like any newborn baby, he was as helpless as can be.

The maternal instinct hit Mia instantly, and she rose from the mahogany tinted sofa to grab Marcos. I handed her the baby, and she sat back down. She lowered her shirt, and Marcos began to feed.

"Still is amazing to experience the second time around with him." I grinned. "I love being his daddy."

Mia was all smiles, too. "I love being his mother," she said. "I want you to know though, I haven't forgotten about our conversations. About our issues."

"Me neither," I spoke, never wavering from eye contact. Mia's big brown eyes met mine, and I detected her utmost sincerity. "Listen, Mia—"

"Yes?"

"I'll be the man I need to be," I said. "I know I've put you in danger now, and I will never forgive myself for that. I've been a bad man, but now I know I can be a good man."

"I appreciate that, Scott," she said. "We were terrified. You let us down. It is going to take a very long time to fully forgive you. I need to know I can trust you again someday." She hung her head, as if she had been holding onto those words for days and just now had let them go.

Of course, her words stung, but the time for me to defend myself was long past. "I know. I never got a chance to say I'm sorry." As I uttered that last word, she beamed from cheek to cheek. A solitary tear rolled down her face, slowly but firmly. I continued, "I know I have so much to apologize for. I'm sorry for neglecting you all. I'm sorry for causing you to doubt our marriage. I'm sorry for not show-ing up as a father. I'm sorry for going into debt with the mob. Most of all, I'm sorry for putting you, Francisco, and Marcos in danger. That is something I never intend to do again."

Mia wept, the teardrops falling down her face now in abundance, and I joined her in the sob fest. "It's okay, *mi marido*," Mia said. "I just need one thing from you."

"Anything."

"Tell me when you are struggling with drinking," she responded. "I'm not a mind reader. But I know you strug-gle."

"I will." I nodded. "I promise."

"You might not know, but I know," Mia said.

"What do you mean, 'you know'?"

"I know you've been drinking every day."

I was baffled. "How do you know that?"

"Scott," she said. "You may think you are sly and sneaky, but you're not." As she uttered those words, my mind played on a loop the past few years of our marriage. Since Francisco was born, Mia had either been pregnant or breast-feeding ninety percent of the time, so I took that upon myself to believe it meant she was a lock to be the designated driver. I used to convey that sentiment with words like "well, you can't drink so I will!" Suddenly, the last five years of our marriage didn't seem so peachy to me as I recalled the number of times I'd looked like a drunken moron in front of Mia.

She continued, "I did a search online a while back that had a headline like 'Signs Your Spouse is an Alcoholic'. You fit most of them: binge drinker, secret drinker, finding excuses to drink. Lying and concealing drinking. Getting defensive when confronted about your drinking. You hit all of them spot on."

"Why didn't you say anything to me?" I asked.

"Because," she explained, "you need to know when to ask for help. All I can do is tell you what I see. Plus, I made some calls."

"Calls?" I went tense. "To who?"

Mia showcased her signature smile. "I'll tell you all of this eventually."

Then it hit me like a ton of bricks. It's not that Mia wanted to avoid a conversation with me about my drinking; she'd been trying to figure out a way to approach it. She was so loving and caring that she had been preparing for this conversation before my alcoholism had a chance to get her kidnapped. I married the best woman in the world for me.

"I love you, Mia." That's all I could say to her. Yes, it was true, but I was utterly speechless in her wisdom. She was powerful beyond words.

"I love you, too. Now get better. I won't trust you again until you do."

Sitting down in the most comfortable chair in our home, with the person I was most comfortable with in the entire world, I fidgeted with my thumbs trying to come up with words that tied together in the form of a sentence. It was like being back at the University of New Mexico campus in December of 2008.

"I missed you." It was true. I remained at a loss for words beyond that, unable to fully articulate the depth of her significance to me. The profound impact she held over me in that moment was incredible.

Instead, she flipped the tone of the conversation back to me. "This is your phrase I am using on you, but *figure out a plan*, Scott." Marcos unlatched then, and Mia uttered, "Looks like someone has a poopy diaper." She stood up abruptly and brought our second son to the diaper changing station in the nursery.

A mere three seconds after my wife left the room with Marcos, I pulled my cellphone out of my left pocket. The home screen opened, and I clicked the green phone icon in the bottom left corner. Under the contacts icon, I selected the name Ana De Leon.

The phone buzzed a few times, and then my sister-in-law answered. "Hello?" she called out.

"Ana?"

"Scott?" she said. "What's going on? Are you okay?"

"Yes, yes," I assured her. "I'm just fine. Everyone is okay."

"All right," she responded. "Boy, what an ordeal that was. I am so glad you and Mia and Dad and the boys are all safe."

"Me too."

"What's up?" Ana asked.

"I need help. Specifically, your help."

There was a long pause on the other end of the line, and then she replied, "Scott, you have no idea how long I've been waiting for this phone call. Mia, too."

Her words caused me to break down a bit on the inside but I maintained a hard exterior. "I'm a really bad guy, Ana," I said. "I can't do life again until I kick this thing." Ana had been sober five years, and I knew she had grown immensely as a person in the time I'd known her. She had come a long way since chirping me the first time we ever met. She would be an amazing mentor to me.

"It's okay, Scott," she said. "I promise. We'll get you better."

"I can't, I just can't—" I blew my cover. I cried out in anguish, "How did you do it?" It's not that I didn't think I could. I needed to hear how she accomplished such a feat. Five years of sobriety is a terrifying prospect, a cruel reality in which I would need to be prepared to endure to protect my family. Their value to me surpassed any measure of effort. I had two boys who would look at me as their first role model. I had to be that man for them, and time was running on empty.

"It's the hardest thing I've ever done, Scott," Ana said. "You have to do this for you. If you're doing it for Mia, or doing it for the boys, it's the wrong choice."

"Teach me what that means."

"Scott, do you know what the first step of Alcoholics Anonymous is?" she asked.

"What, that crazy program where everyone smokes cigarettes, drinks pots of coffee, and sits around complaining about their mundane lives?" I said. "Nope. I don't have a clue."

I anticipated a courtesy laugh at my feeble attempt at humor, but she was silent. "It's that we admit we are powerless over alcohol," Ana explained, "and that our lives have become unmanageable."

"Isn't that what I'm doing right now?"

"Yes, in a way," she said. "It makes me believe you're ready for the program."

"Do I have to do this program?" I cried out. "I'm strong as is. I can do this my own way."

"Let me ask you something," she said.

"Shoot."

Ana drew in a long, deep breath, and inquired, "How is your way working?"

That was another shot in the gut, but I needed it. I knew she was right, though, as I gazed down at my recently repaired right hand, the ring finger reattached by way of an excruciatingly painful hospital visit the night before. "It's not."

"So follow it," she responded. "What do you have to lose?"

"I guess."

"Do you love my sister? My nephews?"

"You know I do."

"Then you have to do hard things for them," Ana said.

I laughed a bit, but acknowledged what she was trying to convey. The hard choice here is to be sober, and the simple decision is to continue drinking. There was a clear right and wrong way to go about this. "Yes, I do."

"All right, I'm coming up to Denver," she said. "Are you ready now?"

"I am."

"Good. How many days sober are you?"

"Three," I said. "No, four now. I don't remember. They are all molding together."

"Great. Let's do this," Ana said. "Can I stay with you all?"

"Of course," I said. "Ana, I am speechless. Thank you so much."

"Don't mention it," she said. "This is what us alcoholics do for one another. Now, are you ready to do the hard work?"

"Yes!" I shouted.

"I'm leaving soon," she said. "I'll see you at seven."

"Thank you, Ana," I said.

"Do you know what, Scott?"

"What?" I asked.

"I know that someday you'll do this for someone else," she said.

"Do you think so?"

"I know so. You picked the right door."

"Great." I smiled. "We'll see you at seven then."

I hung up with a renewed sense of being. My family was so important to me, and I would never let them down like I had. Here's to a new and improved Scott Sharpe, one day at a time.

Chapter 38

Kissing his daughter and grandchildren goodbye, Ramon hopped into his truck and began the trek home. The first few hours were uneventful, and he even dialed Adriana to let her know he was on his way to her. She cried out in thanks to God.

Dashing down Interstate 25 at a little higher speed than normal, the adrenaline still flowing through his veins, Ramon removed his white cowboy hat he retrieved from the janitor's closet and rolled down the window of his old GMC Sierra. He drove by Raton Pass and proceeded to fly by the little yellow sign: "Welcome to New Mexico, The Land of Enchantment". To his left were flowing, descending mountains calling out to passing by tourists. Colorado blue spruces and pinon pine trees dotted the mountain skylines. A group of silver radio masts stood watch over the forest green hills like a vigilant guardian. And though he had over two hundred miles remaining in his journey, Ramon let out a giant sigh of relief. The worst was over, and he'd be home to Adriana soon.

He thought a while about Chayton, the man whose help saved the lives of many. Because of his heroism and selflessness, Mia, Francisco, Marcos, Scott, and Ramon would all return home safely. He gave his life for them, and Ramon would never forget him.

He considered the identity of the witness. In all his moments reviewing every trivial detail, a confession from a mob associate seemed to be the likeliest outcome that granted Ramon his freedom. Elmer could not have done anything to prove his innocence, although him noting Ramon was handcuffed probably helped his case. Was it Mr. Blue Tie? Did Darrell, the scared former college football player, say anything? Had Keith Stephens decided to come clean? Did Chayton document everything before he was murdered? The evidence incriminated Ramon in many ways and here he was, riding down Interstate 25 in his beloved truck a free man. He was heading home, unaware of who the person was who gave him his greatest gift.

While lamenting the events of the days prior to police, Ramon was informed Chayton had no next of kin. He had survived the deaths of both his parents, his sister, his wife, and his son. He had no family to speak of. In response Ramon offered to take the body, found in Keith Stephens' truck in the Whitehawk Casino parking lot, home and bury it. The coroner told him that's not how they treat murder victims, and that he required a full autopsy and the funeral likely wouldn't happen for a few weeks. It was a sad final page of a sad final chapter in Chayton's life. He may receive justice in the form of expensive courtroom proceedings, but they couldn't replace his existence.

Somewhere between Wagon Mound and Las Vegas, New Mexico, about one hundred miles south of the Colorado border, Ramon called Adriana again on his scarcely used cell phone.

"Is everything okay?" Adriana answered in Spanish. After everything he had been through, it was natural for his wife to fret over his safety and whereabouts.

"I'm good," he affirmed her. "But I want to talk to you about something important."

"Of course."

Ramon began, "There's something lost in this whole story. *Someone* lost in this story. I don't want to forget about him, either."

"Okay," Adriana was a tad bewildered. "And who might you be referring to?"

"His name is Chayton," Ramon explained, "and he saved my life. He helped Scott determine which room the mob—"

"The mob?" Adriana shouted. "What do you mean, 'the mob'?"

"I'll get to that later," he said. "In fact, I'll tell you all those details another time. I promise you this."

"Sure, love. So tell me about this man."

"This man is—I mean, was—one of a kind. He helped Scott figure out which room Mia and the boys were in. He led us there. He gave his life for us. He told Scott it was because, years ago, he had lost his own son and wife to a drunk driver on the reservation. Without him, I wouldn't have been safe, and neither would Mia and the boys."

"That's amazing, Ramon." The man cherished when his wife addressed him by name, because of the adage that using someone's name, especially your spouse's, reflects a deeper level of adoration and attachment.

"Yes," he said. "I want to go to his funeral."

"Of course," she responded. "When is it?"

"The coroner says after an autopsy is taken, we can make arrangements. Maybe two weeks from now?"

"That sounds great, Ramon. You need to go."

"Thank you, Adriana."

"What did you say his name was?" Adriana asked.

"Chayton."

Ramon heard Adriana's long, manicured fingernails clacking against the keyboard of her laptop.

"That's sweet," she said.

"What's sweet?"

"The name Chayton comes from the Lakota tribe and means 'falcon'."

"Falcon like the bird?" Ramon asked.

"That's right," Adriana said, and read off the computer, "a falcon, 'known in Native American cultures for focus, intelligence, and speed.'"

"He was focused and intelligent. I don't know if he was fast. I guess it's a fitting definition." The married couple laughed through their phones.

"Do you know what your name means, Ramon?"

"No, Adriana." He laughed. "That sounds like a question you would ask. You know, like in a game. What was that old thing you used to pass around for dinner guests?"

"They're icebreakers, honey. That's how you can get to know someone easily."

"Exactly," Ramon said.

"Anyway, take a guess at what your name means," Adriana responded.

"I don't know. It's of Spanish origin, I know, but that's it."

"Yes, it's Spanish," Adriana said, "but it means 'protector' or 'guardian'."

Ramon blushed. He knew where this conversation was bound. It was headed in the direction of compliments, and Ramon hated compliments. His daughters recently had thrown unnecessary affirmations his way, and each flattering remark escalated in mushiness. They started with simple phrases like, "Thank you for opening the door for us, *padre*" and evolved into grand declarations like, "You are the reason I'll find a good man to marry one day."

He said nothing to Adriana. The silence was deafening. He let a few moments pass and said, "What are you making for dinner tonight?"

"Ramon," Adriana responded, "that is the worst response you could have come up with. You're avoiding the subject at hand."

He laughed because he was conscious of her accuracy. "Go on then."

"Ramon Francisco De Leon," she began. "You are the ultimate protector and guardian."

"Thanks."

"I mean it. You show up for our family time and time again. I love you beyond words."

"I love you too, dear."

Adriana paused for a moment and then said, "I know you are driving, but I want you to open your wallet. Quickly, quickly."

He obliged, slowing his cruise control speed to 79 miles per hour, four miles over the limit. Upon unfastening his busy billfold, Ramon suddenly realized what Adriana wanted him to do. She wanted to tug at his heartstrings.

"Open the second compartment," she demanded.

He obliged, and in the confines of his black wallet lay that notorious, faded yellow Post-it, the one that read, "Thanks for protecting us, Papa. I love you. Love, Mia." The I's had hearts written above them, the bottom line of the lowercase Y extended to loop over the right side. He had shown it to Scott the first time they met, as if to say, "take care of my baby."

Ramon cried. Even though she was married and had a family of her own, Mia was forever his little girl, and his love for his little girl was uncompromising. He had proved as much over the past few days. She may not wear the same pink ribbon, or call him *papa* in the same soprano tone, but she was forever his little girl.

One of his teardrops fell on the left side of the note, right above the word "for". Instinctively, while Adriana sat silent, letting him process, another world away, Ramon pulled over on the shoulder of Interstate 25. Though it was an unseasonably warm seventy degrees outside, he fired up the heat in his car and blasted the level high. He held the yellow Post-it up to the vent. As the handwritten note dried, tears continued to stream down his face. Ramon Francisco De Leon, mister tough guy, protector and guardian, was bawling.

Epilogue

With the aid of his trusty, worn-out *bastón*, Ramon had been plodding along for many miles now. Judging by the sights of civilization and the varying chimes of busy vehicles ahead, he figured he was approaching the city limits of Bernalillo. He would rest when he made it to the Highway 550 bridge that was settled above the murky waters. He would cross going west to east so he could see both sides of the waterway.

The soothing sound of the river brought Ramon a serenity he had not felt since his last visit. It seemed as if an eternity had passed since then. His daughters were safe—all four of them—as were his two grandsons and his wife. Ramon convinced himself he acted as the good man would. He killed a human being, again, but knew the rescue mission was a success. The man he had killed was a bad man, and the humans he had saved were good humans. Sometimes bad men need to be sacrificed so good humans can survive. That's the ugly truth of life.

He was still physically recovering from the events of two weeks earlier, but Ramon had never felt better. He removed his sandal and, though it was a crisp fifty-degree morning, stuck his toes in the ice-cold, murky waters of the Rio. It felt good to truly be *home*. Mexico may have been home, Adriana may have been his soulmate, but the river remained his peaceful sanctuary. He would always run to her.

As he approached the Bernalillo bridge, Ramon reflected on his existence. When his very being was in danger days earlier, he didn't have quite the time to slow down. In moments of life endangering panic, he had heard that one's life may flash before their eyes, but he hadn't experienced anything of the sort. As Scott had later told him, Ramon was simply living that day off pure adrenaline.

He also once again considered Chayton's short existence. His thirty-eight years would be marred by tragedy and death. His mother and father passed away within a year of each other when he was in his teenaged years. He went to live with his grandmother on the reservation when he was eighteen. She died a year later of cirrhosis. He met a girl on the reservation, and they got married. They had a son. One day, his wife and son bought tickets to a movie and never made it out of the reservation. What a sad existence Chayton led, but what an awfully meaningful life he had.

Chayton's late wife was Arapaho, and even though he was Lakota it was written in his wishes to be buried next to her. The service was a lovely tribute to the man, attended by Scott, Mia, their sons, Ramon, Adriana, their daughters, and a few other select employees from the Whitehawk Casino, among them Ariel. Ramon chuckled when he saw the young woman, wondering how far into the *Longmire* mystery series she had read. The manager of the casino stopped by and offered each attendee his heartfelt condolences.

Ramon's pocket suddenly vibrated. He set down his *bastón* and pulled out his cellphone. He didn't recognize the phone number, or even the area code for that matter.

He spoke to the mystery caller, "Hello?"

"Is this Ramon De Leon?" It was the voice of a youthful man, that much Ramon was sure.

"It is."

"Ramon, you may not remember me, but my name is Darrell. We met two weeks ago."

Darrell. Ramon instantly recognized the speaker on the other side as Bart Thompson's bodyguard. His heart sank. "What do you want, Darrell?"

"I'm calling to apologize."

Ramon rolled his eyes. "What did you think was going to happen that day, Darrell?"

"I don't know. I didn't understand the danger when I started working for them."

"You want my advice?" Ramon asked. "Quit the job today."

There was a short lull in the conversation before Darrell answered, "I did, sir."

"Great. Sounds like you're on your way. So why call me?"

There was another momentary pause. "I just wanted to tell you."

"Well, thanks."

"You see," Darrell started. "I left the room right at one-thirty, just like you said and—"

"Okay."

"You were right, sir. I wasn't trying to play with no gun to my head. Your words made me think about my life and where I was headed."

Ramon released an elongated breath to the point he could hear the static through the speaker of his phone. "That's very nice, Darrell, but your men kidnapped and tried to kill me and my daughter and her sons."

"Which is why I told the truth."

"Told the truth?" Ramon asked. "To who?"

Now it was Darrell's turn to take a deep breath. "At one-thirty, like you said, I got the hell out of that room. I wasn't trying to get killed in there. I found a place to hide. Hid there for damn near twenty-four hours. When the coast was clear, I rode over to the police station. I turned myself in and told the cops everything. That you and your son-in-law were innocent men. That I was an accessory to the crimes."

Ramon froze right there on the Rio. He understood the magnitude of what Darrell was saying, that *he* was the witness who granted Ramon his freedom. "You told them about us?"

"Yeah," Darrell responded.

Ramon fidgeted with his white cowboy hat. "So you're the reason they came in and released me?"

"I guess."

Ramon performed the sign of the cross. "I ought to be thanking you then."

"Not necessary, sir," Darrell said. "I'm going to do my time and start my life over, like you said. They say I'll only have to serve a year in exchange for the information I gave. But I'll be free of the chains after that."

"This may be weird to say considering how we started this call," Ramon said, "but I'm proud of you."

"Thank you, sir."

"Keep your head up, Darrell."

"I will. Goodbye, Ramon."

"Goodbye."

Ramon's focus shifted back to the river. A fish jumped up to the surface for a moment, and he recognized the beast as a blue catfish due to its distinguishable whiskers. He laughed, because he knew lying around some room at the house was the book Ana gifted him years earlier, *Wildlife of the Rio Grande*. He would verify his suspicion when he returned to his other home.

Ramon knelt, offered up his thanks, rose from the sludge, and started the walk home. It was a wonderful day to be a good man.

Acknowledgements

First off, I need to acknowledge my family for their constant championing of me as an author. To my wife M, my best friend, your support from day one has been awe-inspiring. Not only have you never wavered in your belief of me, but you actively encourage me. I will continue to thank you the rest of my days. To my daughter I and my son C, Daddy loves you two so much. Keep smiling. Cherish every second of life. The world is a whole lot better of a place with you both in it.

To all those who helped me edit, format, and publish this book, your assistance is truly appreciated. Among many others, a special thanks to Bill, Leilani, Yasir, Mary, and Akadil. *Run to the Rio* could not have been completed without your efforts.

Please send me an email at joe@joeeganbooks.com to initiate a discussion, regardless of any criticisms or reservations you may have about *Run to the Rio* or anything I've ever written. I am an open book.

Lastly, I want to thank you, the reader. Books are an incredible part of life and with your support I can continue to fulfill my dream as an author. If you would compose a short review for *Run to the Rio* on Amazon and Goodreads, it would be a massive help for me. I am a David in a world of publishing Goliaths, and I need every bit of exposure I can get. Every review matters. Thank you all.